Don't miss these other exciting novels by
Vickie McKeehan

The Pelican Pointe Series
PROMISE COVE
HIDDEN MOON BAY
DANCING TIDES
LIGHTHOUSE REEF
STARLIGHT DUNES
LAST CHANCE HARBOR
SEA GLASS COTTAGE
LAVENDER BEACH
SANDCASTLES UNDER THE CHRISTMAS MOON
BENEATH WINTER SAND
KEEPING CAPE SUMMER
A PELICAN POINTE CHRISTMAS
THE COAST ROAD HOME
THE BOATHOUSE
THE BEACHCOMBER
SANDPIPER MARSH

The Evil Secrets Trilogy
JUST EVIL Book One
DEEPER EVIL Book Two
ENDING EVIL Book Three
EVIL SECRETS TRILOGY BOXED SET

The Skye Cree Novels
THE BONES OF OTHERS
THE BONES WILL TELL
THE BOX OF BONES
HIS GARDEN OF BONES
TRUTH IN THE BONES
SEA OF BONES
FORGOTTEN BONES
DOWN AMONG THE BONES
BONE MESA

The Indigo Brothers Trilogy
INDIGO FIRE
INDIGO HEAT
INDIGO JUSTICE

INDIGO BROTHERS TRILOGY BOXED SET

Coyote Wells Mysteries
MYSTIC FALLS
SHADOW CANYON
SPIRIT LAKE
FIRE MOUNTAIN
MOONLIGHT RIDGE
CHRISTMAS CREEK

A Beachcomber Mystery
MURDER IN THE DUNES
MURDER IN THE SUMMER HOUSE

Sandpiper Marsh

by
VICKIE McKEEHAN

beachdevils
PRESS

Sandpiper Marsh
A Pelican Pointe Novel
Published by Beachdevils Press
Copyright © 2022 Vickie McKeehan
All rights reserved.

Sandpiper Marsh
A Pelican Pointe Novel
Copyright © 2021 Vickie McKeehan

All rights reserved. No part of this book may be reproduced, scanned, or distributed in any printed or electronic format without written permission. Please do not participate in or encourage piracy of copyrighted materials in violation of the author's rights. Purchase only authorized editions.

This book is a work of fiction. Names, characters, incidents, locales, and dialogue are drawn from the author's imagination and are not to be construed as real. Any resemblance to actual events or persons, living or dead, businesses or companies, is entirely coincidental.

beachdevils
PRESS
ISBN-10: 8834824893
ISBN-13: 979 8834824893
Published by
Beachdevils Press
Printed in the USA
Titles Available at Amazon

Cover art by Vanessa Mendozzi

You can visit the author at:
www.vickiemckeehan.com
www.facebook.com/VickieMcKeehan
http://vickiemckeehan.wordpress.com/
www.twitter.com/VickieMcKeehan

Welcome to Pelican Pointe

Sandpiper Marsh

by
VICKIE McKEEHAN

beachdevils
PRESS

Prologue

Three days earlier
Pelican Pointe, California

Thick with April's showy signs of spring, the sun glistened on top of the rippling sea. The lavender had come back stronger and taller than ever, blossoming along the beach, spreading its scent from the cliffs to the pier. The fragrant purple flowers had taken over the sedge and sage. But there was still hope for the poppies. The warm weather and sea air promised to give the orange buds their most vibrant color yet. Hints of yellow yarrow pushed up through the sand amid the tall seagrass, stretching their tips toward the sun.

The wildflowers grew around Beckett Callahan as he watched the waves. The swells after last night's storm were today calm as glass. He noted their march onto land was as gentle as a baby kitten. But he knew the dangers of taking the waves for granted. Even now, dark clouds formed on the horizon. Would another storm like the one that battered the coast the night before be strong enough to make its way to shore by nightfall? Probably not. But the winds could change for sure.

And if living on the coast had taught him one thing, he knew how unpredictable Mother Nature could be. The mighty ocean would hold on to its secrets in sun or rain. If it sent its monster waves crashing over the rocks to make a statement, he hoped people would have sense enough to stay out of the water.

But there was always someone ready to defy the odds. Like the siren's call to the rocky shore, the surf called to the foolish and the veteran in equal measures—the trap too tempting to avoid. Its mystical lure could provide hours of fun before morphing into dangerous riptides that could suck you underneath the waves in a heartbeat.

No matter how many signs went up warning against swimming or surfing during high tide, there was always one person who ignored its dangers. Maybe they believed they could conquer the forces of Mother Nature even though Mother Nature had a way of kicking ass and always coming out on top. Any battle remained one-sided. As in war, one side always came out the victor. And Mother Nature held her title like a queen, no matter what season. She danced. She played. She toyed with the novice the same as she did the skilled swimmer. And when the war was over, the sea won every time.

Beckett knew something about the fanciful mysteries beneath the ocean, the yarns the sailors told. As a former Navy SEAL, he'd battled the elements. At times, he'd fought a faceless enemy. He'd seen enough death and destruction to last a lifetime. His goal these days was simple. He wanted to help people.

So when Chief of Police Brent Cody sent out a call at six in the morning to find a missing teenage boy, Beckett and his golden retriever Brodie showed up to help the family.

The kid, a thirteen-year-old named Knox Williams who believed he was the next Kelly Slater, snuck out in the middle of last night's storms to catch the waves at high tide. Knox never returned home. As daylight emerged, so did the worry.

Beckett knew Knox's surfboard had washed up under the cliffs in two broken pieces. But there was no sign of the boy.

As the wind whipped across the beach, scattering Beckett's coffee-colored hair around his face, he considered the sad outcome. Each hour that ticked by, they were likely looking at recovery instead of rescue.

Beckett called to Brodie and headed back to the pier where he'd left his truck. He spread out a topographical map of the shoreline on the hood of his pickup and recalculated time and distance. His amber-flecked green eyes scanned the 3-D images of the coastline before turning his attention to the sonar images he'd taken just two hours earlier. He recalibrated the tide data, updated the wind currents, and entered the new calculations into an app he'd developed himself. That's when he realized something was off.

At six-three, he was long-limbed and had a fluid way of moving that personified self-confidence but not cocky. He stood shoulder to shoulder next to the other half of Terra Search & Recovery—his older brother Birch—older by eleven months.

Beckett shook his head. He elbowed Birk—a nickname his mother had used since they were kids. "We're looking in the wrong place. The last known sighting isn't logistically feasible. That little hidden cove, the one by the B&B, is where Knox ended up. The distance is right and the only place Knox might've been carried to shore. The sonar images tell me he's not in the water. The storm currents show the tides would've been strong enough to sweep an unconscious boy upstream that far along the coast. I'd bet money on it. He probably bounced around the rocks, which might've left him unconscious."

Birk, another ex-Navy SEAL and a mirror image of his younger brother, didn't doubt Beck's numbers. Knowing Beckett was the geekier and nerdier of the two, he accepted the information as fact. "Then we should take the boat and check out the cove—the sooner, the better."

"Don't you want to hear my spiel about why I think Knox is at that location?"

"Didn't I just hear it? Waste of time to go over it again. I trust your data," Birk mumbled, zipping up his wet suit again. "Want to know what I'd like? I want these kids to stop doing stupid stuff, thinking they're invincible. I'm tired of coming across dead bodies. I don't feel much like finding another one today."

Beckett glanced over at Kathy Williams, Knox's mom, who clutched a teddy bear to her chest. The distraught woman stood next to Chief Cody, listening while at the same time unable to take her eyes off the water. "She's probably worried sick right about now."

"Damn," Birk uttered and lowered his voice. "You don't think she heard me, do you?"

"Nah. My guess is Brent's explaining the odds. If only we could find this kid alive."

"We won't find him standing around here," Birk groused, checking his watch. "It's not even eleven o'clock yet. Let's get the lead out."

Beckett whistled for Brodie to follow, and the two men headed for the *Brigid*, their thirty-foot cabin cruiser equipped with sonar they kept docked at the pier.

They took off heading north, pulling a torpedolike device behind the *Brigid* to pick up a wider angle of the water.

While Birk stood at the helm, Beckett kept his eyes trained on the twelve-inch display as they maneuvered through the current. It was like mowing a lawn. If you covered every square inch, you didn't need to worry you'd miss anything.

Beckett knew the shape of a drowning victim. He'd seen enough of them to recognize the distinctive image on sonar. Because the body was dead weight, it descended through water in an upright position with the chest facing the surface. But when the feet hit bottom, the knees collapsed, causing the body to roll on its back with the arms outstretched.

"So far, I'm not seeing a body," Beckett advised.

Birk said nothing as he rounded the coastline into the cove. But he picked up a pair of binoculars to scan the beach. That's when he spotted a boy curled into a ball. "I see him. There! He's facedown on the sand."

"He washed up on shore!" Beckett hollered. "Go get him, Brodie!"

The dog's tail began to wag. As soon as the *Brigid* drew close enough, the Retriever leaped into the water, swimming the remaining twenty feet to get to the kid.

"Make the call," Beckett directed right before jumping over the side after Brodie. The dog beat him to Knox and promptly licked the boy's face.

From where Knox lay on the sand, it looked like the teen had been conscious at one time because he'd thrown up enough salty-tasting water to choke a horse.

Beckett got down close to the teen's mouth to check for breathing. Holding his hand in front of Knox's face, he detected shallow wisps of air. "He's alive! Come on, Knox, stay with me, kid."

He rolled the teen onto his back and lifted his chin to begin CPR. But Brodie leaned in and began to lick Knox's face a little harder this time.

Knox's eye's fluttered open. His lips were slow to curve at the sight of the golden retriever. "That tickles."

Beckett whooshed out a sigh of relief as Birk walked up with the medkit. "Never mind. It turns out dog slobber works better than smelling salts every time."

One

First week of May
Pelican Pointe, California

There was nothing quite like a quaint B&B with access to a private cove and miles of beautiful coastline to kick off her summer vacation. It was an idyllic spot for Dr. Colleen Ecklund until she moved into the furnished house she'd rented in town. She had to remind herself that this venture wasn't a pleasure cruise. She'd stay five days at the B&B to unwind, kick back, and recharge until it was time to begin her research.

She was no stranger to hard work. It always came with a sacrifice or two. The plan was to spend her entire summer doing research. The research was necessary if she wanted to pursue her dream job—a short-term goal with a long-term reward. Or so she hoped. These days everything revolved around research. The more papers she wrote meant a better chance of getting published in all the scientific journals. The more articles that appeared in print, the greater her chance was of landing a job at the Coastal Blue Trust, a place where she wanted to work more than anywhere else.

The brutal semester teaching biology at Redwood State University had finally ended. It had been her first foray into a classroom environment since earning her doctorate. Every day she had to stand in front of students and get them excited about science—biology in particular—showed she wasn't cut out for the job. Not even a little bit. Research was her thing. Dealing with first-year students—their campus life, their problems, their never-ending antics, their complaints, their dreadful work ethic—five days a week had given her a newfound appreciation for all the teachers she'd encountered along the way. She realized now that educators were nothing short of saints or miracle workers.

But the job wasn't for her. She preferred spending her days outdoors in a wetsuit, diving out past the tides, reforesting seaweed in the kelp beds, studying their growth patterns while watching how the water toxicity killed off some species—and writing about it. Geeky, you bet. Nerdy, absolutely. But it was doing wetland research where she found her greatest joy.

It hadn't hurt that she grew up running around the shoreline at Lake Tahoe. Her parents worked as park rangers at the nearby Tahoe National Forest. The family hadn't had a lot of money. But she never lacked for anything to do.

There were trails to explore. Fishing with her dad. Plenty of water sports to keep her occupied. But it was schoolwork where she excelled. Conducting science experiments as a child, she learned she had a knack for biology and chemistry. By the time she started high school, those subjects had morphed into a love of the ocean and anything to do with marine biology.

Most weekends, while her friends were enjoying themselves—Colleen or Kelly as her parents called her—had her nose stuck in a book, usually studying anything that grew in or around the water. While her friends found marine life incredibly boring, she found everything about the subject fascinating. As she got older, she became more interested in science than fashion or makeup. On any given day, she could tell you the exact PH level of Lake Tahoe. She could talk about how sea urchins single-handedly depleted the kelp beds, stripping them barren, crippling the habitat for native fish, and leaving nothing for the fish to eat.

It was no surprise when she landed a full scholarship to UC San Diego and then applied for grants and student loans to stay long enough to get her doctorate. But after graduation, she couldn't find a job as a researcher. With rent, credit cards, and those loans to repay, she took a teaching job at the only university that made her an offer—Redwood State.

Her summer goal was to land a research fellowship using her studies on ocean acidification. She intended to spend her summer hard at work proving that reforesting kelp could protect the coastal ecosystem and help sea life continue to thrive. Our food source might one day depend on it. If the kelp beds disappeared, where would shrimp, crab, abalone, oysters, and other types of fish hang out and flourish? What would happen when these food sources needed protection from the toxic carbon dioxide sucked out of the air and absorbed by the water?

So far, research showed that the rising acid levels were bad all-around for marine life and their habitats in general. Replenishing the kelp forests and seagrass meadows were the best options for keeping sealife flourishing in their low-acid environment required to survive.

This wouldn't be her first visit to Pelican Pointe. In March, she'd spent spring break here, running tests on the tidepools, scoping out the local marsh, hoping the sea urchin population would fit her research criteria. Once she'd figured out how perfect the surrounding wetlands served her kelp and eelgrass studies, she booked a room for May, filled out an application for a short-term rental in town, and began planning the next four months of her life.

Her bad luck was that the rental had needed a few renovations before she could move in. According to the landlord, it needed new flooring, a paint job throughout, and a new refrigerator.

Patience, she reminded herself, was the backbone of a scientist. She pulled her compact pickup—a 2010 Chevy Colorado—past the apple-green sign and into a paved driveway lined with cypress trees.

After parking next to the stately Victorian, she cut the engine. Through the open truck windows, the cool ocean air told her she was no longer in the foothills of the Cascades. After the long, four-plus-hour drive in traffic, she got out and stretched her back, then went around to the rear, opened the well-worn Tonneau cover, and yanked out her laptop bag and a backpack.

Tilting her head toward the house, she admired the architecture through pale blue eyes shaded by a pair of cheap sunglasses. The old homestead did have a fairytale quality. Not that she believed in that sort of thing. But she couldn't deny the throwback style of the castle-like Queen Anne, its picturesque bay windows, or the lacey millwork that hinted at just a touch of gingerbread.

No, it wasn't a hardship to wait it out here in such a scenic setting with its spectacular ocean views.

Tall at five-nine, she climbed the wooden steps to the wraparound porch and rang the bell, something that hadn't been there before.

Her hair, more honied brown than golden, wound through the back of a university ballcap in a messy ponytail. She wore a well-worn gray sweatshirt from her SDSU days and a faded pair of jeans, frayed at the knees, scuffed work boots on her feet broken in years ago from wear and tear in the field.

"Dr. Ecklund," Jordan Harris said in greeting, joined by the woman's hundred-watt smile. "We're glad to have you back."

Kelly's lips curved toward the innkeeper, an attractive woman who always seemed incredibly put together. "Good to be back. You know you can drop the 'doctor' tag, right? I'm not a fanatic about it. This summer, I'm just plain ol' Kelly."

"You earned the title," Jordan pointed out. "It's a show of respect."

Kelly noticed that Jordan had chopped off her hair and sported a long bob. She waved a hand around her own face. "I like what you've done with the new look."

Jordan grinned again and fluffed her caramel-colored hair. "The Snip 'N Curl got a brand-new hairstylist. I was Tess Knightley's guinea pig. She whacked off five inches of dead ends, said it made me look ten years younger. I'm not so sure about that." She led the way into a redesigned hallway and living room before asking, "Still planning on wading around in Sandpiper Marsh this summer?"

"That's the place with the highest acid levels," Kelly remarked, turning in a circle to study the new digs. "Wow, you guys have been busy. Looks like you've made quite a few changes since my last visit. Is that a new door to your private quarters?"

"We enlarged the space, started weeks ago. And we've been busy upstairs with little renovations here and there. Repainted and refreshed guest rooms, replaced old plumbing, and remodeled the bathrooms. I'm putting you in our largest suite—the Nautilus."

Delighted by the news, a giggle escaped past Kelly's lips. "Last time I was in the Sand Dollar."

"You were. But for returning guests, we like to show our appreciation by pampering them with a few surprises. By the way, we had a bit of excitement a few days ago. People are still talking about Knox Williams almost drowning. Thank goodness Beck and Birk found him at the cove still alive."

"The cove below the cliffs here?"

"Yes. Unfortunately, Knox tried to surf during a massive storm. It was our good fortune that Beck and Birk didn't give up. After not finding Knox's body on sonar, they kept looking. They came along at the right moment and found him alive. I don't even want to imagine another outcome. Any longer spent out there in the heat, and that child might've—"

"Yikes. I get it. I'm glad it turned out the way it did. Is the boy okay?"

Jordan smiled. "Yes, thank God. But I don't think Knox will be doing that again any time soon. After his rescue, he spent the night in the hospital with an IV drip. Oh, he's fine now. His thirteen-year-old pride suffered some, though."

A frisky champagne-colored puppy bounced into the hallway, playing with a ball. "Who is this little guy? You didn't have him in March. He looks like a bundle of energy."

Jordan let out a sigh. "A new member of the family. We had to do something after Quake passed away. You remember Quake, right?"

"Indeed I do—a sweet dog, a lovable mutt. I'm so very sorry. How are the kids taking it?"

"Not well. Hutton and Scott are heartbroken. They grew up with him every step of the way. Quake even helped Scottie learn to walk at nine months."

"That's the downside of loving a pet—letting them go when their time is up. It's heartbreaking. Believe me, I know. What happened to Quake?"

"I'm afraid old age caught up with him." Tears welled up in Jordan's eyes. She tried to blink them back, but the tears trickled down her face. "Quake could barely walk from arthritis, had trouble going up and down the stairs. Those last few months, Scottie practically carried him around everywhere he went. But the end came suddenly. Nick woke up one morning to take Quake out for his pee break and discovered him lying in the hallway outside Scott's room. The poor thing just stopped breathing. It's almost as if that dog knew the end was near and tried to get to a place where Scottie wouldn't find him like that. We were all devastated."

Kelly nodded in sympathy and knelt on one knee to rub the pup's ears. "I haven't had a dog since mine died right after high school graduation. A Yorkie terrier mix that I named Lilly Pad. What can I say? I was eight when my dad brought her home. I loved that little ball of fur and cried myself to sleep every night for two weeks after she died. I was seventeen by then, and still, her death hit me hard, so I know what the kids are going through."

Jordan tipped up the dog's chin. "The kids named this one Quigley. Aren't you a good boy, Quig?"

"Quigley looks like a cross between retriever and Labrador. What do they call those? Goldadors or something?"

"You know your dogs. Quigley's a mix with a little Husky tossed in for good measure. Cord Bennett, the town vet, found him at six weeks old, eating out of trash cans along the pier. The theory is that someone probably dumped him out on the highway, and Quigley wandered into town all by himself. Poor little thing."

"Quigley won't be eating garbage now," Kelly said with a grin. "If I remember from last time, mealtime here is a joy. Do you have a full house this weekend?"

"We've been booked solid for months, which is why I hired a sous chef right out of culinary school. Cassidy Kennison doesn't mind doing all the other chores that come with running a B&B. She helps out with meals, changes linens, cleans like a tornado and runs errands for me. It was either hire help or discontinue lunch and dinner. I just couldn't bring myself to do that. Promise Cove has always been a full-service B&B. I'd like to keep it that way."

"Nothing wrong with hiring help. I don't know why you waited so long. Does she live onsite or commute from town?"

"Cassidy took the studio above the garage. And it's worked out beautifully for all of us." Jordan noticed Kelly's lack of luggage. "Where's the rest of your stuff?"

"I have a suitcase in the truck with my clothes in it. But my mom and dad are bringing down the rest of my things when I move into the house. Remember I booked a room for them as a surprise."

Jordan nodded as she checked the bookings on a computer. "I've got it. You check out, and they go into the same room as you. And before I forget, Logan says it looks like four days now instead of five. Feel free to leave a day early if you need to settle at the house sooner."

"Thanks. I appreciate that. My mother will love staying here. I've talked this place up enough for weeks."

"That's what we love to hear. Let me get you checked in," Jordan prompted. She handed off a card key to The Nautilus. "As you can see, we even got rid of the old-fashioned keys. With key cards, we're upscale now. Dinner's at six. Beef stroganoff on the menu tonight with veggies and salad."

"Sounds wonderful. I think I'll settle in and then take a walk around the grounds before dinner."

"You go on up. Doors are labeled. Your room is at the end of the hallway. Enjoy your stay."

"I intend to," Kelly vowed as she headed up the staircase. "See you at dinner."

She was not disappointed in the room. Mint green colors and off-white shiplap greeted her as she breathed in the smells of vanilla and lavender. She let out a little sigh when she discovered she had her own bathroom with a walk-in shower.

After tossing her gear on the antique dresser, she stared at the beach-themed artwork mounted on the walls—primarily old photographs. Some scenes she remembered from her last visit, while others were new to her. But one picture stood out from the rest. Underneath the photo of a man dressed in a National Guard uniform was a plaque that read, "David Scott Phillips, Founder, Died in Service to His Country."

Kelly sucked in a breath, reminding herself that, like many old houses, this place came with a sad history despite its idyllic surroundings.

Not one to sit still for long, she changed into a short wetsuit, then grabbed her backpack that held the test tubes she took everywhere. "Time for that walk to stretch my legs and gather new water samples. Let's hope nothing's changed since March."

Kelly walked past the grassy courtyard intending to head straight to the beach. But the flowerbeds bursting with pops of color and aromatic blossoms stopped her in her tracks. She took out her phone and snapped photos to send back to her mom in Tahoe. Because her mother had a passion for gardening, the texts were a series of pictures of the three-foot-tall bromeliads.

Look at these! They come up past my knees!

It didn't take long for a reply from her mom. *OMG. And look at the purple peonies and all those daylilies. Why doesn't my garden ever look like that?*

Down, Mom. Yours will get there. Give it time.

Yeah. Right. Maybe in my dreams. Glad you made it there safely.

I'm fine. Getting ready to test the water at the cove.

You're supposed to be unwinding for the next few days. Relax for once. Enjoy your downtime. Move-in day will get here soon enough.

Looks like that might be happening a day earlier than we planned. Are you and Dad okay with Tuesday?

Tuesday's perfect. Your father plans to stop in Napa Valley to see an old friend anyway. It's why we've decided to leave out of here early in the morning. But whether your move-in is Tuesday or Wednesday, we'll have plenty of time to stop at your apartment and grab your equipment.

Thanks for doing this. I can't believe I didn't have enough space in the pickup for everything.

You have a lot of equipment. You know your father will make it work. He always does, so stop worrying. He's convinced all of it will fit into the trailer.

But you have your own stuff to bring.

It's fine. Your dad convinced me a long time ago to travel light. Anyway, we've taken the entire week off to see you and this Pelican Pointe. It'll be a nice change of pace for us.

I hope so. Take care. Talk to you tonight.

Even after ten years since leaving the nest and moving out on her own, Kelly still liked keeping in touch with her parents. It helped her feel grounded to know she could reach out to them via text or phone call and always get a reply. She was lucky that way. And they'd always been supportive—not with money—but something so much more vital, unconditional love.

She headed down a familiar pathway, past dogwood trees dripping in pink buds, sweet-smelling magnolias laden with cream-colored flowers, and wild vines heavy with berries just beginning to ripen.

Signs of spring were all around her as she walked into the grove of cypress—a flock of birds, probably plovers—scattered out of the underbrush to protect their nests.

At the cliff's edge, she used the stairs to make her way down the steep climb to the cove below.

As soon as she reached the stretch of beach, Kelly kicked off her sandals, sinking her toes into the pristine sand glistening under her feet.

She spotted the dog first, a friendly rush of furball that charged toward her like a bull at full speed. In the distance, someone shouted a command to stop.

But it was too late. The golden-haired pooch, tongue hanging out, tail wagging, almost knocked her to the ground.

"Brodie, no!" Hollered a man wading through the water, leaving a skiff ten yards offshore. "Sorry about that."

"No problem," Kelly mumbled as she fought to stay standing. Privacy lost, she reached her hand out to rub the dog behind his ears. After all, she could hardly ignore a fluffy sixty-pound canine with adorable brown eyes currently licking her face.

In a gesture of no hard feelings, she waved at the man. But as he drew closer, she studied his sharp boned face, the hint of stubble, the relaxed way he moved. She could see those sexy green eyes flickered with amusement as the situation unfolded. Her annoyance level ratcheted up slightly when he shot her a sleepy grin instead of minding his dog. "Your friend here seems to enjoy attacking people."

"Sorry. Brodie thinks he's still a puppy. Almost a year old and he still thinks everybody wants him in their lap," Beckett justified, closing the distance. He knelt on the sand to get a good hold on Brodie's collar, tugging him off the woman's leg. "We've tried extensive training, but Brodie got kicked out of school."

Kelly decided the owner was as charming as his dog. "Aww. It's okay Brodie. You just need a tutor." She eyed the man. "That's your job."

"Believe me, I'm trying. You must be one of the latest guests to check-in at the B&B."

Kelly nodded. "As of twenty minutes ago. You?"

"Nah, I live in town. I'm Beckett Callahan. Beck for short if you prefer."

"Kelly Ecklund. No, I think Beckett suits you better. The name reminds me of that guy on those *Quantum Leap* reruns."

"My mother's a distant cousin of Samuel Beckett, the Irish-born playwright. Don't ask about my middle name."

Kelly saw an opportunity and lifted a brow. "Barclay is your middle name?"

"How on earth did you know that? Most people these days don't even know who the guy is."

"Samuel Barclay Beckett won the Nobel Prize for Literature in 1969."

She was smart, Beckett decided. More than impressed, he perused the woman. Tall and model-lanky, she wore a pale blue wetsuit that matched her eyes. The wind whipped her ballcap off her head. With the reflexes of an athlete, she caught it in mid-air, revealing glossy honey-brown tresses underneath.

Kelly noticed he kept staring at her. It made her wonder if she had something on her face. "I'll be out of your way as soon as I take these water samples," she explained, digging into her backpack for a test tube.

Beckett's eyebrows knitted with interest. Some people had a fear of dirty ocean water. But he'd never seen a surfer test the water before wading in. "You take water samples before you surf?"

She detected a southern drawl somewhere in that easy tone of his. The words seemed to roll off his tongue like vanilla-flavored syrup. "I do. I need to know the acidity of the water."

He gave her a weird look. "Before you surf in it?"

"Not exactly. I study marine life, aquatic grasses, tide flats, that sort of thing. I'm assuming you like seafood as well as the next person. Right? Now me, I love a good Dungeness crabcake and a tasty shrimp cocktail. I'd like both food sources to live another sixty or seventy years. But right now, there are all kinds of creatures in that water—shrimp, crab, lobster, to name a few—dying off as we speak because the water temp keeps rising along with the acidity. When that happens, shrimp, clams, and crabs won't survive in their natural habitat. Replanting aquatic grasses might be the only way to reforest the seabeds and help with their survival."

"You don't say? You've come to our little neck of the woods trying to save the shellfish, save the planet, is that it?" Beckett noted, eyeing the tall, willowy female in a brand-new light.

Kelly didn't intend to apologize for her work. It wasn't the first time she'd faced ridicule about her research. "Make fun all you want, but this is what I do. It's important that we find a way to save the dwindling estuarine invertebrates." Realizing she'd climbed onto a soapbox, she huffed out a breath. "Along with their food sources. *Their* food sources mean our food sources continue. It circles back. If that means getting laughed at, I'm okay with that."

"Whoa there. I didn't mean to downplay the importance of what you do. I remember now that Jordan mentioned a biologist intended to stay for the summer. I never asked for specifics."

"Ah, I see. You assumed male. A lot of people hear biologist and assume that. What else did Jordan say?"

Beck's lips curved. The innkeeper had failed to mention the Ph.D. was female *and* a total hottie. But he kept that to himself as he clipped a leash onto the dog's collar and got him to plop his butt down on the sand. "Stay. This is Brodie."

"We've met—intimately. He planted several wet kisses on me," Kelly murmured as Brodie once more tried to continue the foreplay.

For a distraction, Beckett tossed a piece of driftwood twenty feet away so the retriever would fetch. Once Brodie darted after the stick, Beckett angled toward the biologist. "Brodie's been known to pick out the prettiest woman on the beach and fix me up."

His wasn't the most creative pick-up line she'd ever heard. She glanced around the deserted cove. "Brodie does all that, does he? It seems I'm the only female around this afternoon."

"But he got the beautiful part right, didn't he?" Beckett said, pointing off to the horizon. "See that island out there in the distance?"

Her eyes followed his track. "Sure. Jordan calls it Treasure Island. What about it?"

"It's a great place to catch fish, crab, shrimp, you name it. You can sit around a firepit, kick back and enjoy the stars."

"And?"

"Ever had crabcakes cooked over an open fire?"

Kelly let out a laugh. "Not recently."

"Then you're missing out on one of the best meals around town. And since you're trying to save them from extinction, it makes sense that you should sample what the locals have to offer."

Brodie returned the stick, and Beckett threw it out again.

Kelly noted the man was a smooth operator. She'd give him that. "I don't have much time for a social life."

"Now that's a downright shame. Because people around here are usually the friendly sort, the kind that won't think twice about asking you to supper."

"I'll keep that in mind. Are you staying at the B&B?"

"As I said before, I live in town."

"No, I meant for dinner. Tonight. What brought you here?"

Beckett shook his head. "I'm here to get interviewed by the TV station out of Santa Cruz. They wanted the exact spot in the frame as the backdrop where we found Knox."

"Oh, right. You're the one who saved the boy. You and your brother."

"We got lucky."

Before Kelly could respond, she heard voices behind her, the chatter coming from an attractive platinum blonde holding a microphone and a grumbling cameraman trying to catch up. The reporter, in five-inch heels, tried to navigate the sandy beach, wobbling her way toward Beckett.

Kelly watched with amusement as Brodie dropped the stick and turned his attention to the reporter. She could see what was about to happen and felt sure Beckett should have seen it coming, too. The retriever timed his jump like an Olympic high jumper, sending the blonde down for the count onto the sand.

"Get that animal away from me," the blonde shouted.

Kelly smiled over at Beckett and lowered her voice. "Looks like that's my cue to get my water sample and get out of here. Good luck with the reporter. She looks like she's in a much better position to sample the local fare."

Two

Beckett sat in his home office answering emails. Now and then, Brodie, sprawled out in front of the fire, would lift his head, waiting for the signal it was bedtime.

But a restless Beck wasn't ready for sleep. He read each email twice, then forwarded the ones requesting help finding a missing family member to his brother. Between the two of them, they received calls from all over the country asking for help locating someone who'd disappeared. Every time a rescue story went viral, the traffic on their website increased, their inboxes overflowed, and their phone messages doubled.

They'd started Terra Search & Recovery five years earlier after their sister Brigid vanished one night while attending UC Santa Cruz. Brigid, a sophomore at the time, left the group of people she was with during a night out with friends. Her family had been searching for her ever since without success.

Whenever tips came in via their website, they checked out every lead. It's the reason the entire Callahan brood had packed up and moved cross country from their home state of Virginia to set up shop closer to where Brigid had vanished.

While his parents settled in Santa Cruz, Beckett had preferred the smaller town atmosphere in Pelican Pointe. Birk had been late to the party, deciding to pick up and move a year after everyone else. But then Birk kept to himself, held his secrets close to the vest, and traveled a lot throughout the world. Beckett rarely asked for details. And Birk wasn't the type to share unless backed into a corner. The less he knew about his brother's off-the-book jobs, the better.

But tonight, Brigid wasn't the reason Beckett couldn't sleep. His thoughts kept drifting to a particular biologist and his reaction to her. He wasn't usually as spontaneous with women he'd just met. But there was something about Kelly that appealed to him, even though she wasn't exactly his type. A fashionista, she wasn't. Compared to the reporter, some people might even describe Kelly as plain. But they'd be wrong. Just because she hadn't worn expensive heels or makeup didn't make her a plain jane. Far from it. She hadn't needed paint to enhance those eyes. Those mistrusting glassy blue eyes all but sparkled mischief and mayhem. And what about those high cheekbones? And that pouty rounded mouth? Maybe in her former life, she'd been a Viking princess.

Brodie's head popped up about the same time the dog let out a deep snort, warning an intruder had dropped in for a visit.

"Probably not a princess," a male voice stated from across the room. "More like a Viking warrior."

"Jeez," Beckett groaned, scrubbing his hands down his face. "What is wrong with me? Sentimental babble always brings out the ghost of Scott Phillips. Every time. By now, I should know better. The ghost who comes around without an invitation to remind me that I'm not fifteen and horny anymore."

"You're a long way from fifteen, but just as horny," Scott cracked, his tone teasing. "Attraction between the sexes is as natural as breathing."

Beckett swallowed hard. Since moving into his house several years ago, he had encountered these incidents off and on. Each time it happened, Beck swore he'd move. If only he'd listened to the locals. They'd tried to convince him the place was as haunted as a graveyard after midnight.

So what if he'd fallen in love with the house on Sandy Pointe, the Mission-style two-story Revival with its arched doorways and old-world glam. He should've listened to reason when Logan Donnelly warned him it might come with a resident ghost.

"What is it you want?" Beckett asked the man who'd died almost two decades earlier.

"I just thought you'd want to know Dr. Colleen Ecklund is the kind of self-assured woman who can handle herself in a tough situation."

"Colleen?"

"Nicknamed Kelly."

"Look, I just asked her to share crabcakes with me. It wasn't a marriage proposal."

"Crabcakes are a start. But soon, she'll need a favor, a friend, someone she can trust. When that happens, you'll share more than a meal. Don't make the mistake of pushing her away. She's strong but not unbreakable."

"What the hell does that even mean?"

"It means Kelly Ecklund is about to get the rug pulled out from under her."

On those words, Beck watched the infamous Scott fade away. He thought about picking up his glass, the one he'd used for a nightcap before bed, and hurling it against the wall in frustration. But what purpose would broken glass serve other than spending the half-hour it would take cleaning up the mess?

He checked his temper but raised his voice to a shout, "I'll somehow hunt you down for this. Find somebody else to haunt."

In the years he'd been living here, Scott had never once warned him about another person. Were his palms sweating because he'd just had a conversation with a ghost? Or was his heart racing at the idea Kelly might be in trouble? Either one caused the hairs on the back of his neck to feel like a nest of camel spiders had taken up residence on his skin.

His gut hadn't felt this uneasy since the firefight in Ramadi.

Beck got to his feet and decided it wouldn't hurt to take a drive out to the B&B. Just in case. Just because. If things looked okay from the street, knowing Kelly and everyone else inside were safe and sound, he could rest easier and maybe get to sleep before dawn.

Kelly had taken the time to unpack, folding her stuff neatly into the dresser drawers. A short stay didn't mean she had to live in an unorganized mess.

She dressed for bed in a pair of pale blue cotton pajamas, then leaned back against the headboard, balancing her laptop on the pillow next to her.

Tapping the keyboard at a fast and furious pace, she described the sad condition of her latest find—Panulirus Interruptus—also known as the California spiny lobster she'd discovered on her walk along the beach after dinner.

The ten-inch specimen suffered from a severe case of epizootic shell disease. She'd found it riddled with protozoans and nematodes. Most damaged were the dorsal carapace and abdomen. Fascinated at finding such a lobster this far north when it usually stuck to warmer waters near Baja, she sent a photo of the damaged crustacean to her former professor and mentor at UCSD.

Appealing to Dr. Baylen Wright—the country's leading authority on marine life—to spend some time in the area during the summer months made sense. She suggested he might want to explore the reason for the lobster's change in habitat. She also proposed they co-author a paper on the subject. Surely other scientists might want to know why and how the spiny lobster ended up north of Santa Cruz. No doubt, rising ocean temperatures had something to do with it. But hard evidence outweighed supposition. She vowed to find the reason.

Either way, Baylen's input would lend credence to her own research, boosting its value and increasing interest. After detailing everything she wanted to say in the email, she hit send.

A nagging curiosity had her changing browsers to Google the name Beckett Callahan. That's how she learned about the ex-Navy SEAL and Terra Search & Recovery. The search for the missing sister had dragged on for five long years.

Depressed to discover someone could vanish like that without a trace, she checked the time on her laptop and decided to make a quick call to her mom. When she didn't get an answer, she texted instead.

Gone to sleep early, I see. Good for you. Be careful on the road tomorrow. It's the weekend, so there will be a lot of traffic between Tahoe and Napa. Let me know when you pull in there for the night. Have fun. Just don't drink too much of the grape. See you soon! Love you guys!

She barely finished texting when exhaustion took over. Sinking into her pillow, she snuggled under the comforter and fell asleep with the phone still in her hand.

Images of a dark-haired man with green eyes invaded her dreams.

Like a scene from a movie, Beckett Callahan's rugged face looked back at her. The island setting as the backdrop seemed so vivid. They danced around a campfire to the strings of Vivaldi. The flames flicked high and hot. Hazy smoke floated around them. The scene was like a Caribbean vacation or maybe a Hawaiian luau. But this was no raucous party atmosphere. It was just the two of them, enjoying the mood, the romance of each other.

Kelly could feel the heat move through her when his strong arms wrapped around her waist. His hard body swayed with hers to the music. His full mouth knew a thing or two about slow, deep, sultry kissing. He took her to heights she'd never known. Unlike some men she'd been with, this one took his time, getting to know every inch of her body.

It was unfair to compare, she told herself, while at the same time wanting more. So much more. Being held like this in the arms of a man like Beckett was a glorious feeling. Too glorious. Heady with lust, she could feel herself sink into the sand, his body hard on hers. Complete surrender put a smile on her face and took her to all those places she'd wanted to go but never knew existed until that moment.

She sunk deeper into sleep, still feeling the adrenaline rush from the dream. But somewhere in her subconscious, she realized that it wasn't real. She was alone. That was her reality. Forever alone, she willed herself back on that beach, back to the island, trying to bring the scene with the man into focus once again.

Disgusted with himself for making a wasted trip out to Promise Cove, Beck sat behind the wheel of his pickup and stared up at the house. He realized pretty quickly that everyone inside had gone to bed hours earlier. There were no lights on anywhere. He felt like a fool and a little like a stalker.

"This is what I get for listening to a ghost," Beckett said aloud. "I'm gonna start looking for a new place to live."

"It won't do any good," Scott reminded him from the passenger seat. "No matter where you go, I'll just show up there."

"You're joking, right? If you're this know-it-all ghost, how come you won't tell me what happened to Brigid?"

A pained look crossed Scott's face. "I can help you on your journey, but it's impossible to hold all the answers. It's one of the reasons you'll need Kelly. She's good with puzzles. Help her. You help yourself. One thing, though. Brigid is not alone."

Not a patient man when it came to riddles or games, Beck was about to fire back a heated reply when, once again, Scott vanished, and he sat there in his truck talking to thin air. "Yeah, that's a neat trick. When the questions get tough, it's easy to go poof."

Frustrated, he shot his middle finger and aimed it where Scott had been sitting. Which only ramped up his annoyance at himself. Maybe he was headed for some kind of mental collapse. Maybe he'd finally cracked and was in the throes of a complete nervous breakdown.

Feeling foolish, he slid the pickup into gear. In one fluid motion, he stepped on the gas. All the while, though, his eyes—sharp as a marksman's—scanned the countryside looking for the elusive Scott. As he headed south back toward town, he thought he heard laughter. He reached over and cranked up the volume on his stereo system. He let Guns N' Roses blast their way through the cabin. With the windows rolled up, *Welcome to the Jungle* drowned out anything else he didn't want to hear.

Three

Kelly slept late—the first time since Christmas vacation. She woke to a dead phone that needed charging. Assuming that was why she hadn't heard from her mom, she plugged it in and was disappointed to find her voicemail empty and no text messages.

She tried calling her mom again and left another message. There was no reason to call her dad because Daniel Ecklund hated cell phones. Her father was old-school, more the two-way radio type. No matter how she'd tried to persuade him to join the high-tech world, the more stubbornly he had refused.

She told herself not to overreact. There was a good reason her mother hadn't called. They'd probably gotten on the road at some ungodly hour like four-thirty this morning and lost track of time. But even then, it wasn't like Luella Ecklund not to text back.

Telling herself everything was fine, she took a hot shower to wake up. Afterward, she made herself get dressed first before checking the phone a second time.

After putting on a clean pair of jeans as faded as the old pair, she grabbed a powder blue turtleneck and yanked on her boots.

Standing in front of the mirror, Kelly pulled her hair back into the proverbial no-fuss, no-frills ponytail and headed downstairs for breakfast.

A bubbly twenty-something Cassidy Kennison greeted her in the dining room with a warm smile and an eager attitude. "Can I fix you an omelet?"

"Sure. What do you recommend?"

"The Denver omelet's been popular this morning."

"Great, I'll take that."

"You got it. Toast and hash browns, okay?"

"That'd be great. Am I the last guest to eat breakfast?"

Cassidy nodded. "But that's okay. You're not on a schedule. I'm here to cook whenever you're ready to eat."

Ten minutes later, Cassidy returned with the best-looking omelet Kelly had ever seen. Thick and fat with plenty of ham and cheese tucked inside, her first bite proved the chef knew her way around a stove. "This is delicious."

"Thanks. It's my specialty. What do you have going on this morning? Any plans?"

"I'd like to drive by the house I'm renting in town, then scope out the area where I'm conducting my experiments, get a better feel for the place."

"Since you're hanging around until the end of summer, we could do something together one night if you'd like. We're about the same age. I don't know many people here, and the nightlife is pretty tame."

Kelly thought of Beckett and his invitation the day before. Unlike then with Callahan, this time she wasn't so quick to say no. "Sounds like a plan."

"Great, then let's exchange phone numbers."

"Good idea." Exchanging numbers meant picking up her phone to key in Cassidy's. She couldn't help but take the opportunity to swipe for messages. Again. But there were none. A deep-down worry began to take over. She felt that something was off. But she wasn't sure what to do. What had changed with her parents between yesterday afternoon and this morning?

It dawned on her who to call—their longtime next-door neighbor had a key to the house. She'd bet money that nosy Alice Van Alstyne would know when they pulled out of the driveway to the exact minute.

She finished her breakfast and went outside on the wraparound porch to make the call. Mrs. Van Alstyne answered on the third ring. Kelly explained the reason for the call.

"Oh, honey, your mom and dad left out of here last night pulling that trailer, probably close to seven-thirty."

"But according to Mom, they weren't supposed to leave until this morning."

"I don't know what to tell you. I saw them load up myself and drive off. And Luella asked me to collect their mail while they were gone. Maybe Dan got a burr up his butt and took off early. You know how your dad is sometimes when he wants to get where he's going in a hurry."

Kelly couldn't deny that. Most times, her father had a laidback outlook on life. Other times though, when he wanted to stay on a schedule, he could get downright pushy about it. "I suppose he might've wanted to get a jump on traffic."

"There you go. I bet you hear from them any time now. Luella wouldn't want you to worry like this."

"You're right. Thanks, Mrs. Van Alstyne."

Kelly ended the call, but she didn't feel better about things. Why on earth would they have left before bedtime? Then she answered her own question. She could hear her dad insisting they get down the road a little farther, even if it was late on a Friday night. It didn't make a lot of sense to her, though.

She stared at the phone in her hand. Would leaving one more voicemail for her mom make any difference? She decided it couldn't hurt.

Mom. Call me. Or text. Something. Where are you guys? Did you make it to Napa? Let me know where you're staying.

Feeling frustration build if she sat around here any longer, she'd go nuts with nothing to do but worry and check her messages. She had to get her mind off the idea that something had gone wrong and switch gears. After all, her parents were two competent adults, perfectly capable of handling a situation. They weren't elderly, she reminded herself. Daniel and Luella Ecklund were as active in their mid-fifties as they had been in their thirties, possibly more so. They were in excellent physical condition. They hiked. They biked. They worked in rugged terrain. Their jobs took them all over a National park, managing burns, overseeing recreational areas, and dealing with year-round traffic issues. These were two people trained to handle a crisis situation.

Which meant, they were more than likely just fine.

Kelly kept telling herself that as she collected her backpack and laptop bag from her room and headed into town.

The drive through the countryside showed off magnificent cliffs on one side dotted with hardy ice plants and rolling fields on the other. She passed an organic farm with a busy fruit and vegetable stand. But she didn't stop. Maybe on the way back *after* she'd heard from her parents, she'd pick up a little box of strawberries, and some vine-ripe tomatoes and save them for when her mom and dad arrived.

Checking on the rental would definitely make her feel better. And she needed a distraction to stop thinking the worst. When the old lighthouse came into view, she sighed, knowing she was almost there.

She had fallen in love with this quaint beach town back in March. The boardwalk, the pier, the lighthouse, the houses, the shops, and even the people seemed friendlier than the neighbors she had in Hayward.

Not that she could explain it. The vibe seemed different all around here.

One pass through Athena Circle told her that several contractors were still working on the bungalow. A pair of painters had given the white stucco a fresh coat and power-washed grit and grime off the red brick trim. And this on a Saturday. That was nothing like her apartment building manager. If anything broke on a weekend there, forget about getting it fixed until sometime later the following week.

She pulled to the curb and parked her pickup in the middle of the block. Pleased to see things progressing for herself, she needed fresh air. Shouldering her laptop bag, she locked the truck out of habit and decided to walk.

Heading toward Ocean Street, she took a right at the corner. Everything seemed within walking distance—the beach, a bookstore, even a coffee shop.

When she spotted a forest green pickup parked at The Perky Pelican with the Terra Search & Recovery logo on the side, she decided she needed an iced coffee. What could be more spontaneous than accidentally bumping into Beckett while grabbing a frappe?

But once Kelly entered the shop, she realized Beckett wasn't there. This pickup must belong to the other Callahan. The website had pictured two brothers with similar bios. But the older of the two, Birch, had a much more serious-looking face. That's how she could tell them apart. At that moment, she decided this one seemed unapproachable, best left alone. He sat at a corner table nursing his coffee cup and reading a file folder or maybe several stacked on top of one another.

She felt like ducking out the door, but the woman behind the counter beckoned Kelly closer with her wide smile. "Hi, there. I'm Paula Bretton, the owner. You're the biologist replanting stuff in the ocean over the summer. Kelly Ecklund. Right?" Paula's lips curved wider at the shocked expression on her customer's face. "It's a small town. You'll get used to it. Word travels faster than a lightning strike. What can I get you?"

Kelly studied the forty-something woman who wore her cinnamon-colored hair in a long bob. "Large espresso frappe with milk and ice, no syrup, no whipped cream."

Paula turned to get started, reaching for the large-sized blender. "I remember that order from March. It's kind of unusual. Can't say I remember anything else about you, though."

"I sort of blend in wherever I go," Kelly said with a grin.

Paula sputtered with laughter as her hands stayed busy working the blender. "I didn't mean it like that. It's just that last March, we had a lot of spring breakers—college students—in here. You sort of blended in with them."

When the door to the shop opened, Paula poured the frappe into her biggest to-go cup and pushed it toward Kelly. She waved at the next customer. "Hey, Beck. Birch's been waiting for you. Fifteen minutes. Can I get you the usual?"

Beckett nodded, but his eyes drifted to the biologist. Despite Scott's warning from the night before, Kelly looked perfectly fine. Better than. "How's it going?"

Kelly sipped her iced drink and studied the man's face. "I'm okay. You look a little tired, though. Rough night?"

Beckett chuckled. "You wouldn't believe me if I told you."

"Oh, I don't know. As a scientist, I'm more open-minded than you might think. In fact, I was hoping you could tell me about the kinds of cases you take, maybe go into more depth about the rescues you do. I looked you guys up last night on the Internet."

"Really? What prompted that?"

"Let's just say I had a chance to sleep on it, and I'm reconsidering my crabcake options."

"Imagine that," he replied as Paula handed him an oversized ceramic cup with foam artwork on top shaped like a leaf.

"What's your usual?" Kelly asked.

"Cappuccino. Yours?"

"Espresso frappe," she answered. "It's totally different than a sweet Frappuccino, that syrupy drink in a bottle."

"Let me guess. No flavoring or whipped cream, just espresso, milk, and ice with a bitter taste."

"Very observant. Define bitter. It's coffee, not a milkshake. The frappe is a popular drink in Greece. Is that how you find people? By being observant? Your website mentioned you'd discovered over a hundred missing persons."

"Not all of them are found alive. Unfortunately." Beckett pointed to his sour-faced counterpart in the corner. "I do have help. It's a partnership. Kelly meet Birch. He answers to Birk since I was old enough to talk."

Birch overheard that last part. "Which makes me wonder why he always keeps me waiting."

"I had a phone call that ran long. That Bay Point dad with the missing teenage son. He wanted to know when we might be able to get up there. You want me to cut it short with a grieving parent?"

Birch let out a sigh. "There's always a reason you're late. You could've texted."

"Don't mind Mr. Grumpy Pants over there," Beckett cautioned. "Birk always needs something to complain about. Birk, this is Dr. Kelly Ecklund, the biologist. She's in town for the summer hoping to reforest the kelp beds."

"Nice to meet you. That's a tall order," Birk stated, sizing the woman up and down. "I guess saving the planet has to start somewhere."

"Isn't he a peach?" Beckett fired back.

"I've encountered worse," Kelly admitted. "Nice to meet you, Birch. Unusual name, by the way. Birch, the tree, has sixteen different species native to North America. From the round leaf variety—Betula Uber—found in Virginia to the Betula Glandulosa found in the mountainous regions of California. When manufacturers aren't using birch to make furniture, it's a popular wood used as firewood because it doesn't pop and crackle. Let's say if you were out in the woods trying to evade detection and wanted the fire to quietly burn, not sizzle or pop, you'd look around for birch. The bark makes excellent kindling because it burns, whether frozen or not. It's lightweight and flexible, making it popular with Indigenous Peoples who discovered everyday uses for it—bowls, utensils, canoe construction, and obviously building their houses. You know, wigwams."

For once, Birk appeared speechless.

Kelly lifted a shoulder and pivoted back to Beckett. "Just saying. Anyway, whenever you finish your meeting with Birch, could I talk to you about something? I'll be over in the opposite corner on my laptop."

"Sure." Intrigued, Beckett watched her walk away before plopping down across from his brother.

"Good God, she's a female version of you," Birk decided. "A regular walking encyclopedia, a know-it-all with facts and figures at the ready. Where the hell did you meet her? Obviously not bad to look at, either."

"Obviously."

Birk tossed four file folders toward his brother. "These cases we can handle. No problem." He laid a hand on four more. "This stack is a *maybe* because of logistics, which might be feasible if we could figure out a way past the issues. The rest are a big fat, no way. We just don't have the right equipment to tackle those."

"And what about Lee Esterman, the Bay Point dad? His daughter Lila has been missing five years now, along with Wes Scofield, the boyfriend. You and I both know those kids likely ended up that night in the San Joaquin River."

"Then maybe we go up there first of next week and take a look."

"That's what I was hoping you'd say. I'll call Lee and arrange to have him meet us at Threemile Slough."

Birk bobbed his head toward Kelly. "Go on. I know you're dying to find out. Go see what the hottie wants."

"She is something, isn't she?"

Birk cracked a grin. "Want me to pass her a note in study hall?"

"Bite me," Beckett whispered, getting to his feet. He beelined toward Kelly's table, trying not to seem eager. "What's up?"

Kelly licked her lips and closed her laptop. "I know your sister went missing five years ago. I'm sorry about that. The question I have is, how long before you knew, or anyone knew, that Brigid was really missing? I mean, how long did it take anyone to start worrying or thinking something was wrong?"

When Beckett remained standing, Kelly sat up straighter. "Look, I'm not trying to bring up a hurtful time for you and your brother. I want to know for a reason, which I'll gladly explain if you just take the question seriously."

Beckett sat down and rubbed a hand over the back of his neck. "Her roommates alerted our parents back in Virginia that she didn't come home that night. They called and talked to Mom, then Dad got involved and called Birk, who called me. My father is the one who phoned Santa Cruz PD to report her missing. By this time, Brigid had been out of contact with anyone for about ten hours. Now, what's this about?"

"My parents. I haven't heard from my mom since yesterday afternoon. That was right before meeting you at the cove. Mom and I texted several times back and forth. The plan was originally to leave Tahoe on Saturday morning, then drop by my apartment in Hayward to load up the trailer with the rest of my equipment, stuff that wouldn't fit into my pickup. But then, yesterday afternoon, Mom mentioned something about stopping in Napa Valley first to see one of Dad's old friends. This morning, I couldn't reach my mom. I called a neighbor lady I know. It's the same neighborhood where I grew up. Anyway, I found out from Mrs. Van Alstyne that they left South Lake Tahoe last night at seven-thirty, pulling the trailer."

"Is that unusual for your mom not to text or call?"

"It is. I'm an only child. I'm relatively close to my parents. We talk at least once a day. Even when she's at work, Mom will text me about something funny that happened or send me a link to a newsworthy story or a cartoon. And even though Dad doesn't bother with a cell phone—he's the old-fashioned type of guy who uses his two-way radio instead—he's a great park ranger. Both my parents work at Tahoe National Park. They know a thing or two about the roads, the weather, the elements. I simply can't wrap my head around why my mom hasn't bothered returning my voicemails or texting me back."

She held up her phone. "It's almost noon. And nothing. Radio silence since yesterday afternoon. And I'm starting to freak out. Why didn't I ask the name of the friend in Napa? I can't even follow up on that. Why wasn't I more curious about their side trip?"

"What route were they taking? Do you know?"

"The route they always take. Highway 50, straight through to Sacramento, then a jaunt up to Napa. If Dad pushed it, they could've gotten to Napa by eleven, eleven-thirty at the latest, depending on traffic last night."

Beckett frowned. "On a Friday night, 50 is usually packed. Not to mention that it's a curvy, twisting road in daylight under the best of conditions. Starting on a road trip at night might not be the best idea, especially if they have trouble seeing the road. How old are they?"

"Mid-fifties. And they're in relatively great shape, with no underlying medical conditions that I know about anyway. They're park rangers. They live an active lifestyle."

Beckett took out his phone and brought up a map app. "Doesn't matter. Parts of 50 is a two-lane roadway, especially leaving the Tahoe Basin."

"For someone who isn't a native of the state, you seem very knowledgeable."

"I've been all over California, probably dived in most man-made lakes and a lot more of the rivers. What do you want me to do?"

"I want your advice. If it was your parents, would you raise the alarm or just keep hoping that everything's okay?"

Beckett looked straight into her pale blue eyes. "You're probably not asking the best person. Since Brigid went missing, I'm not exactly the wait-and-see type. If you feel something's wrong, then it probably is."

"Do you recommend calling the Highway Patrol and reporting them missing?"

"I'll do it. I have a buddy in Sacramento. He'll put the word out. I need names and their date of birth. What kind of vehicle are they driving?"

"Daniel and Luella Ecklund. Daniel's birthdate is June 29th, 1962. Luella's is March 26th, 1964. They're driving a crew cab Ford F250 2012 pickup pulling an enclosed silver/grayish trailer that Dad built himself. The truck is copper and tan in color with a Yosemite license plate background, plate number 2Y57425."

Impressed, Beckett keyed in the information, so he'd have it on hand. "You know all that off the top of your head?"

Again, she held up her phone. "Personal data keyed into my notes for emergencies just like this. I never thought I'd have to use it."

"Let's go outside to make the call," Beckett suggested, stopping at his brother's table to let him know the latest.

Birk followed them outside and stood next to Beckett's truck, where Brodie waited in the front seat. "Could I make a suggestion? Before we contact Steve Pollock, let me see your phone, Kelly."

Kelly handed it over without comment. She watched as Birk scrolled through her messages and counted how many times she'd tried to contact her mother. "If you have any other ideas, I'm all ears."

"Sorry, but I had to check," Birk said, handing her back the phone. "Pollock is our guy at the state patrol.

He'll want to know details like that. How many times have you tried to reach your parents?"

"Yeah, he will," Beckett verified. "The thing is—"

"The thing is, I should head up there myself," Kelly finished. "I know the way like the back of my hand. I'll just backtrack from Hayward and head to Sacramento. Once I reach Highway 50, it's a straight shot—"

"No," Beckett heard himself say. "First things first. Pollock will check for any accidents reported along that route last night. That's the first step. Then we take it from there."

Birk eyed Beckett. "He means *we* will take it from there. We're both licensed pilots with access to a jet. No, we don't own it. But the man I work for is very generous. He lets us use it for long-distance Search and Rescue missions. Flying will get us to the area faster than a car trip."

"Right now, there's something you need to do first," Beckett cautioned. "Call your mother and tell her what's about to happen. Leave a detailed voicemail, then follow up with a lengthy text message. That way, if we're dealing with an innocent miscommunication and they're drunk out of their gourds somewhere in wine country, she'll know you're freaked out and hopefully will call you back right away."

It made sense, Kelly decided, stepping a few feet away before redialing her mother's number. "Mom, this is Kelly. Every hour that goes by without hearing from you is freaking me out. I'm about to contact the Highway Patrol and ask for their help. If you get this message, you need to tell me that everything's fine. Otherwise, I'm launching a search party on my end. Call me back. *Now.*"

"That's perfect," Beckett stated. "Good job. Now, we wait a few minutes to see if she responds."

They waited twenty minutes longer. But Kelly's phone remained silent.

Four

"We're looking for guardrail damage," Beckett explained to Steve Pollock. "Anything along Route 50 heading west to Sacramento that might show a car went over the rail last night between seven-thirty and eleven-thirty. Or any signs of an abandoned pickup with the hood up. Maybe the truck had engine problems. They could've pulled off the side of the roadway, then got out to walk for help."

"That will take time. You're talking about a hundred plus miles to cover. And before you ask, I've already checked the hospitals. There were no accident patients admitted anywhere in the vicinity. And there are a lot of small towns in that area with rural clinics. I checked them all. Nothing. I sent the word out to my officers patrolling that section of 50 to look for any signs of the truck and trailer."

"Thanks. We'll be up there by the end of the day."

"I'm not sure what you think you can do that we haven't," Pollock stated.

"For one thing, we're attempting to track Luella Ecklund's cell phone to get a ping before the battery dies."

"Let's have the number," Pollock snapped. "I can do that."

Beckett cut his eyes to Kelly's and smiled before rattling off the information. "Keep us up to date. We're on our way."

Watching Beckett jump into action, Kelly's worry became full-blown fear. They'd already passed the twelve-hour mark without hearing anything from her parents. She was beginning to believe something terrible had happened.

She needed to find their truck.

The next hour seemed a blur. While Kelly texted Jordan and made her aware of the situation, Beckett prepared a short flight path from the local airstrip to Sacramento's smaller executive airport nearest to Highway 50.

The plan came together fast. Once they reached Sacramento, they would rent a car and head toward South Lake Tahoe, checking the route along the way.

The business jet turned out to be a sleek Cessna Citation XLS with a nine-passenger capacity, the interior designed in classy white and gray upholstered seats.

"Where's Birk?" Kelly asked, settling in next to a window.

"We never fly together. It's a business risk type thing," Beckett pointed out. "Birk will stay behind, look after Brodie for me. He'll also work the communications angle, re-contacting the hospitals and maintaining the link to Pollock."

"I didn't realize. I don't remember you saying anything. I just assumed Birk took separate transportation to the airport."

"It's a policy we follow religiously. That way, if anything happens, one of us is left standing to continue our work."

"I could've driven," Kelly grumbled. "They are my parents. I wouldn't want to put anyone else at risk."

"I'm a good, thorough pilot who doesn't get distracted," Beckett declared with a grin. "I don't take risks, and I don't plan on crashing any time soon."

"Good to know."

"Then sit tight while I go over my preliminary checklists. It's a quick hop to Sacramento. Like thirty minutes or less once we're in the air. You can sit up front if you'd like."

"I don't want to distract you. I'm a little nervous about this whole thing. One minute I'm sitting in the coffee shop, and the next thing I know, I'm on board a jet."

"Understandable. But you won't distract me. You could, but I'm a focused pilot once I'm airborne."

"The last thing I want is to distract you," she uttered, barely above a whisper. She watched him put on a headset, watched as he flipped buttons, and went into pilot mode with air traffic control.

They waited for clearance from the tower and got underway twenty minutes later, roaring down the runway at a fast clip.

"You're not afraid to fly, are you?" Beck asked after he'd leveled off at twelve thousand feet.

"Not usually. I didn't realize until this minute that I prefer a much larger aircraft, though."

Beckett burst out laughing. Knowing he needed to keep her mind off what they might find along the roadway, he wanted to distract her. "What's your worst flying experience?"

"That's easy. I got stuck sitting on the runway in Tampa for four hours once during a thunderstorm. Once you board, you're stuck with no place to go until the tower says you can take off. I never knew that. Then once we were in the air, it was a bumpy ride all the way back to Reno. The woman who sat next to me kept thumbing her rosary just in case. That's how bumpy the flight became. And Lake Tahoe doesn't have a hub, so I had to fly through Reno then drive through snow to get home in time for New Year's Eve."

"When was that?"

"Ages ago. My winter break to Florida when I was twenty, then home to see the parents before starting the spring semester."

"At?" He already knew because he'd looked her up online, but he asked anyway to keep her talking.

"UCSD. Great place to live, San Diego. I spent ten years of my life living there."

"I almost ended up in San Diego," Beckett began, "when my family decided to come west. Beautiful city. It offers everything a person could want in nightlife, eating out and beach living. But when my parents went with Santa Cruz instead, I knew I needed to be closer. And I realized I wanted a smaller atmosphere, smaller than what Santa Cruz offered. I went out of my way to stay away from a major metropolitan area. The small-town environment is much better for me, anyway."

"So you like Pelican Pointe?"

"I love it. So does Birk, when he's home."

"What exactly does Birk do?"

"Ah, that's the question, isn't it? All I know is he does investigative work for the guy who owns this jet."

"Like background checks?"

"Yeah, that sort of thing. We both use our Navy SEAL training to dive and find people who go missing. Our expertise is in locating people in or near the water. It all started when we found this guy's brother—missing for twenty years—in a pond less than a mile from his house. He'd been there the entire time."

"The owner of the jet's brother?"

"Yup. He was so grateful he staked us to all the equipment we needed, gave us the use of his plane any time we needed it, and helped us get Terra Search & Recovery going."

"Who is this guy?"

"Doug Wolfson. One of the richest men in Silicon Valley."

"I'm not rich, but I'm very grateful you're doing this—helping me find my parents."

"That's our thing."

"How long were you in the Navy?"

"I signed up right before high school graduation, so I put in a dozen years. It was just a coincidence that I was home on leave when Brigid went missing."

"Home is Virginia, right?"

"Yup. It was. Brigid vanishing like she did, tore the rug out from under all of us. I personally know how it feels when a loved one disappears, and there are no clues to finding them. It's gut-wrenching, watching your parents die a little inside every time the phone rings and there's no news."

"So you opted out of the military to help locate Brigid?"

"Not at first. I thought law enforcement would come up with something. Do their jobs. But after three months of nothing, Birk and I decided to intervene. The only way for us to find Brigid was to devote our resources full-time. So that's what we did. We came out to California and showed up on Santa Cruz PD's doorstep. I don't think the cops liked it very much. They still don't. But we've been there ever since. But hey, you do what you need to do during a situation like that, right?"

Enough about him, Beck decided and directed the conversation back to Kelly. "What got you into science? You teach at Redwood State, right? You're a professor when you're not replanting the kelp beds?"

"I haven't started replanting anything yet," she declared with a nervous laugh. "Kelp isn't actually a plant. Plants have roots. Kelp doesn't. It's marine algae that use photosynthesis, much like a plant does. Although when it reaches the ocean's surface, it grows level to the water, floating like a carpet that shades the seafloor. It grows upright because each giant kelp stem or leaf contains a gas-filled pod that floats. The California coastline has lost ninety percent of its kelp forest. It's mostly grown in aquaculture operations these days."

"Wow. Really?"

She blew out a breath realizing she'd gone on and on. "Sorry. But I love science. I've always enjoyed the idea of carrying out an experiment and getting a result, good or bad, finding out what makes things grow, live, thrive. It's what I like best."

"Did you always want to teach?"

"Oh, God, no. My first year teaching was a nightmare. I found out quickly that the kids were pretty much there to fulfill a science requirement. Biology falls into the required coursework for science credit. They didn't care anything about biology or science in general. That's why I prefer sticking to research."

"So, you're not happy as a professor? Why on earth not?"

"Well, I wouldn't say I'm unhappy. I'm just not a very good teacher. I admit it. Over half my students landed Cs as a final grade, some even lower. That doesn't exactly reflect well on my teaching skills, now does it?"

"You can't force them to learn."

"No, but it was obvious early on that other professors in my department were better at it."

"How long have those guys been teaching, though? Decades?"

"Sure, but you'd think I could at least get my kids excited about the basics. I couldn't."

"But it sounds like you reached forty percent of them. That's not bad. That shows some of those kids were there to learn. You should focus on the successes."

Kelly's lips curved. "You're an optimist, the glass half full kind of guy, right?"

"I guess I am."

Kelly's cell phone sounded, and the noise made her jump. "Sorry. I don't recognize the number, but I'm answering it anyway. It could be about my parents. Hello?"

"Is this Kelly, the daughter of Daniel Ecklund?"

"It is. Who's this?"

"My name's Markus Pauley. I live in Napa Valley. Your parents and I had a meeting scheduled for this morning at ten-thirty. They didn't show up for it. I wanted to know if maybe you knew if they'd changed their minds."

"About what?"

"About their upcoming retirement. I'm a financial planner. I've been advising them for a few months now on what to do once they retire. That's how I had your number in their files."

"I don't understand. Mom and Dad are ten years away from retiring. I know because they discussed it when I was with them at Christmas. The plan was to work another ten years. What happened? Did you talk them into something?"

"No. No, it's nothing like that. They're gearing up for *when* they both retire."

"I see. All I know is my parents didn't stand you up on purpose. That much I do know. They left for Napa last night and no one's heard from them since yesterday. We're trying to find out what happened to them."

"Oh, wow. Keep me informed. Will you? Your mom and dad are a hoot. I'd planned to take them on a tour of wine country while they were here. Let me know what happens."

Kelly hung up in a mood. "I don't understand this at all. My parents never said a word about seeing a financial planner."

"Do you tell your parents everything?"

"Of course not."

"Then why should you expect them to tell you every little detail about their lives?"

"Good point."

"Buckle up. We're on final approach."

Kelly watched him at the controls, adjusting the flaps and slats. She could feel the aircraft slow down, hear the landing gear drop beneath them. When the plane descended out of the cloudy haze, she got her first look from the air at the sprawling capital of Sacramento.

Beckett set the plane down and cruised to the end of the tarmac, then headed toward a private hangar.

"That was very smooth," Kelly remarked once they were ready to open the door. "You are a good pilot. I never once felt afraid up there. And all that talking you did was a great idea. It kept my mind off my parents."

"That was the goal."

Within minutes of their arrival, Beckett's phone dinged with a text from Birk.

Pollock found the truck down an embankment using Luella's cell phone pings. The fire department is on the scene now, cutting the top off the truck's cab to reach them. According to firefighters, they're alive. Dehydrated but alive.

But before giving Kelly the news, Beckett needed more information, so he texted back, asking a series of questions for clarification.

Birk obliged, detailing everything he knew.

Beckett read the last of Birk's messages on their walk across the tarmac to the rental car kiosk. "Here's the deal. There's good news. Thanks to your mom's cell phone, the state patrol located your parents. They found the pickup and trailer thirty-five miles east of Sacramento. It seems your dad's truck plunged ten feet down a narrow canyon where it's been sitting out of sight in the brush for the past fifteen hours. When they crashed, the airbags deployed. Luella's cell phone apparently went flying out of reach, landing somewhere in the backseat of the crew cab. Neither one could get to it. They kept hearing it ring and ding with messages repeatedly but couldn't get out of their seat belts to answer. They were trapped inside the cab, unconscious for the first several hours from the impact. But don't worry. The paramedics say they're in good condition, considering the circumstances. They think your father suffered a few cracked ribs. Your mom has a knot on her head and some bruising. But they're okay. Rescuers had to cut the roof off to get them out. But they're free. They're on their way to the hospital now, which is where we're going."

Tears welled up in Kelly's eyes as she slumped against him. "Thank God they're alive. I was so scared. Thank you for getting the right people involved so fast. If not for you and Birk, I wouldn't have known what to do. I'd still be in the car driving up here. I'd probably be driving up and down that stretch of 50 going crazy."

He tilted her chin up. His arms went around her waist for support. Her hair smelled like sunshine and magnolias. "It's okay. I'm glad we could help."

Standing so close, the warmth between them inched up. Their eyes met. A brief moment of lust hit as Kelly stayed where she was. She didn't want to move, or the moment might end. Feeling the strength in his arms made for a yearning she hadn't felt in a long time. She wanted his mouth on hers.

He lowered his head before fitting his lips to hers. The kiss was an even slower fusing of taste until it deepened into a surge of pleasure.

The roar of a FedEx DC-10 taking off overhead broke the moment.

Beckett ran his fingers down her ponytail before stepping away, huffing a sigh. He turned on his heels, heading toward the row of available SUVs. "We'd better pick up the rental and get on the road."

Kelly trailed after him as he pointed to a white Chevrolet Tahoe. "That'll do. I love express membership."

She rolled her eyes and made a chopping slash through the air at the back of his head. Men. They could switch gears without so much as a backward glance. Going from a shared *hot* moment to babbling about a stupid SUV wasn't what she expected. Maybe she'd misread the signals. She slid into the front seat and decided if he could act as if it had never happened, then so could she. "Which hospital?"

"Mercy General." His demeanor was all business as he keyed in the destination on the GPS to get directions. "It's twenty minutes away, depending on traffic. We might even beat the EMTs there."

They got bogged down on 518 near the zoo and sat bumper to bumper with other rush-hour traffic wanting to get home. The delay meant they had to talk to each other.

Beckett was the first to speak. "What happened back there between us was a mistake. It shouldn't have happened. I would never take advantage of a vulnerable woman who let down her guard and is under stress."

"Oh, so now we're going to discuss it, are we? And call it a mistake? I thought maybe you'd stick to the benefits of express car rental."

"Hey, not every car rental experience is the same," Beckett cracked. "Trust me. When you travel, it pays to be a gold member, to get the best available ride. You'd be singing a different tune if we'd got stuck with a Mitsubishi, one of those economy jobs where you feel like a sardine crammed into a piece of metal. It's happened before."

"Listen to yourself going on and on about renting a car. Jeez. What happened between us was physical attraction. Lust. Plain and simple. For that brief moment, you wanted me and I wanted you. It's a natural occurrence between consenting adults, even without margaritas or mojitos."

"What I felt back there didn't seem plain or simple. And I haven't had tequila in quite some time."

"But what you felt was a mistake? Look, I get it. There's no reason to continue down this path. If you say it was a mistake, then fine. I can live with that."

Beckett narrowed his eyes on the road, staring at the car ahead of him. Why couldn't females be less complicated? Why did they always take things the wrong way? Why couldn't he have kept his trap shut?

The awkward silence hung in the car for the next half hour as they inched their way to the hospital.

Five

Beckett hated everything about hospitals probably because he'd woke up a time or two in one. The smells were always off-putting.

Walking past the entrance to the ER, Kelly noticed his reaction. "I don't like hospitals either."

His eyes cut to hers. "Ever been in one as a patient?"

"Yeah. A car accident when I was sixteen put me in Barton Memorial for overnight observation. You?"

"Shrapnel to the back from an IED blast," Beckett murmured as they walked up to the front desk and got in line. "That was the first time. The second was from a high-velocity round in the leg. Damn near bled to death."

Kelly's mouth gaped open. "You are a fascinating man. Promise me that you'll sit down for a drink one day and tell me how that happened."

"Sure. But it's no big secret. SEALS go after insurgents. We perceive targets and go after them. They often hide in remote mountains or tightly packed, hostile regions throughout a combat zone. One of our jobs was to help train whatever special forces exist locally. We usually make ourselves known to the area tribal chiefs, gather the resistance, then take them on live missions. It's the best way for them to learn how to fight. So there are ample opportunities to take on small arms fire. And that's not even counting all the times your helicopter might get shot down."

Kelly stared at him. "How long were you in the hospital?"

"The first time I stayed a week, piece of cake. The second was about a month if you count PT. Physical therapy. I don't walk with a limp, though, so there's that. After the second incident, that's when I went into training stateside."

"Incident? More like a life-threatening event," Kelly corrected right before it was her turn to speak to the admin behind the glass. "Paramedics brought in my parents. Truck accident. Ecklund. E-c-k-l-u-n-d. Daniel and Luella."

The employee looked up the name on the computer. "You'll need to take a seat. Your parents are in separate treatment rooms. I'll let the doctors know that family is here. He'll be out soon to give you an update."

"There's no way I can see them now?"

"You'll have to wait."

Kelly traded looks with Beckett. "So much for hurrying through town. You think it's like the movies where you simply rush through the ER door and the staff lets you right into the room to stand by the bedside."

Beckett chuckled, looking around the waiting room. "If only. There must be twenty people here waiting for word on a family member."

"You don't have to stick around. You can take the rental car and head back to the airport if you want."

"And leave you here? How will you get back?"

"I'll figure something out. There's always Lyft or Uber. Depending on how my mom and dad are, I need to get my equipment out of my apartment while I'm up this way."

"Where is this equipment?"

"Hayward. I borrowed some of it from school. But the rest is from the stuff I've collected over the years, used sonar, calibrators, meters, that sort of thing. The baby sea kelp and eelgrass are scheduled for delivery on Wednesday of next week at the rental house. It'll work itself out. Everything will be fine with some organization."

"Are you trying to convince you or me? You use sonar in your work?"

"Sure. Why?"

"No reason. I just realized that maybe I don't know what it is you do. Exactly."

"I have tools for measuring water temperature, acidity levels, and PH balances. I always use my sonar to check the ocean before diving into the water."

"That makes sense. When the time comes, I'd like to help you do that kelp planting thing, even if it's not a plant."

"Really? Okay. That would be awesome. Not many people realize it, but seaweed accounts for fifty percent of the world's oxygen."

"I don't know what's wrong with those students of yours, but you make me want to crack open a textbook."

"That's sweet of you to say."

A doctor in green garb called out, "Who's here for the Ecklunds?"

Kelly cleared her throat. "That's me. Us. They're my parents. How are they?"

"Under the circumstances, they're both doing remarkably well. Your father sustained several bruises to his ribcage from the airbag. No broken bones, though. X-rays confirmed that. Your mother hit her head on the side window glass. It's a miracle she doesn't have a concussion. It could've been a lot worse. We're giving them IVs to hydrate. And due to their ages, we'd like to keep them under observation for the remainder of the day."

"Does that mean they can go home later this evening?"

"It does if everything remains stable over the next few hours."

"Great news. Can I see them now?"

"Sure. We're putting them in the same room for as long as they're here. Let them get settled first. Then the nurse will come and get you."

Kelly exchanged an exasperated look with Beckett. "I'm serious. You should go ahead and get back home—after you meet my parents first. Who knows how long you'll need to hang around for that? I want them to meet the person responsible for saving them."

"I didn't find them," Beckett pointed out.

"Sure you did. You called the right people."

Before debating about it, a nurse approached them and led the way down a corridor.

Kelly stepped into the room to see her mom stretched out on one bed while her dad was asleep in another. They looked battered and pale, their faces swollen. An oxygen tube helped them breathe while a machine registered their vital signs. Because her dad had dozed off, she went over to her mother and hugged her. "Mom, I'm so glad you're okay."

"Oh, Kelly, it was horrible. Your father drove off the road to avoid hitting a deer. It happened so fast. We went straight over the side in the dark. The truck's totaled."

"Don't worry about that now. Just focus on getting better. We can always replace the pickup and trailer. I brought someone I want you to meet. Beckett Callahan. He's the owner of a Search and Recovery outfit. He's the one who alerted the Highway Patrol to where you might be. He's the reason we found you."

"It was a joint effort," Beckett explained, moving closer to the other side of the bed. "Nice to meet you, Mrs. Ecklund. Your daughter made us aware of the situation this morning. I'm glad we could help."

Tears welled up in Luella's puffy eyes. "Call me Luella. I'm afraid we realized rather quickly that Kelly would need to get worried about us before anyone found us. We were that deep into the ravine. And it wasn't even daylight yet. This morning I woke up in the dark. I saw that your father was still out cold. Or asleep, I couldn't tell. I couldn't even reach across to help him. I couldn't get to my cell phone. I kept hearing it ring and ding, but I couldn't reach it. I was so scared and worried. Thank God you found us when you did."

Beckett squeezed the woman's hand. "You just rest yourself. Take it easy. You'll be back home before you know it."

Kelly's gaze went from her mom to Beckett. Her heart felt as though it flipped in her chest. He was so kind. Had she ever known anyone like him before? She didn't think so.

In the next bed, her dad tried to sit up. "Kelly?"

"Dad." She closed the distance and wrapped her arms around him gingerly at first, then squeezed a little harder. "I'm so glad you're okay."

"Me too. There for a while, I thought your mother and me might be goners for sure."

"And you worry about my driving," Kelly teased before turning to Beckett again. "Dad, I'd like you to meet Beckett Callahan. He's the one who put your Search and Rescue into motion."

"Good to meet you, Mr. Ecklund."

Dan extended his right arm in an awkward attempt to shake Beckett's hand. "None of that Mr. Ecklund stuff. Call me Dan. We're grateful for your help."

"I'm just glad it turned out this way."

"So am I," Dan said with a chuckle. "I'm sorry we didn't make it to Hayward to pick up Kelly's stuff. Give me time to get my truck replaced, and I'll get your equipment to you.

"Stop that. Don't worry about me," Kelly admonished. "You're heading straight home after leaving here and taking it easy. That's an order. You both are lucky to be alive. You were taking the rest of the week off anyway. So now take the time to recoup. Get well. Keep those ribs from cracking."

"How will you manage?" Dan muttered.

"Seriously? When the time comes, I'll rent one of those U-Haul trailers. Now, please stop worrying about me. I'm a grown woman who can take care of myself. I've been doing it for years now. I'm worried about you guys."

From the other bed, Luella lifted her head. "Call one of your aunts. LeeAnn's closest. She'll see to it we get home tonight."

"I'm here to do that," Kelly protested. "I came all this way. Beckett even flew me over here in a corporate jet to help you guys."

"We'll get you back to Lake Tahoe, get you settled before we take off," Beckett promised.

Luella waved off that suggestion. "No need to disrupt your plans when LeeAnn can do it. All my sisters live within driving distance. But LeeAnn lives just five miles from us. As soon as she finds out we're here, she'll be here anyway."

"Are you serious? I don't believe you guys," Kelly reiterated. "I'm standing right here, ready and willing to help."

"But you have things to do," Luella stated. "You need that equipment down in Pelican Pointe. Looks to me like you have this big strong guy willing to assist. For once, let him. You want to land that job at the Coastal Trust, don't you? Then don't waste a minute of your summer messing around with us."

"Mom—"

"Colleen, do not argue with your battered mother," Dan cautioned. "She's been through enough."

"You guys don't even have transportation," Kelly pointed out. "Besides, I'm here now. Aunt LeeAnn isn't. My stuff isn't going anywhere. It can wait until next week when I'm in the house."

Luella laid a hand on her aching head and looked at Beckett. "Arguing with her will give you a headache every time."

"Tell me about it."

Luella's lips bowed up. "She gets that stubborn streak from her father. Me? I'm as agreeable as a baby kitten."

"More like a baby lioness," Kelly fired back. "I'm not sure why you're so opposed to my help. By the way, some guy named Markus Pauley called from Napa, checking up on you guys."

"That sounds like Markus," Dan stated. "Did you tell him what happened?"

"I didn't know what happened when he called. Mom talked like the guy was an old friend. Instead, he described himself as your financial planner."

"He planned to take me fishing," Dan said. "I'm taking him on a tour of Tahoe National Forest."

"We planned on taking a tour of the wine country," Luella corrected. "Markus is setting up our retirement accounts."

Kelly made a mental note to check the guy out before they had time to make any more financial decisions. "How long have you known Mr. Pauley?"

"He came highly recommended by one of our coworkers. There are about ten of us who decided to use him to set up our retirement accounts."

For some reason, Kelly didn't like the sound of that. Before she could ask anything else, though, her aunt, LeeAnn Sullivan, breezed into the room.

"I saw you guys rescued on the news," LeeAnn reported. "I texted everybody to watch while they hauled your truck out of that ravine with a crane. How on earth did you manage to run off the road like that?"

"Hello to you, too," Kelly uttered.

"Hey, sweetie, how are you?" A bubbly forty-something, LeeAnn, wrapped her niece in a hug. But soon, her attention turned to Beckett. "And who is this?"

Kelly made the introductions, embarrassment washing over her. But Beckett seemed to take the antics in stride. He cracked jokes with the aunt and made fast friends with the parents while keeping the families' theatrics from taking over. She wasn't quite sure how he managed it.

The nurse on duty wasn't happy to see so many visitors in the room. "Somebody has to clear out."

LeeAnn looked at Kelly. "You go. I'll see that they get home and get settled. I've made all the relatives aware they'll need looking after over the next couple of days. We've got it covered. With all our kin, there's no short supply of help."

"Fine. I give up," Kelly replied. "Beckett and I will head back to Pelican Pointe."

"We're an hour and a half away from Hayward," Beckett pointed out. "I might as well help you with your equipment. Will your stuff fit in the back of the SUV if we put the seats down?"

"But what about the plane?"

"We'll load up in Hayward and circle back to the airport."

"That sounds like a lot of unnecessary traveling. I appreciate the offer. I do, but how about letting me figure something out for next week. I need to get into the house first. The innkeeper's great, but I doubt she'd want me hauling a bunch of stuff into my room upstairs. Think about it. I have a lot of equipment. Besides, I don't want to move it twice."

"Are you sure? It's no trouble."

Kelly shook her head. "Believe me, it's trouble. The only reason my parents were picking up my stuff is because I'd booked them a stay at the B&B." She turned back to her mother. "The offer still stands when you feel like traveling."

"We appreciate it, but after this ordeal, I think I want to sleep in my own bed for the next dozen years or so. I may never leave the Tahoe area again."

"Okay. Let me know if you change your mind." She said her goodbyes and walked out of the hospital two hours after they'd arrived.

"Sorry about that thing with my family. Sometimes, they can get a little bit crazy and a whole lot weird," Kelly explained once they walked outside. "Today was apparently one of those times. They seemed more upbeat about getting into a car accident than I expected. They downplayed the whole thing."

"Maybe they didn't want you to worry," Beckett reasoned.

"Maybe. But it seemed weird that Mom wanted her sisters there instead of me."

"How many sisters does she have?"

"Five. One lives in Reno. The rest live in the Tahoe area."

"In a case like that, I don't think it's all that weird for her to depend on her sisters to step up. Besides, your mother seemed concerned about you landing this other job."

"Coastal Blue Trust. I doubt that happens. I've applied to them several times before, and they've always found a reason not to hire me. I'm not sure why I keep chasing after that dream. Come fall, I'll probably end up back at Redwood State."

"Would that be such a bad thing?"

Kelly lifted a shoulder. "No. It's a job."

"I wouldn't worry too much about the family dynamics. As I said, families can be weird. You've met Birk."

Kelly found that funny. "At least Birk makes sense. Here I thought I'd be helping them get back home. Instead, they're sending me on my way. How weird is that? How weird is this thing with the financial planner? Should I be worried about this guy?"

"You should definitely check him out, find out if he's legit. Are you sure you don't want to get your stuff while we're this close?"

"Positive. The solution is simple. As soon as I get the keys to the house, I'll unload my truck—making more room for my equipment—then head back up to my apartment to grab my stuff. It's not a big deal. Do you know anyone who wants a free three-day stay at the B&B? It's already paid for."

"I'm sure Jordan will refund the money."

"You think so?"

For the first time today, Beckett realized Scott's warning about Kelly needing help had been dead-on. "Do you believe in ghosts?"

"Talk about a segue. Um, I'd have to say not really. I consider myself open-minded, but I'm not sure I'm that flexible regarding the paranormal. Why?"

"It's a long story."

Kelly glanced at her watch. "I'm not going anywhere. You're my ride back to Pelican Pointe. Might as well entertain me."

Six

It was dusk by the time Beckett landed back in Santa Cruz. They'd watched a beautiful sunset over the ocean before touching down. But it wasn't the romance of a full moon rising that had the most significant impact. Discussing a ghost with a skeptic proved a powerful way to get to know someone.

"Wait a minute. You're saying that this guy keeps showing up at your house, popping in and out, and you have an actual conversation with him?"

"Don't look at me like that. Scott Phillips haunts the entire town. If you don't believe me, ask around. Ask Jordan. The man was her first husband."

"Oh, my God. You're talking about the guy in the photo in my room—the National Guard soldier who lost his life in Iraq. That's your ghost?"

"It's not just me. Everyone who's been in town for any length of time has encountered Scott Phillips."

"Interesting. You're talking about the entire town experiencing multiple sightings of the same man who died so long ago?"

"That sums it up. Scott showed up last night and said you were in trouble. I drove out to the B&B to see if you were okay."

Kelly's mouth gaped open. "I've never had anyone do that except maybe my parents. That's why you looked so tired. You were worried about me. And in your mind, all this happening today confirms what this spirit guide said to you."

"How do you ignore a warning like that when it comes to pass?"

"Beats me. I've never had an up-close personal encounter with a spirit guide before. Although, it's prevalent in Native American culture. I will say the first time I saw the guy's picture on the wall, his face seemed eerily familiar."

"Stick around here long enough, and you'll get the chance to talk to him yourself."

Kelly wasn't convinced but realized there was no changing Beckett's mind.

Before they started on the trip back to Pelican Pointe, Beckett decided on the spur of the moment to drive by Brigid's last known hangout before she disappeared. The bar known as Clever Pete's had taken up a corner in the downtown section near the infamous boardwalk. But the place no longer existed. It had gone out of business two years earlier and was now a boarded-up reminder of Brigid's last night out.

It still held special significance for Beckett. "Talk about haunted places. Clever Pete's is it for me. It angers me every time I see that place. How could her friends just let her leave like that without going with her?"

Surprised that he'd chosen to talk about his sister, Kelly took advantage of his mood. "Since learning about her disappearance, I admit I've had questions along that line. Did you track her mobile phone?"

From behind the wheel, Beckett took his eyes off the road long enough to send her an incredulous look. "Of course we did. The last known ping was a place known as Shark Fin Cove, a remote, secluded spot with a rock that looks like a shark fin, hence the name. It has this spooky old mining tunnel nearby that quite frankly gives me the creeps. The day we got that information, Birk and I spent twelve hours searching that tunnel, then went back again the next day and searched another twelve hours. We never found a damn thing."

"I'm familiar with Shark Fin Cove. I've been there before taking samples."

"Where haven't you been taking samples?" Beckett commented, cracking a grin. "There were several issues with Brigid's case we had to overcome." He ticked off the problems. "We didn't have her phone or her purse. At first, we didn't have her passwords to any of her social media accounts. That was a roadblock for weeks. By the time we finally cracked the code and got access, the cops told us to back off. Three months went by, which to us meant the cops were part of the problem. During that time, they shared zero information with the family. Still don't. Plus, they had a theory. They kept repeating how she'd had too much to drink that night—in other words, drunk—and she'd gotten lost in an unfamiliar neighborhood, which is total BS. Brigid had lived in Santa Cruz for two years. She knew every retail outlet, every corner of that place, every popular hangout, including the touristy beaches."

Something about the wording the cops used bothered Kelly. "Unfamiliar neighborhood? Since when does anyone refer to Shark Fin Cove as a neighborhood? That wouldn't be how I'd describe its remoteness to town because it's not easy to find. I doubt you could hike up the steep trail to get there if you were intoxicated. I know I couldn't do it. And I'm a lightweight when it comes to drinking but a very experienced hiker. Why would your sister leave a bar and go there at night anyway by herself? She must've been with someone else who had transportation. How else would she get from downtown Santa Cruz to Shark Fin Cove? That's roughly ten miles."

"Exactly. Over rugged terrain. That's what we thought. But the cops had a different take. They said she probably wandered along the road by herself until she somehow reached the cove. A CCTV camera picked her up around midnight in the parking lot of a burger joint walking southbound."

"But the cove is in the opposite direction. It's north of Santa Cruz. And just because she appeared to be alone doesn't mean that she was."

"Try using that logic with the police," Beckett muttered. "They'll laugh in your face."

Kelly chewed the inside of her jaw. "Then there's the other scenario. Someone could've snatched her off the street and taken her to that remote location with sinister intentions."

"As a family, we believed Brigid met with foul play, that someone did something to her. But the cops decided that she walked that far by herself, then fell into the water and got swept out to sea. I kid you not. That's what they decided. The riptides in that area make it difficult to surf or swim. Without a shred of evidence to the contrary, it was hard to argue with their logic. However, I don't think Brigid would be that stupid even if she were three sheets to the wind."

"It must be maddening to go through that experience. It's hard to believe a person could simply vanish without a trace."

"Happens every day. Are you hungry?"

"Starving."

"What about sharing a pizza once we hit town?"

"Sounds like a plan."

"We'll take the pie back to my place. If that's okay."

"I just need to get my truck. I don't want any of the neighbors having it towed."

Beckett let out a laugh. "I think you'll find the people in Pelican Pointe friendlier than that. By now, word has gotten out that you're renting the house. They know what truck you drive. And why you're here. They probably know what happened to your parents today."

"I only told one person."

"Think about that for a minute. That's not true. You phoned Jordan. Sure. But Birk knew. Paula Bretton at the coffee shop probably got wind of it. She overheard us talking. When people pick up their caffeine fix, you're the newest interesting info to pass along."

"Jeez. Really? Paula didn't strike me as the nosy busybody type."

"Most everyone gets caught up in everybody else's business. Case in point, did you know Paula's been seeing the guy who runs the T-shirt shop?"

"I don't know who that is," Kelly admitted. "Newcomer here. I'm familiar with the souvenir shop, though."

"His name's Malachi Rafferty. His band plays every weekend at The Shipwreck."

"So now it's your turn to show me how it works—the gossip mill?"

"For better or worse, it's the way of small towns. I need to call Birk and let him know I'm back. He can bring Brodie home, or I can stop by and pick him up. We'll swing by and get your truck. You follow me over to Birk's house before we pick up the pizza, then on to home." Getting it all worked out in his head, he grabbed his cell phone, punched in his brother's number, and left a message when there was no answer.

"Should we call in the order so the pizza will be ready by the time we get there?"

"Sure." He handed her the phone. "Order what you like. I'm flexible as long as it has pepperoni as the base."

She snickered with laughter. "I can live with that."

"So you're not a vegetarian?"

"Nope. I am a vegetable lover, though. But who doesn't love a good pepperoni pizza?"

"Along with Dungeness crab and shrimp cocktail," he added.

"So you were listening?"

"Every word. You were using your professor's voice when you lectured me on the benefits of kelp forestation."

"I was not lecturing you in my professor's voice," Kelly insisted. "I was simply stating the problem in a clear and concise manner."

"You were lecturing," Beckett repeated, handing her his phone. "Order some of those cheesy breadsticks while you're at it, will you?"

"Sure. Who doesn't love cheesy sticks?"

Beckett slowed his speed as they passed the city limits sign. "Three stops to make before we eat. Do you have a dog back in Hayward?"

"No. I miss having one around, though. I love dogs, grew up with one until he succumbed to old age the way Quake did at the B&B. One day, maybe, I'll get another."

"When you get ready for one, I know a place. The town vet started a shelter for all the strays in the area. The current number sits around twenty at the moment. But the number climbs every day. Every one of them could use a good home."

"I rent, remember? And I'm only here for the summer," Kelly reminded him. When she saw an opportunity to change the subject, she pointed down the road to Athena Circle. "Don't forget I need my truck."

He veered toward the bungalow, noting its spruced-up look. "Looks like Ryder and his crew are putting the finishing touches on the place. I bet you'll get the keys no later than Tuesday."

"Let's hope. I'm excited about moving in. Lead the way to Birk's," she said as she hopped out of his pickup.

"Birk hasn't acknowledged my voicemail yet. Let's grab the pizza and eat first."

"Fine by me."

Kelly got her first look at Beckett's home on Sandy Pointe half an hour later. The place seemed like a throwback to a classic style found deep in the Tuscan wine country. It wasn't the apricot stucco finish that gave it that Mediterranean vibe, but the arched windows and the limestone courtyard. It made her think she had arrived at an Italian villa.

"Where's the vineyard?" Kelly asked in mock praise.

Beckett let out a laugh. "That was my first thought, too. The only vineyard in the area is the one Caleb and Hannah run—Dancing in the Moonlight Vineyard. This house has a nice backyard but the only thing growing out there at the moment is a couple of olive trees still in a bucket on the patio."

Kelly sputtered with laughter. "My kind of gardener. I saw a bottle of wine with that label at Murphy's Market, touting a locally grown connection. Is the stuff any good?"

"How about if I open a bottle and you can tell me. I've had it on hand since Christmas." He didn't mention that the reporter had given it to him as a gift.

"When it comes to wine, I don't mind being the guinea pig," Kelly joked, glancing around at the sparsely furnished living room. "How long have you lived here?"

"Almost three years. I rented from Logan before buying. Why?"

She grinned and followed him into the kitchen. "Looks like my first apartment off-campus. You're missing a few key pieces of furniture, aren't you? Where's the sofa? I see side chairs but no couch."

"I put all my money into a king bed and a big-screen TV, then outfitted my office," Beckett explained. "I'll give you the tour after we eat."

He found the bottle of merlot in the back of the pantry. "Maybe it's supposed to be served chilled."

"Not much of a wine connoisseur, huh? I'm sure it's fine served at room temperature. I'm not picky. I've been known to drink Chablis out of a box."

Beckett began to work the cork out of the bottle. "Word around town has it that this wine is made from some special kind of grape, not seen since the 1930s."

Kelly flipped the lid up on the pizza box, scanned the slices, and scooped one up. "Okay, I'll bite. What makes a grape special?"

"It hasn't been around for decades. But the infamous Scott Phillips somehow managed to get his hands on a vine and sent it to Caleb and Hannah to start their vineyard."

Kelly's eyes danced with mischief as she plopped into one of the chairs at the kitchen island. "When the man was alive?"

"Nope. Years after he died."

"Somehow, I knew you were going to say that." Intrigued but unconvinced, Kelly grimaced at people believing anything so outlandish. "You're suggesting this ghost somehow found this illusive vine and sent it to the couple who just happen to have a place to grow it? That's some powerful ghost?"

"That's the folklore around here. Hannah insisted the story be included on their website. It's also up on the wall in the tasting room at the winery."

"Maybe there's something in the local water that promotes this kind of hysteria. It's a fascinating story for anyone interested in the paranormal. I'm surprised Pelican Pointe hasn't appeared on one of those reality ghost-hunting shows."

"How do you explain that Scott knew you'd need my help before you did?"

She opened the box containing the breadsticks and the marinara sauce, dragged a piece of cheesy bread through the sauce, and took a bite. "Look, I'm not an expert on ghosts. I don't know how that works. I'd need to study the data if there is any. I know there are two camps—one believes ghosts are for real, and one believes it's a bunch of hooey. There's usually no middle ground."

"Ever had an encounter with one?"

"Not that I remember." She kept munching on the breadsticks but frowned.

"What?" Beckett asked. "Did you think of something?"

"Well, I did have this one weird incident that happened at an aquaculture convention held at UC Santa Cruz a couple of years back. It freaked me out. I'd gone there to hear this speaker give his take on shallow water cultivation, specifically regarding seagrass and how to maintain the acid levels to get the best yield. Anyway, after the lecture, I was on my way back to the hotel. I had to cross this bridge to catch the shuttle in the parking lot. It was the first week of December, so it had already gotten dark outside."

Beckett's gut twisted at the notion she'd been in harm's way and alone. "Are you about to tell me someone followed you?"

"From the Sciences Building. Yeah. I didn't think much about it until I realized I was the only person around. I made it to this spooky bridge. Picture a foggy December night in central California and walking across this bridge in the dark."

"Let me guess. After the lecture, you'd hung back later than everyone else so you could ask follow-up questions?"

Kelly gave him a sheepish look. "Well, of course. I'd paid for the lecture out of my own pocket, so I wanted to get my money's worth. I'd walked about twenty yards from the building when I realized this dude kept getting closer and closer to me. I reached the bridge, and that's when the guy made his move. It happened fast. The guy reached out to try and grab me, and that's when this other man popped out of nowhere like he jumped out of the bushes or something. But remember, we're on a bridge, so there are no bushes. He sort of tackles this weird guy. The man who followed me suddenly fell down onto the wood, muttering something like, 'what the hell was that?' Whatever *it* was, it was enough to scare him off. The guy took off running, I mean, as fast as he could run to the other side of the bridge. I turned to thank the other guy who'd come to my rescue. But he wasn't there. One minute this guy is right beside me, and in the flash of a few seconds, he'd disappeared."

"Why do you remember this incident so vividly?"

"Two reasons. One, I almost got mugged or worse. And two, the guy who came to my rescue was dressed for the beach, not a chilly December evening."

Beckett felt his gut tighten. "Could I hazard a guess as to what he had on? The man who saved you?"

Kelly let out a sigh. "I see where you're going with this. But it's ridiculous to think like that. This was Santa Cruz, not Pelican Pointe. And just because the guy didn't hang around for a 'thank you' doesn't mean squat. He could've been late for a meeting."

Beckett smiled. "He wore a pair of khaki shorts in December, no jacket, but had on a light blue Oxford button-down shirt with the sleeves rolled up to the elbows. A yellow T-shirt underneath said, 'The surf's better in Pelican Pointe.' Am I right?"

"I don't remember what the yellow tee said."

"So it was yellow?"

"I think so. That doesn't mean—"

The doorbell broke up the disagreement.

"That's probably Birk with Brodie," he said, strolling to the front door.

A few minutes later, the jumping attack dog appeared in the kitchen doorway. Brodie spotted a visitor. The retriever bumped around chairs, tail wagging until he reached Kelly.

"I smell like pizza, and you smell like you just had a bath."

"That's because he has," Birk grumbled. "Took him for a walk on the beach, and the next thing I see is Brodie chasing a bunch of plovers all over the sand before jumping into the freaking water. He smelled like fish, so I had to hose him down."

Beckett slapped his brother on the back. "Thanks, man. Now I don't have to shower him off."

"You owe me," Birk grunted, eyeing the pizza. "Got enough for three?"

Kelly pushed the box toward Birk. "Sure. Help yourself. I filled up on cheesy bread. Beckett and I were just discussing Scott the Ghost."

Birk plopped down on one of the other stools. "And you think he's living in the *Twilight Zone*?"

"Something like that. Have you ever seen him? Scott?"

"Scott is everywhere in this town. Wait long enough, and you'll see him, too." Birk eyed her reaction before bursting out in laughter. "The look on your face is priceless. You have a lot to learn about Pelican Pointe. This town was a wide spot in the road until Scott Phillips came back here to live in that house on the cliffs."

"The B&B?"

"Yep. The story goes that Scott inherited the house from his grandparents. When he married Jordan, he brought her here to live with the idea of turning it into a B&B so that he could spend more time with his family. But then, the Iraq War happened. Scott left to serve with his unit in the National Guard, leaving Jordan behind, pregnant with their first child. Scott died in Iraq. He didn't make it back. But his spirit lives on throughout Pelican Pointe. That's the short version."

"That's a nice story," Kelly remarked. "Maybe he's not dead."

"Very difficult to fake your death in a war zone with two dozen witnesses who saw the Hummer blow up from an IED blast," Birk offered. "There are too many variables that click into place."

"We're all not crazy," Beckett injected. "Everyone in town seems to have a Scott story to tell. Besides, I could take you out to the cemetery to see Scott's headstone." He angled toward Birk. "Should we tell her how we were so skeptical after arriving in town that we hacked into Scott's military records?"

"I wouldn't mention that to too many people outside this room," Birk cautioned with a sly grin. "It might get back to the wrong people."

"I'm not telling anyone anything," Kelly vowed. "I owe you both a debt of gratitude for how you handled finding my parents. I'm not in the habit of turning on my friends. Thanks again for what you did. If not for you, my parents might still be hanging upside down in the cab of a truck they couldn't escape." She could see that declaration made both men uncomfortable, but she didn't care. "If you ever need anything from me, just ask."

Kelly glanced at her phone to check the time and got to her feet, causing Brodie to give her a sorrowful look. "I need to go. It's been a long, stress-filled day. I'm running on fumes here. Thanks for the pizza."

"My pleasure. I'll walk you out," Beckett said. "Does Jordan expect you back tonight?"

"I texted her before we picked up the pizza. All I want now is a hot shower and maybe sleep for the next twelve hours."

"You're heading into Scott country," Beckett warned as he opened the front door and stepped out into the courtyard.

Kelly grinned. "Sounds like I've been in Scott country since I got here." She leaned in and planted a kiss on his cheek. Her eyes lingered on his face. "You take care."

"You too," he managed to say as he watched her get into her pickup.

Birk came up behind him. "I haven't seen you this smitten since Carrie Davenport gave you a series of hickeys in the backseat of her cherry-red Mustang."

Beckett waved Kelly off before cutting his eyes to his brother. "I'm not sure why but I feel a connection to her."

"We're not talking about Carrie."

"No," Beckett spat out. "Kelly and I have almost nothing in common. A professor of biology who doesn't enjoy teaching yet seems good at it wants to spend her summer watching kelp beds grow."

"And you want to spend your summer watching Kelly watch kelp beds grow."

"When you put it that way, it sounds pathetic."

"It wouldn't be the first time," Birk levied. "The Scott thing clearly threw her logical mind into overload."

"It did, didn't it? I wouldn't mind seeing her face the second time she spots Scott and realizes he was that same guy in Santa Cruz. Why hasn't he appeared to her like he has other guests at the B&B?"

"Give it time. She's barely been here twenty-four hours." Birk frowned. "Wait. What guy in Santa Cruz?"

"Come on back inside and finish your pizza while I wow you with an unbelievable tale from two years back."

While they rehashed Kelly's encounter with a mugger, she drove the road back to Promise Cove in a lighthearted mood.

She had received a text from her Aunt LeeAnn saying her parents were back home safe and tucked in for the night. It sounded like her aunts were on top of things. She felt like a weight had lifted.

With the window rolled down on the truck, she breathed in the crisp ocean air. For the first time all day, it wasn't her parents who occupied her brain. No, a worry nagged at her regarding Beckett Callahan. She liked the guy and enjoyed his company. They could easily have a summer fling without hurting anyone, keep things casual, and move on when their time together ended.

But was it what she wanted?

Kelly pulled her truck into the long driveway and cut the engine. She had a feeling Beckett liked to keep things at a distance, especially his women. She'd caught a glimpse of the card attached to the wine bottle he'd opened earlier. Some woman named Kimberly had written the sentiments about a relationship they'd had around Christmastime. Hadn't the blond reporter's name at the beach been Kimberly?

"That's over," Scott said from the passenger seat. "Their relationship started after he did an interview with Kimberly between Thanksgiving and Christmas last year. It didn't last long."

Kelly sucked in a breath and cut her eyes across the bench seat. The man sitting next to her appeared as real as he'd been that night in Santa Cruz. Speechless, she stared for several long seconds. "You're not real. I'm imagining this. It's all in my head. The power of suggestion has me seeing you, but you aren't really sitting here."

"Keep telling yourself that. And yet, I'm talking to you. Ask me something. Go ahead."

"Hold on. I'm still trying to get my brain to engage. It was you that night on the bridge in Santa Cruz."

"Yeah. That was me. I usually don't leave Pelican Pointe, but River Amandez gave a lecture that night about the Chumash Museum she heads. River is Brent Cody's wife. I felt like I should be there to hear what she had to say. I love history, especially how this area started out thousands of years ago. Anyway, I was there for River. But then, after the lecture, I spotted that jerk on the bridge."

"I see. So there are times when you leave your comfort zone?"

"This isn't about me. When you think about the world in general, it seems it's this huge unconnected blob of space. But it's not at all. Human beings invariably connect with others. You like theories. Try the six degrees of separation. The world isn't that big after all. See, you had a connection to Pelican Pointe two years ago and didn't even know it."

"I don't believe in ghosts," Kelly stated.

"That's a shame because here I am. Are you hallucinating? I doubt it. You drove from town out here without any signs of delusion. I allowed you to get to your destination before speaking up."

"That's very considerate of you."

"I thought so."

"What do you want?"

"Ah. There's always that question. Did you ever think you might be all wrong to work in research?"

"I'm all wrong for academia. That's why I want to do research," she pointed out.

"You do excel at research. Although it might not be the kind you originally thought you'd do."

"What other kinds of research are there?"

"You'll figure that out for yourself. Eventually. I know you think you're saving the world's food source by replanting the kelp beds. But there are other more pressing ways to help civilization thrive. Improve the soil. Develop better drought-resistant crops. The list is endless."

Panic trickled down her spine. "You're suggesting I change my research at this late date?"

Scott smiled. "I want you to consider a new outlook, new possibilities, and maybe other ways you could help people. Consider branching out. Is that such a strange idea?"

"It is when I'm thirty, and I've been doing this same thing for years now. Why do I have to change? I like what I do."

"There's no need to fear doing something different. Change is part of life. Broaden your horizons. That's all I'm suggesting."

"That's easy for you to say." Kelly's head felt like a mallet was at work inside her brain. "Look, I've had the most exhausting twenty-four hours ever. My head feels like it's about to explode."

"Give it time with Beckett," Scott said before pointing to the front porch. "Jordan heard your truck drive up. She'll be opening the front door any minute now."

Sure enough, Kelly watched Scott evaporate, then two seconds later, Jordan stepped out onto the wraparound porch.

"Are you okay?"

Kelly grabbed her backpack and got out. "This is a very bizarre place."

Realization hit Jordan. "Who were you talking to just now? I heard voices."

"Figures. I questioned whether Scott existed today. I guess he had to put in an appearance to make a believer out of me."

"I'm sorry if he scared you."

"Oh, no. I'm used to ghosts popping in and out then telling me how my life's work has been wrong up to now."

"Scott said that?"

"Oh, yeah. Your Scott isn't shy about putting in his two cents, even if no one asked his opinion." With that said, Kelly stormed off into the house.

Seven

After finally picking up the keys to the rental late Monday afternoon, Kelly got her first look at the renovated space. It didn't disappoint. They'd used recycled lumber—Tuscan maple—to refurbish the hardwood floors.

As she walked from room to room, the walls popped with color—from pale blue to sea green and trimmed in soft white—the ocean theme was a cheery, soothing break from the bland apartments she'd called home for so many years.

The place was so not what she'd expected that she felt like she'd scored a major rental coup. With all the homes she could've rented, this one seemed ten times nicer than all the rest.

That first night she spent organizing the beach house into her summer home. As she went about unloading her truck, she left the doors open to air it out from the smell of fresh paint and new flooring.

She had to rearrange the furniture to accommodate the stuff she'd brought with her, deeming the second bedroom her office. There were laptops to boot up, books to unpack, and equipment to get working.

It didn't take long to fill up the two-bedroom, nine-hundred-square-foot cottage that came fully furnished with the bare essentials—a sofa, a small kitchen table and two chairs, a full-sized bed, a washer and dryer unit in the bathroom, and a massive bookcase with lots of shelving.

The décor leaned toward mid-century modern—another term for thrift store finds. That was fine by Kelly. She liked vintage. And every piece of furniture made a statement.

She especially liked the couch, upholstered in a bold but delightful teal color, just the right size for the modest living room. The little kitchen had white cottage cupboards with glass doors and scant drawer space. But, as promised, a brand-new Smeg refrigerator with a bottom freezer sparkled in the corner, stunning in pastel green. On the opposite wall, the cutest café table in walnut continued the mid-century modern look with two upholstered mustard yellow chairs.

In her mind, the only thing the place needed was a few little touches here and there to make the house feel like a home.

The landlord had bought a brand-new mattress. But she didn't have the proper size sheets for the bed, so she ended up going shopping for new sheets and a comforter. She spent an entire evening exploring the shops in town.

After picking up a set of indigo dishes and coffee mugs at the thrift store, she moved from shop to shop, ending up at a garden center called The Plant Habitat. She perused the aisles, selecting six of the hardiest houseplants she found on sale—an assortment of sansevierias, a ZZ plant, a couple of dracaenas, and a basket filled with golden daffodils. Nothing made a house feel more like a home than greenery and colorful flowers.

Kelly's last stop of the day was to buy groceries. At Murphy's Market, she stocked up on a list of inexpensive things to eat like ramen noodles, peanut butter, and plenty of mac and cheese. Since her grad school days, she had budgeting her money down to a fine art.

On her first night there, she convinced herself that Scott would surely make an appearance and they could finish their conversation. But the ghost stayed away.

The next day she drove back to Hayward for the rest of her equipment and finalized the deal on subletting her apartment to a co-worker's mom in town to visit her daughter for the summer. Renting out her unit hadn't been part of the plan. But it made sense financially and might stretch her money further.

The out-of-state lab had come through for her, sending a batch of sunflower sea stars bred in captivity. Before bringing kelp into the equation, she would release the starfish into the marsh, hoping they would dine on the purple sea urchins destroying the kelp.

On the heels of that delivery, UPS dropped off several storage containers filled with her Macrocystis pyrifera. She used the back deck to store the shipments of sea stars and the kelp without taking up space in the house. Hoping to keep everything out of harsh sunlight and thus keep it alive, she used a tarp she found in a storage shed at the side of the house to protect the delicate invertebrates until she could deposit them into the ocean.

Although she stayed busy getting things set up, by the fourth evening, she realized how lonely she felt. She had no one to talk to. Beckett had left town with his brother to spend two days searching the San Joaquin River Delta, looking for the bodies of two teenagers who'd vanished five years earlier.

She'd started out missing the dinner conversations with the people at the B&B. There was always something going on there, gossip to track or new events popping up. But now, she could admit that she also missed talking to Beckett more. She even missed that awkward encounter with Scott.

That night after supper, she realized she needed to walk off this mood. She could either sit on the porch and admire the flower beds overflowing with sunny yellow blossoms or take off across Ocean Street to the pier and let the beach work its magic.

Feeling a bit down, she decided the walk would burn off more depressing vibes. But after stretching her legs and jogging along the sand, her mood didn't change much. She strolled along the beach until she came to the wetlands the locals referred to as Sandpiper Marsh. This was her research field, where sea urchins had eaten all the kelp down to a nub, where the acidity level was so high that certain types of sea life had died off. It's the reason she'd embarked on this journey, convinced that it would help land her a better job. But why didn't she feel happier about it?

She watched the sandpipers pecking at the shoreline for their dinner, snapping up tiny crabs as they dug up the little crustaceans buried in the sand. She usually enjoyed birdwatching. But tonight, it just seemed sad to watch the predator devour the crabs trying to get away.

After finding a dry place to sit on the rocky outcrop, she kicked off her shoes and dug her toes into the sand. Listening to the waves, the noisy pelicans, and the sound of the sea should have been more comforting. But tonight, a melancholy came over her she couldn't explain.

She'd let one encounter with Scott get inside her head and amplify doubts already there. Why? She'd always loved the ocean. What was wrong with trying to save it?

She heard a commotion behind her. Before she could react, she had sixty pounds of furry dog in her lap, trying to lick her face. She giggled and went nose to nose with the dog. "Brodie, where did you come from? What are you doing here?"

"I knew Brodie would find someone to rescue," Beckett said with a laugh. After a gut-wrenching day, he'd hoped to find her here. And sure enough, she was sitting all by herself on a rock, wearing a pair of white shorts that showed off the tan of her long legs and a cropped pink top.

"When did you guys get back?"

"About an hour ago."

"Any luck finding the teenagers?"

"It took us two hours of diving near Threemile Slough. But then we spotted the pickup lodged in debris almost a hundred feet down. The location was very close to where a witness spotted them last, off to the left of the recreation area. It's a known lover's lane or was back then. The remains were still inside the Silverado pickup belonging to the boy's dad."

"That's the kid who was driving, right?"

"Yeah. Two sixteen-year-old farm kids, Lila Esterman and Wes Scofield, out on their first date, Memorial Day weekend, the night of the 28th, five years ago."

"A sad ending to a long ordeal for the family. Do you think foul play was involved?"

"Nah. Not this time. The couple had left a party together around midnight. Wes probably had a little too much to drink. A camper spotted the truck headed past the boat ramp speeding toward a dirt road nearby. Since the kids were on their first date, they were likely looking for a quiet spot to make out. Wes probably missed the turn, an inexperienced driver, booze involved, and went right into the water. They never had a chance to escape the cab."

"I didn't realize the San Joaquin fork of the river was that deep."

"It can be up to two hundred feet in certain places. These kids went missing in the deepest part of the channel, where it creates a maze of sloughs and dangerous currents."

"Where the Sacramento River meets up with the San Joaquin. I've been there. Murky waters for diving."

"And this time of year, the water level rises because of snowmelt. The temperature of the water was ice cold. Not many people realize that. And where the tributaries narrow toward the port at Stockton, it's even more dangerous. In warm weather, there's probably a drowning victim in that area once or twice a month. You watch. We'll be called back there before the summer's out to fish out another body." He took a long hard look at Kelly's face. "What's wrong? Are your parents okay?"

"They're fine. Thanks for asking. They're being spoiled by a stream of aunts, coming and going."

"Then what is it? You look like you need cheering up."

She let out a nervous laugh. "I moved into the house and got a little sad here by myself. I'm not usually so glum."

"I know what you need. A good meal."

"I ate a PB&J for dinner."

"No way. Now that's what's sad. How about if I buy you breakfast at the Hilltop? A stack of pancakes, some bacon, maybe a side of eggs to go with it?"

"I suppose I could eat."

"There you go. Did you hear that, Brodie? Time to eat."

The word "eat" got the golden retriever to jump off Kelly's lap. She tried to get to her feet, but in Brodie's excitement, he wagged his tail so hard that he almost knocked her down.

"I wanted Brodie to become a rescue dog, but as you can see, he's just a plain ol' fun-loving chowhound. He didn't take to the training, too undisciplined, the trainer said."

Kelly took hold of Brodie's chin. "What does the trainer know anyway? You could be the smartest dog in the world just waiting for the right motivation."

Beckett grinned. "Yeah. Right. On most days, Brodie's motivation is a T-bone steak flavored biscuit."

When they opened the door to the Hilltop Diner, Kelly thought she'd stepped back in time. The restaurant had a 1950s malt shop motif that looked like it had been around during James Dean's reign. Its black-and-white-checkered floor showed its age. Yellow splotches here and there in the linoleum marred the pattern. But customers didn't seem to mind. The dinner rush had wound down to a few latecomers.

With menus in hand, Margie Rosterman, the owner, a redhead in her early sixties, directed them to an empty booth. She took their drink orders as Dolly Parton and Kenny Rogers harmonized on the jukebox.

"I'll have an orange juice," Kelly mumbled, perusing the choices.

"I want a chocolate shake made from chocolate ice cream and chocolate syrup with plenty of whipped cream on top," Beckett ordered. When he got a hard stare from Kelly, he added, "I burned up a ton of calories today. I'm so hungry I could eat most of what's on this menu."

"Good thing we don't have a limit on orders," Margie teased and left to get the drinks started.

As Beckett got comfortable, he assured Kelly the food was first-rate. "Don't mind the way this place looks. Pick anything on the menu, and I promise you won't be disappointed."

Kelly looked around at the interior.

As restaurants go, the place wasn't big. Margie had managed to make the most of what dining space she had. The small counter had room for eight. She'd squeezed in another eight mismatched tables and an odd assortment of chairs. Along the front windows, four roomier booths could hold six people if they crammed in next to each other.

Kelly judged the Wurlitzer jukebox probably hadn't seen a playlist update since the late 1980s when Dwight Yoakum sang about guitars and Cadillacs. As if Kelly had conjured up the singer, the tune changed to Dwight's *Thousand Miles*.

"I'm sensing a country and western hangout," Kelly cracked. "Are the omelets any good?"

"One of Max's specialties," Beckett declared. "The eggs won't taste like rubber if that's what you're worried about."

"Then I'm having a veggie omelet with the works and a side of crispy bacon and hash browns."

Margie returned with the drinks and nodded in approval. "We have tomatoes right off the vine, fresh spinach, and fresh chives. Max is back there unpacking the mushrooms now."

"That's what I'm talking about," Beckett noted, closing his menu. "Make it two."

"I love a couple with a good appetite," Margie said with a wink. "Want toast with that?"

"Toast would be great."

Margie took off for the kitchen as Kelly studied Beckett's face. She noticed the dark circles under his eyes. "After the kind of week you've had, I think you could use some cheering up yourself."

"I wouldn't say no to a movie," Beckett replied. "Kick back and watch something that makes us forget about everything. I drove by the Driftwood earlier. They're showing *About Time*. You know, the rom com about time travel."

"Now that surprises me. I would've thought you'd want a good shoot 'em up."

Beckett smiled. "No thanks. I've had my fill of war and gunfire sounds. I don't need to see a bunch of actors recreating it on-screen."

She winced. "Sorry. That makes sense. I should've brought my bike. We could've gone for a ride around town."

"How much did you see of this place when you were here in March?"

"Not much. I spent most of my time around Promise Cove and Sandpiper Marsh. I ate my meals at the B&B because they came with the package. I didn't really experience much of the local flair while I was here." Kelly glanced out the window to check on Brodie, who was not thrilled about being left in the pickup.

Beckett followed the track of her eyes. He could tell she liked dogs by the easy way she acted around Brodie. "I'm sensing you're a dog lover, right?"

"Who doesn't love dogs? And with my busy schedule, I've had to put dog ownership on the back burner, along with a lot of other things. Marine biology requires a lot of fieldwork. And most times, you're traveling with a group of other grad students who don't care much about having a dog around. Then you get a job, and you're gone all day. Doesn't seem fair to the poor dog leaving it alone so much of the time. So, yes, I love dogs, but I haven't had one since high school."

"If you get this job as a researcher, would you still live in Hayward?"

"No, Coastal Blue is headquartered in Morro Bay with a state-of-the-art lab, second to none."

Margie delivered their platters, huge omelets laced with cheese and stuffed with vegetables, strips of bacon on the side, and hash browns cooked to perfection. The food smelled heavenly. "Here you go. Two veggie omelets. Enjoy."

"Thanks," Kelly murmured, picking up her knife to butter her toast. "This looks delicious."

Beckett barely let the dishes hit the table before devouring everything on his plate, then eyeing what remained on hers. "Are you gonna eat your toast?"

She snickered and pushed the bread toward him. "Help yourself."

"When do you start your research?"

A warm feeling moved over her. Maybe talking about her work would drag her out of the doldrums and give her that incentive she needed. "UPS dropped off the last of my Macrocystis pyrifera this morning, so I'm ready to start planting once the conditions are optimal."

"That's the kelp, right?"

"Yep. I sent out drones today to capture the most current images of the marsh and the surrounding water. The data confirmed what I feared—another thirty percent kelp loss since I was here in March. That's an incredible rate of deterioration. I'm hoping my batch of sunflower sea stars I got yesterday will devour the purple sea urchins before they can destroy my baby algae, and the kelp will get a chance to grow. Think about it. I could turn around the barren kelp field in Smuggler's Bay in less than three months and track different results by August."

He pushed his plate away and decided he loved listening to the nerdy side of Kelly. "You mean the starfish will eat the sea urchins dining on the kelp. And if the kelp thrives, it's a win-win situation for the ecosystem."

"The ecosystem could use a win. The sunflower sea stars once thrived in the waters between Alaska and Mexico. But when the ocean's temperature got hotter beginning around 2013, the starfish started to die off from a marine pathogen. They turned into blobs."

"Seriously? Did you make that up?"

"No, I didn't make it up. It's called wasting syndrome. The sea stars waste away and become blobs. Without the starfish, the sea urchins took over. Their populations exploded. As a result, the sea urchins decimated the kelp beds. Scientists estimate that as many as five billion starfish died during that time. The animals never recovered. That's why sunflower sea stars are grown in labs these days—in hopes of bringing them back to their glory days. But that's only happened recently. A lab on San Juan Island found a way to successfully breed the sunflower sea star species in captivity from embryo to one-year-old specimens. It's been done with other types of starfish but not this classification. The good news is that these new lab-raised guys seem tougher than their predecessors. They can survive in warmer ocean temps. This is the kind of breakthrough marine biologists have been waiting for, well, me anyway."

Fascinated, Beckett shook his head. "And you have these baby sunflower sea stars in your possession right now? The lab sent them to you?"

"Sure. I'm working in conjunction with the lab to perform what's known as a controlled test over the summer. If it's successful and the sea stars dine on the urchins as they did before, then my paper will be published. That's when things will begin to pop. It moves on to the next phase with state and federal regulatory approvals. We could reestablish the starfish population in this area, maybe turn things around, correcting the imbalance. There was a great deal of red tape just to get this far. Why do you ask?"

"Because releasing those sea stars into the ocean sounds a helluva lot more exciting than going to a movie."

"You want to help me release them—tonight?"

"I thought you'd never ask. The sooner the starfish land in the water, the sooner they can start eating the sea urchins. Right?"

Kelly cracked a grin. "I like you. We'll need our wetsuits for this."

"I like you, too. I keep my wetsuit washed and pressed, ready for action in the truck at all times."

"So do I. Then what are we waiting for? Let's do it. Oh. Wait. I had chartered the *Sea Dragon* to take me out on Saturday. Simon Bremmer runs Argonaut Tours and has me down for all day on Saturday."

"But I have the *Brigid*. That means you won't need the charter."

"I wasn't sure if I should ask. And besides, I wasn't sure you'd be back by the weekend. Booking the *Sea Dragon* made sense at the time. I could still use the *Sea Dragon* to plant the kelp, though, sticking closer to shore."

Beckett signaled for the check and took out his wallet to pay. "It's up to you. But if Birk and I don't get called away and we're in town, I don't mind helping you with the kelp. And if you're worried about Simon Bremmer, don't be. I know the guy. He'll understand. Plus, you'll free up some cash by using the *Brigid* for free."

On her budget, that sounded like too good a deal to pass up. "Sure, if you don't think Mr. Bremmer will hate me for the cancellation."

"I don't think he'll mind at all. This time of year, Simon usually has to turn away business. Besides, the B&B keeps him hopping most of the time."

"By the way, you were right about Scott. I saw him and even had a conversation with him. It was the eeriest thing I've experienced since high school when I got dragged into going on a ghost tour of Tahoe's Biltmore Hotel. Talk about weird."

"That didn't take long for Scott to show his face. When did this happen? While I was out of town?"

"Nope. The night I left your place. The guy waited until I got back to the B&B to pop into the front seat of my truck. Otherwise, you might've been pulling me out of a ditch."

Beckett chuckled. "What did he want?"

Kelly slid out of the booth. "He wanted to make sure I knew that I was on the wrong career path."

"What?"

"Yeah. Apparently Scott doesn't want me saving the planet by reforesting the kelp beds."

"What does he want you to do?"

Kelly looped an arm through Beckett's. "Beats me. He was never specific about that."

"Damn. I hate it when ghosts are vague."

Eight

The sun made its timeless descent across the evening sky, prompting the beds full of golden hibiscus to tuck themselves in for the night.

Standing in the driveway, Kelly took her cue from the blossoms. She stopped to watch the sky explode into a million shades of orangey-reds, pinks, and violets. Even though she could explain the breathtaking sight scientifically, it didn't diminish its postcard quality.

Being around Beckett had lifted her spirits. An hour ago, she'd felt defeated. Now, she tugged his arm and pointed to the sunset. "How's that for a show?"

"Red sky at night, sailor's delight," Beckett provided. "The old adage signals good weather. Since we're about to launch the boat, I'd say it's a perfect sign."

He'd helped transfer the dozens of clear plastic bags filled with starfish into large Igloo coolers for transport, then onto the pickup bed of her Chevy Colorado. A playful Brodie sniffed each pouch and started to sink his teeth into one of the bags.

"Bad dog. The starfish are not chew toys," Beckett informed the pup, pushing Brodie's nose in the opposite direction. "Go sniff the flower beds over there."

When the dog trotted away to inspect the hibiscus, Beckett angled back toward Kelly, staring at the colorful two-inch specimens. "I've observed starfish while diving.

In their natural habitat, they're massive predators. These things get huge, and they're fast. They gobble up food at an alarming rate."

"Sea stars need to be fast to catch their supper. They do enjoy chowing down on an immense array of mussels. But their menu in Smuggler's Bay will primarily consist of sea urchins. I know because I've dived in this area. I've seen very few clams and scallops left. And there are barely enough crabs to keep the birds happy. However, the estimated number of sea urchins indicate they're everywhere within reach of Sandpiper Marsh."

"So this area doesn't have a lot of starfish?"

"Nope. They all died off. It doesn't have kelp either. But thanks to you and me, that's going to change. Did I tell you how much I appreciate the help? I usually do this kind of stuff solo."

"Have you ever done this with starfish before?"

"No, this will be a first. I've replanted kelp, though. I volunteered last summer at Coastal Blue. We reforested the Mendocino and Sonoma coastlines." When she'd hauled the last bin into the truck's bed, she turned to Beckett. "You ready?"

"I'm amped to do this. Come on, Brodie, let's go make history and release some invertebrates back into the wild."

A few minutes later, Kelly pulled up near the pier to unload the truck. She spotted the *Brigid* bobbing in the harbor. "You can't possibly understand how helping me like this jumpstarts my research."

"I think it'll be fun. Now tell me what happened during the haunted Biltmore tour. You didn't finish."

"Forget I said anything."

"Oh, no, you don't. You said you adamantly did not believe in ghosts. But it sounds like something happened back in Lake Tahoe."

Kelly let out a sigh. "It borders on silly now that I look back."

"Are you gonna tell me or not?"

"Fine. Okay. The incident happened after I went on the lame ghost tour, which was so cheesy that I wanted to ask for my money back. But since I was the only one who felt that way, I didn't have the guts to ask."

"You're stalling. Why?"

"If you dive a lot, then you must know that Lake Tahoe is more than sixteen hundred feet deep."

"Yeah. I've dived there. It's the second deepest lake in the country. What's that got to do with the Biltmore tour?"

"Then you know about all the myths and folklore attached to that area. Mainly about how the mafia out of Reno, circa the 1950s, used Lake Tahoe to dispose of bodies."

"I'm aware of the stories. Are you suggesting you saw a ghost at the lake?"

"The day after that ghost tour, I went out there to go hiking, collect rocks, and take water samples. I passed a man on the trail that morning who mumbled something to me about how clear the water was in Emerald Bay. He looked out of place. He wasn't wearing running shoes or jogging clothes but a white suit and white patent leather shoes. White in October. Think about it. He looked like he had just stepped out of a 1960s casino. He seemed real enough at the time. But when he kept talking after I jogged past him, I decided to turn around to get a better look. And he was gone. There was no one there. I was alone on the trail. I decided that I was still wrapped up in leftover fantasy from the ghost tour the night before and headed home, a little spooked."

"So wait a minute. You're copping to having not one but *three* encounters with a ghost. The first was back in high school, the second was with Scott in Santa Cruz, and the third was with Scott out at the B&B. I'd say that qualifies you as a paranormal magnet."

Kelly sputtered with laughter. "Oh, come on. A magnet? How many times has Scott shown up at your house? That points to you being a more powerful magnet than me."

"But Scott found you in multiple locations. Think back. Are you sure this didn't happen to you at some point down in San Diego when you were in college?"

She frowned. "I think I'd remember. Besides, Scott never mentioned we'd connected before Santa Cruz. And he wasn't the man I saw on the hiking trail. What about you? Are there other ghosts who contacted you before you arrived in California?"

"Let's not talk about this now. Okay?"

"You brought it up," Kelly fired back as she studied his face. That's when she realized he'd gone somewhere else. His mood had shifted at hyperspeed into somewhere dark. The change indicated he'd had other encounters he didn't feel like sharing. For several long minutes, he'd grown silent, staring out the passenger window, unwilling to look at her. She reached out and took his hand in hers. "It's okay. We'll switch gears and focus on the starfish for now. At some point, I don't think this topic will go away. I'm here for you when you're ready to talk about it. I'm not going anywhere."

"Good to know. Thanks. What's the plan after we get the starfish onboard?"

Content for now that the dark moment had passed, she took out her phone to refer to her notes. "We set the GPS to this longitude and latitude. Don't worry. It's a mere fifty yards or so to the mouth of the bay."

"That close?"

"Uh-huh. We release the first of our specimens at that point and then slowly drop them closer to shore until we've covered the entire harbor. It's sort of like when you're looking for a dead body. I believe you call it mowing the lawn. You cover more ocean that way. I read that on the Internet. The same thing applies to releasing the sea stars into Smuggler's Bay. Using a grid pattern, we cover more ocean."

"As Birk would say, we're not gonna accomplish anything sitting here on our butts."

They got to work, hauling the containers to the *Brigid*. A relieved Kelly saw Beckett's blue mood change back to carefree, almost joyful.

"I love being outdoors," Kelly admitted. "I think it's why I hated the classroom so much."

"Same here. Part of the joy of owning a business keeps us outside."

"Part of your joy is helping people. I saw it on your face when you received word about my parents. I saw the same thing when you returned from finding those teenagers. You love what you do. You give families what they've been waiting for—sometimes waiting for years—news about what happened to their loved ones."

"Yeah, I'm a regular boy scout," Beckett muttered, starting the engine and steering the boat out of the dock. "Not. You haven't known me long enough to know I need to make up for all the bad things I've done. As a Navy SEAL, I've killed people, Kelly. And I live with that every single day. Ghosts? You bet. I see them all the time up here." He tapped the side of his head. "I don't expect them to ever leave me in peace."

She wasn't sure how to make him feel better, so she did the only thing that came naturally to her—she went into a chatty mode. As they made their way into the harbor, she kept up a steady stream of dialogue. "The last thing I expected to see in Pelican Pointe was ghosts, let alone talk about them, talk to them. Did I mention that Jordan accepts Scott roaming the house and grounds? We had several conversations about it before I left. She takes it in stride. I'm not sure I could do that. Did you know that she couldn't see Scott at first? He showed himself to everyone else but her. Strangers. Guests. Townspeople. That pissed her off. It would me. I wonder how difficult it is living your life knowing your ghostly ex could be wandering the halls. Do you suppose Scott watches Nick and Jordan have sex?"

That seemed to break Beckett out of his funk. "Interesting theory."

"I know, right? And Jordan is doing it with Scott's best friend. Talk about awkward. How do you keep a ghost out of your bedroom when he has access to everything else? It's his house. Or was."

"It's Jordan's and Nick's place now. I'm sure Scott accepts that. It's general knowledge that he watches over his kid, Hutton."

"That's what Jordan said. And last summer, Scott prevented little Scottie from falling headfirst down those steep steps. He was trying to carry Quake to the cove and tripped. So it sounds like Scott looks after all of them, like a guardian angel."

Beckett turned the boat into the harbor. "This is the release point. What do we do now? Toss them over the side?"

As the boat swayed, Kelly maneuvered toward the crates and the starfish. "If only it were that simple. Did I mention that we have to hope the starfish don't eat each other? They do that, you know." She grinned and added, "But at least we shouldn't have to worry about them getting eaten by sharks or manta rays."

"Let's hope not. Otherwise, we're looking at our own horror movie. These little guys should be fine gnawing on the sea urchins and not each other."

"We'll need to acclimate them as best we can from the saltwater they're in now to the bay's temperature and acidity level. I'll need to test the water, then note the conditions."

"How long will that take?"

"Not long," she assured him as she removed several test tubes from one of the containers. Leaning over the side of the boat, she scooped up water, used a thermometer to determine the temp, and then measured the PH level. "Looks like we're good to go."

They took turns releasing the sunflower sea stars at various depths into the bay until emptying the last pouch near the marsh.

"What's next? The kelp?"

"The plan is to introduce seagrass and kelp all along the harbor. Whatever plant inventory remains, we'll place further out near the entrance."

"What's the difference? Aren't seagrass and kelp the same thing?"

"Nope. Seagrass has about sixty different varieties. They belong to the order Alismatales and the class Monocotyledons. In this case, I'm using the Pacific Cymodoceaceae variety." When he gave her a blank stare, she added, "It's the kind that looks like it has feathers on the tips of the stems."

"Oh, yeah. Good choice. I like the look of those."

"I'm also planting Zostera, eelgrass as it's known, hoping to produce a nice, large meadow growing from it. Fish and shellfish love the eelgrass. It's where they like to lay their eggs."

"No kidding?"

"Did you know that seagrass came from terrestrial plants that recolonized the oceans seventy million years ago?"

"No way. Terrestrial sounds alien to me. Wouldn't it be a kick to find out aliens recolonized the ocean?"

Kelly didn't get the joke. "I'm assuming you're either making fun or teasing me."

"No, really. Terrestrial sounds alien."

"You're thinking of extraterrestrial, otherworldly. It's not that. Terrestrial refers to land or having to do with the land. You named your search company Terra so you should know a thing or two about terrestrial. It's the same concept. Terrestrial refers to plants that grow on, in, or from the land. Like aquatic plants grow in water, lithophytic types grow on rocks, and epiphytic types grow on trees."

"What about beachgrass?"

She pointed to the shoreline. "Ammophila. Found all around us growing on coastal sand dunes. Again, a different species altogether. So is seaweed, very different from seagrass."

He could listen to her lecture for hours and not get bored. She named off the classes, the order, and the subtypes of seaweed. Amazed that she had all that information in her head, he kept her talking by asking questions.

It took her several minutes before she caught on. "You already know all this, don't you? I knew you were pulling my leg."

"No, I just like to hear you talk."

"I doubt that. You've been diving for how long? You probably were diving before I learned to drive."

"How old do you think I am, anyway?"

"Pushing forty, I'd imagine."

His face broke into a grin. "Fair enough."

"You aren't the only one who can crack a joke." After he maneuvered the *Brigid* into its space at the dock, a few realities hit. She found him easy to talk to. He was patient with Brodie, the oversized puppy slash lap dog. He could make a joke out of nothing and make her laugh without trying too hard. He was helping her kick off her summer project. He didn't seem to mind when she rambled on about kelp. Yeah, she was falling for him. What female wouldn't?

When his warm amber-green eyes shifted to hers, his lips curved in a soft smile, lessening the lines on his face. He reached out to touch her hair, damp from the ocean's mist. Loose strands framed her face in a glow of golden honey.

Everything about him drew her in, his scent, the strength of his shoulders, his taste. So when his mouth closed over hers, she gave as good as she got. The kiss lingered longer when her hand cupped his neck, bringing him closer.

All Beckett could think about was getting her out of those clothes sooner rather than later.

"We could shower at your place," he whispered, nibbling her neck.

She ran a hand along his chest. "Hmm. Get rid of the fishy smell. I like that idea. I have lavender and vanilla shower gel." In the recesses of her brain, she pictured him naked and wet. But from a distance, she heard someone call out his name.

They broke apart in time to see Birk watching them from the boardwalk. "We got a call from Santa Cruz. We've got a missing ten-year-old girl."

"Rotten timing," Beckett muttered, his brow resting on Kelly's forehead. "Save my place. I promise we'll take that shower together real soon."

She patted his cheek. "It's okay. There's no rush."

"Speak for yourself."

She let out a soft laugh. "I won't say I'm not disappointed. But it'll wait. How about breakfast in the morning if you're back in time? My place. I fix a mean avocado on toast."

"I guess that thought will have to keep me going for the rest of the night."

"Here's something better," Kelly said, pressing her lips to his again.

An impatient Birk hollered, "Come on, Beck, get the lead out. Say goodbye already! You're not going off to war. It's fifty miles away, for chrissake."

Beckett shook his head. "See what I have to put up with?"

She hated seeing him go but realized Birk wasn't about to leave them alone. She laid a hand on his chest. "Go find that kid. If anyone can do it, you guys can."

After spending an hour logging statistics and data into her spreadsheet, it was almost midnight when Kelly jumped in the shower. Alone.

As she soaped up, her mind kept drifting back to the smoldering kiss she'd shared with Beckett. If Birk hadn't intervened, she had no doubt they would've ended up back at her place.

"Damn that Birk," she murmured while towel-drying her hair and getting into a pair of pajamas. "Would it have killed him to wait an hour longer?" But then she thought about the missing child. "Okay, so maybe finding a kid is more important than my sex life."

Talking to herself seemed to be a bad habit of late. Maybe she needed to think about getting a dog. At least with a dog, she could carry on a stream of dialogue and not seem crazy. After all, she was a taxpaying adult now with a job and no longer a student. And having a dog might keep her stress level down, less reason to feel depressed. Deciding she'd look into it, she plopped on the bed to power down her laptop. But something on the screen caught her eye—a local news alert about the missing girl in Santa Cruz.

It reminded Kelly to look up Brigid Callahan on the Internet. She picked up her computer, leaned back against the headboard, and keyed in everything she knew about the missing twenty-year-old. For the next hour, Kelly dropped into the rabbit hole that was Brigid's case. She went from website to website, gathering specifics, then reading different theories on blogs run by amateur sleuths about what happened that night.

Brigid had been drinking on a phony ID which contributed to the cops thinking she was drunk. What college student didn't get drunk after a night out partying with a fake ID?

Kelly thought that conclusion seemed like a rush to judgment without any facts to back it up, not to mention the entire theory seemed too critical of the victim. According to four different bloggers, Brigid had not left the bar drunk but went home early because she'd argued with one of her friends.

After finding the CCTV link of Brigid online taken near the burger chain, Kelly had to agree. She watched the video no less than a dozen times. It didn't seem to her like Brigid wobbled when she walked. Nor did it appear that she was lost. The woman held her phone in her hand the entire time she appeared on camera, walking with purpose, which led Kelly to deem that Brigid seemed sober in the footage.

The gaping holes in the police theory nagged at Kelly. It didn't make sense that a college student would walk all that way to Shark Fin Cove. After an evening of drinking with friends, why would a woman set out to visit one of the most remote beaches in the area by herself? A twenty-year-old usually had a wide circle that encompassed a variety of friends. That assumption made Kelly lean toward someone picking her up.

In addition, if Brigid ended up drowning in the water, wouldn't the tides have carried her down the shoreline? If not that, wouldn't her body have gotten tangled up in the rocks closer to the cove?

Having lived around a lake her entire life, she knew people fell in and drowned year-round. But the body usually surfaced one way or another unless something prevented it from floating to the top. She thought of the teenagers trapped inside the truck cab who couldn't get out. In Brigid's case, she hadn't been driving. One of Brigid's roommates had provided transportation that evening for all of them. So why would Brigid head out to a remote beach by herself? It didn't make sense.

Maybe Brigid knew the person who picked her up, Kelly decided, re-watching the video footage of the student pacing in front of the burger restaurant in the parking lot. Had she been waiting for someone to pick her up and give her a ride? Wouldn't her phone records have indicated that Brigid called for help? Who had she texted or called last?

Kelly liked solving puzzles. But this one seemed riddled with contradictions. And not enough information. The fact that she couldn't explain what happened to Brigid's body was the most troublesome detail of all. And it wouldn't go away.

Not one to speculate without facts, she opened another tab and went to a website that stored tidal information by date and time. She keyed in the data to get the wind and current for midnight. Using the height and weight for Brigid that she found on the missing person flyer, she logged that data and waited for the result. She was shocked at the results. The body should have remained in or around Shark Fin Cove unless Brigid didn't end up in the water.

No wonder Beckett—and most of the websleuths online—weren't fans of the police theory. The meager breadcrumbs left behind were no help at all.

Captivated by the mystery, Kelly decided she needed to put her heart and soul into digging deeper. If not for her own peace of mind, she could at least help Beckett find answers.

Nine

During the forty-five-minute drive to Santa Cruz, Beckett took plenty of razzing from his brother about Kelly until he'd had enough. "Shut up. Will you? This isn't middle school. Act like an adult for once."

"I will if you will. I can't believe you helped her release a bunch of fish into the bay."

"Not fish. Sunflower sea stars that chow down on sea urchins. And why shouldn't I help her? She's trying to do something to help the community, a place where she doesn't even live."

"It's not such a noble gesture if she's writing about it to get noticed for a better job."

"I don't get you. What have you got against her? What did Kelly ever do to you? Just because Claudia Simpson left your crying ass at the altar doesn't mean every woman is the enemy."

Birk let out a sigh, knowing it was true. "I thought we agreed you'd never mention my ex to me ever again."

"I wouldn't have brought her up now if you weren't acting like such an ass around Kelly. I really like this woman. She's funny and she's smart. She's inventive, too. You didn't treat Kimberly this way, and we only went out for a few weeks."

"Kimberly was a ditz. Still is. And I knew you weren't serious about her. This one lights you up whenever she comes into a room."

Beckett's lips curved into a wicked grin. "Yeah. I wonder why that is. Why don't we change the subject to why I got dragged out here tonight? Tell me about this missing girl."

Birk held up his phone and read the alert. "Elena Aguilara. Ten years old. Went missing around three-thirty this afternoon on the way home from the school bus stop. The bus driver swears she got off with the rest of the kids at Liberty and Bay Streets."

"Then that's where we should start. Any sex offenders in that area?"

"Twenty-five or so. There's also a mobile home park three blocks away."

"Did you contact Debra at CCSU?"

CCSU stood for Coastal Canine Search Unit. The brothers had a long association with the nonprofit organization they'd used to search for Brigid. Even if they hadn't located their sister, they'd worked together off and on for several years to find other missing people.

"No, Deb contacted me," Birk returned. "You weren't listening earlier, were you? Debra was rounding up the team thirty minutes ago. They'll meet us in the parking lot at Santa Cruz PD. She's probably already there waiting for us, giving everyone else the best assignments."

"Don't start," Beckett warned. "I'm here now. Besides, if you were in that much of a hurry, we could've taken the boat. Used it to motor around the coastline and docked at the pier in record time instead of towing it down the highway." He took a left off PCH onto Laurel Street, then a right onto Center in the heart of downtown. He spotted the crowd gathered in the parking lot.

"Looks like they got a good turnout," Birk commented.

When someone went missing, volunteer groups from all over the county usually assembled at the direction of law enforcement or sometimes the victim's family. From Boy Scouts wanting to help to mobilizing military helicopters and off-duty police officers into action, there were always people willing to show up and assist, especially when that missing someone turned out to be a child.

Beckett pulled to the entrance. A uniformed cop approached the truck. "You can't park here. This area is reserved for official police business only."

"We're the Callahans from Terra Search & Recovery," Beckett began, producing his ID. "Santa Cruz County Sheriff's Office contacted us to assist. We're here to help locate Elena Aguilara."

"Oh. Sure. You can pull into that corner to the left where everyone else has gathered and get instructions on what to do next."

"Thanks."

"There's nothing quite like teamwork," Birk stated, pointing to where Debra and the other volunteers assembled with their search dogs. "Take notes, Brodie. That's what we expected out of you."

At hearing his name, Brodie woofed in response.

"He just needs seasoning," Beckett said, jumping in to defend his dog. "Isn't that right, boy?"

From the backseat, Brodie leaned in and gave Beck's cheek a tongue bath.

"Okay, okay," Beckett responded, bringing the pickup to a stop next to Debra Rattlin, a thirty-something dog trainer who'd trained and certified every dog she owned to detect human remains and work forensic collection.

Deb had long red hair, porcelain skin, and big brown eyes. She reminded him of the actress Bella Thorne but with a fiery disposition to match the ginger hair. "You know Deb has a major crush on you, right? She always holds back and gives you the best places to search. I don't know why you were worried. She's been waiting two years for you to ask her out."

Birk shook his head. "You do remember this is the same woman who failed Brodie, right? She said he wasn't cut out for Search and Rescue, which certainly put the kibosh on our plans. She wanted us to take that silver Labrador. What was his name?"

"Cyrus. Deb thought Cyrus was smarter than Brodie. What does she know about Brodie anyway? He's every bit as smart at tracking as Cyrus. The least Brodie can add to a search is tracking. Don't get me started. It doesn't matter. I'm not the one she's crazy about. It's you, bro. I've never seen you scared of anything until Debra Rattlin gets within twelve feet of you."

"The woman has commitment written all over her. Quiet. She might hear you. Here she comes now."

"I see you came prepared," Debra Rattlin remarked, pointing to the boat they towed. "I'm not sure this is a water retrieval situation. Unless Elena walked eight blocks to the beach and fell in, or her kidnapper tossed her in the ocean."

Birk winced at the two scenarios as he got out on the passenger side. "Does law enforcement know any more than they did an hour ago?"

"They checked CCTV in the area where the bus stop is. They're doing a door-to-door now. Our assignment starts where she was last seen getting off the bus."

"Is that verified as the girl's last location?" Birk wanted to know.

"Yep. Cops are making the rounds to the sex offenders in the area now."

Beckett joined the two at the front of the truck, holding onto Brodie's leash. "Sounds like they're not wasting a minute this time around."

Debra bobbed her head across the parking lot toward the guy with the microphone handing out assignments. "The panicked parents are standing next to the police chief. They've given us articles of clothing to use that belonged to Elena." She held up five plastic baggies containing an assortment of underwear, socks, and tops.

"In your absence, I volunteered you guys to be with my team. I hope that's okay."

Beckett shouldered his backpack. "Sure."

Deb handed the pair two-way radios. "You know the drill. I brought Pepsi for Birk. They've worked well together before." She angled toward Beckett. "But I'm assigning you another golden retriever—since you're fond of that breed—who's good at what she does."

Beckett looked back at Brodie and let his hand rest on the dog's head. Instead of arguing with the woman's strategy, he nodded. Finding Elena was the objective. "We're good to go."

"That's what I wanted to hear. We'll take my SUV because the dogs are already loaded in the back unless you'd prefer to drive. Different vehicles are fine by me. You can follow me there if you want."

Beckett chose to follow Debra. On the way across town, he laid out his plan to Birk. "Just so you know, I intend to hang back with Brodie and whatever other dog she assigns me and watch the canines, watch their handlers work."

"Debra's not going to like that. In case you hadn't noticed, she had four dogs in her SUV. If one doesn't get the job done, she's not shy about pulling the dog off detail and replacing it with another."

"I know. But this is my chance to prove Brodie is better than she thinks."

Birk twisted in his seat. "Look, Beck, I like Brodie. But he's all over the place. He needs more time before settling into a role where he's been tasked with finding someone missing."

"You think I don't know how important the job is? Of course, I know. How long have we been doing this?"

"I'm just saying that tonight might not be the best time to test Brodie's skill. But if your heart's set on it, I'll do what I can with Debra to cover for you."

"Thanks. It looks like Deb's turning into the spot. I'll park a little further down the street. That way, in all the excitement, maybe she won't notice Brodie."

"Yeah, I'm sure she'll think she's seeing double. You're dreaming if you think that," Birk muttered. "Nothing much gets by Debra. But whatever. Hang back long enough, and she'll get caught up. I'll try to stay between you and her."

"Thanks."

After Debra handed off the golden retriever to Beckett—a dog named Calico—Deb got busy organizing the search, slicing the neighborhood into a grid, and assigning the volunteers their sections.

Convinced the trainer was distracted, Beckett let Brodie out of the backseat of the truck. Holding onto the two dogs, he remained near his pickup while watching the others get to work.

The teams—human and dog—systematically paced the sidewalk, the dogs sniffing for a time around the corner bus stop before taking off after Elena's supposed track home.

Deb had given Birk the Australian shepherd named Pepsi. Beckett watched as Birk and Pepsi followed Deb and her border collie toward the roundabout on LaMonte Avenue.

After letting them get a decent head start, Beckett led both retrievers across the street to the corner. Under the streetlamps, he opened the baggie that held a pink sock and waved it under Brodie's nose first, then Calico's. "Come on, boy. You can do this. Let's go find Elena."

Brodie sniffed deep, excited, tail wagging, then bumped Beck's legs before taking off in a different direction than the rest, with Calico trailing behind.

Eat my dust, Beckett thought, as Brodie looked confident. He couldn't say the same thing about Calico. She looked confused about which way to go. But if Brodie had taken the wrong route, so be it, Beckett decided. They would still cover more ground this way than following the others. At the very least, they would eliminate another slice of the grid.

While volunteers covered the nearby park, Beckett kept up with their progress over an occasional two-way update. Same with the people searching around the bridge near the pier. So many had come out that the radio buzzed with constant chatter.

Halfway between blocks, Beckett lowered the volume. He didn't want anything distracting Brodie from his mission. They hauled ass down the first street and churned their way to the second block, making significant headway into an older section of town. They were approaching an intersection when his phone dinged with a text from Birk.

Heads up. We're circling back your way. Dogs are headed northeast in the opposite direction from where they began.

Beckett keyed in his reply. *Thanks. Brodie and Calico are setting a pace to meet up near Lavatera Way.*

Up ahead, Beckett spotted the trailer park on the right-hand side of the street. It backed up to a retail shopping center. He was only mildly surprised when Brodie headed toward the bare dirt path next to the walkway. The dog scrambled past a row of hedges that lined the entrance to the mobile homes, then scampered up a small embankment, sniffing the asphalt.

Beckett took out the baggie again and let Brodie sniff the sock until the dog seemed satisfied with the scent. Refreshed and reset, Brodie made a beeline into the center of the mobile home park. The dog loped toward a double-wide with an awning over the front windows. It was the fourth mobile home nearest to the entrance.

He watched as Brodie sniffed the carport before switching directions and approaching the steps leading to the front door. The dog plopped his butt down on the pavement, letting out three quick barks in a row, his signal, his alert.

Right behind Brodie came Calico, who reacted the same way.

Beckett's heart raced at the possibility. He called both retrievers back to his side. "I hope you're right this time, guys, because I'm calling this in."

The two-way crackled to life. "I've got an alert at 6507 Lavatera Way. That's a mobile home park called Monrovia Village. The unit space is number four. Request officers get a warrant to search the property."

Debra came back with a confirmation request.

Beckett obliged, letting her believe for now that Calico had gotten the hit and that Brodie was here for the exercise.

A few minutes later, Birk arrived with Pepsi. The Australian shepherd strolled up to the same trailer and alerted to the exact unit. Debra's border collie Sid made it four for four when the collie dropped his butt down next to the same set of steps and then barked three times before licking his chops.

Convinced, Debra called the detective in charge. The trio and their dogs backed out of the complex. For the next half hour, they stood on the corner, waiting for the cops to arrive.

"This is the part I don't like," Beckett told Birk. "I feel like bashing in the door."

"Same here. In our former life, we would have. But we're civilized now. It's not our call." He studied his brother. "Brodie got the first hit, didn't he?"

"Yep. It went down just like I hoped. I told you all Brodie needed was a chance. He never once went off course. He kept his nose to the ground, and here we are."

"When do you plan to tell Debra? Let me know because I don't want to be around when she finds out."

"Let's see if Elena is in there first. Then I'll come clean about it. Deb might not even believe me."

"Remember what Debra told us over and over in training. Trust your dog. Four hits say the child is in there. Now whether it's good news or bad—"

Beckett didn't allow himself to think about the bad. He took Brodie and Calico to the other side of the street and sat down on the curb to wait.

The police found Elena huddled in a back room of the three-bedroom trailer. She was battered and bruised but alive.

After going through an hour of debriefing, Beckett approached Debra in the hallway. He confronted her with the truth about the trailer park. "Believe it, don't, it's your choice. But it was Brodie who got there first. And he didn't have to go four extra blocks in the wrong direction to end up there."

"You're right. I don't believe it. I didn't think you'd stoop so low as to try and use this as a way to get Brodie certified."

"How long have you known me? Almost six years this October? If you think I'd do something like that, then maybe our association should end here, tonight." Beckett turned to go.

But Debra blew out a tired breath. "Wait. No, I don't think you'd try anything like that. Fine. Bring Brodie in Monday morning, ten sharp, and I'll test him again."

"Thanks, Debra. You won't regret it."

"Something tells me I already am."

Ten

Saturday morning, Kelly rolled over in bed to read a series of texts from her mom, including photos of the totaled truck and trailer and pictures of their bumps and bruises. The road to recovery seemed paved with regrets about making the trip at night. Their insurance would cover a certain amount for the loss of the truck. But they would likely need to take money out of their savings to replace it.

After researching Brigid Callahan's disappearance until three-thirty in the morning, Kelly messaged her mother. *Look on the bright side. You're both alive, and you didn't suffer any long-term injuries. I'd say that's a miracle in my book. Count your blessings.*

True. But you know how much your dad loved that truck.

It's just a truck, Mom. You can replace it and make it a fun experience truck shopping with him for another. And as soon as he feels like it, send him out to the workshop and have him start building a new trailer.

Good idea. He's already getting antsy.

Let me know if you need anything or need me to come home.

We're fine. Your Aunt LeeAnn has it all under control. You take care of yourself and finish your work. The job of your dreams is waiting.

Bless Aunt LeeAnn, Kelly thought as she got out of bed to pee.

Still tired, Kelly had stayed glued to her laptop and hadn't fallen asleep until well after four a.m. She didn't like getting sucked into Brigid's case. But it seemed there was no way out of the black hole. Without clear-cut answers, doubts lingered. No matter how she looked at it, she came to the same conclusion. Brigid hadn't gone into the water. And if she hadn't gone into the water, where was she? Was there any chance at all that she was still alive? If not, where was her body? Why hadn't Beckett and Birk found her by now? If Brigid died, what was the cause of death? Was it a hit and run? Had an impaired driver hit her then needed to hide the body? How did her phone ping at Shark Fin Cove if that scenario played out?

On less than four hours of sleep, the questions made her head hurt. Was it too soon to text Beckett? Probably.

Kelly changed out of PJs and into a tank top and shorts. She swiped through her phone to learn the latest news about Elena Aguilara. The girl had been found in the home of a man who'd snatched her off the street. The horror of the girl's abduction sunk in when she realized the ten-year-old was in the hospital, recovering from her injuries.

Thank God for people like Beckett and dogs like Brodie, Kelly thought as she made her way to the kitchen and the coffee pot. She pulled out a bag of freshly ground beans from Murphy's Market and started the coffee, brewing an entire carafe in case Beckett made it in time for breakfast.

The aroma wafted through the whole house and went a long way to further waking her up. When the coffee finished its brew cycle, she took her newly purchased indigo blue mug and strolled to the back window, staring out into the yard. The square concrete patio, drenched in streaks of sunshine at the edge, was a beautiful place to start the day.

She waved to her next-door neighbors, a young couple eating breakfast on their patio with their toddler and newborn baby. She'd have to remember to introduce herself.

The thought hadn't been two seconds in the making before the woman, a stunning redhead, handed off the infant, closed the distance, and introduced herself. "Hey, there. I'm Bree, and that's my husband Troy. He's one of the carpenters who worked on your house to get it ready for you."

"Nice to meet you. I'm Kelly Ecklund. And thanks for the fast work you did, Troy."

Troy wandered over, carrying the bundle swaddled against his chest. "The scientist. Yeah. We heard. We'd love to have you over for dinner sometime."

Kelly thought of Beckett's remarkable clarity in that regard. It was exactly how he'd defined the people here. "I'd love that. Maybe we could do a cookout, some burgers, toss in some crabs, maybe have a fish fry."

"What a wonderful idea. And different from the usual burger slash hotdog fest around here," Bree said, turning to her husband.

"How old is the baby?"

Bree beamed at the question. "Six weeks. We named her Zoe Colleen Dayton."

"That's uncanny," Kelly relayed. "My given name is Colleen, for my grandmother. My parents have been calling me Kelly since forever."

"My mom's name was Colleen," Bree explained. "That's so weird, right?"

When the baby began to fuss, Troy simply handed Zoe off to Mom. "She's hungry again."

Bree nestled the baby into her body. "This girl's got an appetite. I guess we'll catch you later. If you need anything, don't hesitate to holler."

As Kelly watched the couple go back inside, she wondered if she had ever wanted babies. Strolling over to check on her seedlings, she lifted the lids to each box. The grass pods were still in good shape, still submerged in saltwater, but the water level was down from the day before. Their shelf life dwindled each day they weren't in the water. The grasses needed planting today, no later than tomorrow.

As the toddler next door ran around the backyard and squealed in delighted giggles with his dad in pursuit, she couldn't remember a time when she'd played with dolls. Surely, she had carried around a Barbie or two like most other little girls. But she couldn't remember owning a baby doll. Not ever. Why was that?

Before she could think about it for too long, Brodie appeared around the corner of the house four steps before Beckett.

"We knocked but then heard voices in the back. We're celebrating this morning," Beckett said, holding up a bag from the Hilltop Diner. "Veggie omelets again with bacon and hash browns. I figure we could use the fuel before planting."

As Brodie bumped her legs, Kelly laid a hand on his furry head. "Congrats on finding the girl. Both of you did an outstanding job."

Beckett grinned ear to ear. "Did we make the news?"

"You did. The paper had to correct the story, though. At first, it said another golden retriever named Calico had found her. But eventually, they got it right."

"You know what this means for Brodie?"

"He gets a medal?"

"Not yet. Maybe. Brodie gets another chance at becoming a search dog. I plan on spending all day Sunday working with him."

"I can figure something out if you want to start his training today instead of messing with the kelp."

'Nah. Brodie had a good night last night. We're on a high. Getting out in the boat will do everybody good. Hey, we need to eat these omelets before they're stone-cold. Out here or inside?"

"Let's take them inside and sit down. There's no table out here, and we need silverware." She led the way through the back door and went straight to the cupboard.

"Wow. What a cute beach house. I had no idea Logan Donnelly had a flair for interior design. This is so much more than what I expected."

"Well, he must have a flair for vintage. He used mid-century modern to decorate the entire house. Look at the flooring. I've never seen recycled barn wood in such great shape. I just now met the carpenter next door who worked on the rehab."

Beckett took a seat at the table while Brodie curled up at his feet. "That's the Tradewinds crew. Ryder McLachlan, Zach Dennison, and Troy Dayton. They build boats when they're not doing construction work."

Kelly brought over napkins and silverware, then finally sat down to eat. "Interesting town you have here. Troy and Bree invited me to dinner. I countered and suggested a fish fry."

"Excellent turnaround from the day we first met."

"I don't want people thinking I'm not friendly."

"No, we wouldn't want that after the way you shut me down."

"I'm not taking them to the little island for shrimp and crab. But wouldn't it be nice to have an outdoor party like that here?"

"Do you know how to catch fish?"

She took that first tasty bite of her eggs. "I fish. Sure. I grew up around a lake. I'm just not very good at it. I'd hate to rely on what I catch for my dinner. Do you?"

He gave her a sidelong glance. "I have survivalist training in cold climates the same as desert conditions. So yeah. Hunting. Fishing. Camping. They're second nature."

"Hmm. Maybe you should teach me how to survive in the wild. It might come in handy one day."

"Good idea. Let's plan to go camping next weekend."

"Really?"

"Really. Were you ever a girl scout?"

"Sure, till I turned ten. You should know that was a long time ago."

"That old, huh?"

Buttering her toast, she chortled with laughter. "But I have a long history of fieldwork in challenging situations. I spent the summer between my freshman and sophomore year studying the kelp Baja field in Isla Natividad. Mexico. At the southernmost tip of the Macrocystis pyrifera range. It was no picnic."

"Two words. Afghanistan. Iraq. On second thought, add one more. Hell. Both places were hell on earth."

"Okay. Okay. I get it. You win."

He'd already devoured his food.

"Is that why you eat so fast?"

"In war, mealtime is a luxury," he said, flipping Brodie the last bite of his bacon. Grateful, the dog caught it in midair, chomped, then looked over at Kelly for her contribution.

She obliged, holding out half a piece of what she still had on her plate. Brodie, lips smacking, gobbled it up, then looked for more.

"He'll need some water after eating that," she concluded and got up to fill a wide mixing bowl halfway full. She watched as Brodie lapped it up.

When Beckett opened the door for Brodie to head outside, she studied his face and knew something was on his mind. "You want to tell me what's going on? Is it about what happened last night?"

"Let's just say that I'm glad I didn't get my hands on the man who took that kid."

Kelly drew in a hard breath. "Mind if I ask you something? Each time you're called out to hunt for a missing person, doesn't it bring back a lot of painful memories of looking for Brigid? It must flood your subconscious at least to remember what it was like those first few days."

"Sure, sometimes. But you're there, on the ground, hoping to prevent another family from going through the same five-year-long drought of not knowing."

Brodie scratched on the door to get let in, and Beckett angled toward it to open. "What do you say? Let's get this show on the road. I've never planted kelp before, and I'm anxious to see how it's done."

The change of subject was abrupt but not surprising. Kelly started to clean up the mess they'd made on the table but realized she needed to pack a lunch. "Then we'll get to it. But first, I need to make us some sandwiches."

"No PB&J for me."

"That's what I thought you'd say. How about ham and cheese?"

"Much better."

"Virginia baked ham and Swiss on a bed of lettuce and tomato?"

"Now, you're talking. Lots of mayo."

"You got it."

They loaded Kelly's precious cargo of aquatic pods and pulled on their wetsuits and Wellies. The breeze fluttered across their faces as Beckett pulled up to the marsh. They got out and unloaded the crates packed to the brim with kelp. They stacked the baby plants at the water's edge within easy reach of the first location.

Kelly waded into the murky wetlands to look out over the barren estuary, wondering if she'd ever get to see it thrive again.

Salt marshes and sloughs were supposed to be rich habitats for the local and seasonal birdlife. Numerous plants had once thrived in these wetlands, giving fish and small marine mammals a place to call home. The natural vegetation here should have acted as a filter, getting rid of pollution from the water before the tidal flow moved it out into the ocean. This shallow ecosystem should have removed greenhouse gases from the air and captured things like carbon dioxide, methane, and nitrous oxide like a carbon sink. But these days, there just wasn't enough flora and undergrowth to get the job done.

"These particular kelp pods are supposed to tolerate warmer oceans and suck up more carbon in the air. Souped-up in the lab, it's as known as super kelp. We'll see in the coming weeks if this stuff is as great as they touted. Habitat restoration could use a miracle."

"You want to bring this estuary back to life," Beckett said, standing next to her, Brodie bumping his leg.

"Let's hope it's not too late. When I was here in March, I spent some time at the library researching what this area used to look like. You wouldn't believe how lush it used to be."

"You have pictures to document your research, right? Like a before and after redo?"

She nodded. "I'd love it if I could contribute to the after, the dream that it flourishes again as it did before. Wouldn't that be a kick?"

He held up a bag of what looked like large granules. "What's this stuff?"

"Kelp seeds. We're spreading those, too. I took everything the lab offered to give me. See that first ridge of water coming in off the surf? That's the outer rim of our test field. It's shallow enough to give these babies enough sunlight for photosynthesis yet has weak currents that won't wash them away."

"Location is key."

"You bet. That's why we need the *Brigid*. It will likely take us most of the morning and part of the afternoon. Your boat will go a long way to cutting the time down, making this go faster. Bet you didn't know you'd signed up for an all-day chore, huh? Got your sunblock slathered on?"

"Yep. It's in the glove box. Help yourself."

She reached for her backpack and held up her own brand. "I'm good. Thanks." After applying the sunscreen to her face and neck, she took out her camera phone to document the conditions of the plants and the surrounding marsh. "Notice how we're avoiding the areas with large amounts of free-floating sediments and murkier water. We don't want these seedlings having to fight the elements to stay alive."

"But it could happen, right?"

"Unfortunately, yes."

"Then we'd need to do it all over again."

"Well, I don't intend to mess this up."

He seemed to love the water as much as she did. Kelly saw the joy on his face. It was unmistakable as he took his first step out into the estuary. She pushed trays of pods toward him, the trays floating, half-submerged in their wire mesh and biodegradable paper containers.

At first, they were knee-deep in the water, then waist-deep, surrounded by tiny fish and god knows what slithering around their knees. He noted that none of the slimy stuff seemed to bother Kelly, not even the film coating their wetsuits.

They worked the marsh like a grid, setting the root-like structures at the bottom of the stalks—called the holdfast—in place to act as the anchor. They had to press each holdfast into the sandy bed until they could use the biodegradable material to attach the stem.

"Time-consuming but rewarding," Beckett noted when they placed the last of the pods into the sand. "I can't believe how bare the vegetation is below the surface of the water. There's not much growing in this spot. I just never noticed it before. And I've been hanging around here for years."

Kelly beamed in agreement as she began to spread the seeds. Feeling satisfied with the job they'd done, she looked over at him. "Now you see why I chose this place for my research. Ready for the next part?"

"Amped and jazzed."

It was shy of noon when they switched focus to the boat.

He tossed a relaxed arm over her shoulder as they walked back to the truck. "We're lucky to have you. Your work is essential if we don't want to see the ecosystem fail right in front of us. How about we eat as soon as we get on the boat? I've built up an appetite. I'm ready for those sandwiches."

She elbowed him lightly in the ribs. "I could use a cold drink."

"Cold drinks in the cooler already on the boat." He glanced over at Brodie. The dog had found himself a place to take a nap. "Come on, boy. Let's go eat."

The dog bounded up, recognizing the word, and smacked his chops.

"If it's not too much trouble, let's eat away from the pier on the water."

"Sure. Any reason?"

"I just like the peaceful notion of a leisurely picnic, kick back, and think about the bay's future."

Beckett smiled. "I can take the boat out to the edge of the test field. We'll sit out there with our sandwiches, eat lunch, and wave to the people on the dock."

"Wave? They might think we're crazy."

"Who cares? It's a beautiful day to be on the water. As long as this exercise in saving the planet means diving, I'm there every day of the week and twice on Sunday because I love to dive."

"Me too." She lifted her face to the sun and cupped her hand over her forehead to block out the rays. "I won't argue with that. We picked a good day to do this."

They stretched out on the deck with the boat bobbing in the water. They slipped out of the Wellies, propped their bare feet on the railing, wiggled their toes. With the sun warm on their faces, they shared a bag of chips, munched on the chunky ham sandwiches, and washed the food down with ice-cold orange soda from the bottle.

Brodie was happy getting pieces of her sandwich between a few doggie treats Beckett had hidden away.

They lazed in the sun, basking in the warmth of the spring day.

Her legs were tanned, Beckett noted, sexily bronzed and long. Her feet were narrow, probably size nine and a half. She'd painted her toenails turquoise and wore a silver ankle bracelet with a mermaid dangling from it. He gazed up the length of her body, stopping at the neckline on her floral print wetsuit. "How many of those things do you have?"

"What?"

"The wetsuits? How many do you own?"

"Gosh. Probably six. Why?"

He'd like to get her out of this one. "Just wondering."

She sent him a smile and patted her stomach. "Ready to get back to it?"

"Sure. Should I ask to see your dive certificate?"

She rolled her eyes. "I've been diving since I was ten. If you want to see proof, it's back in Hayward."

"Nah, I trust you. How does this work anyway? Use the tanks for diving in the deeper part of the bay?"

"How else would it work? Unless you can hold your breath long enough to hold the pods in place until we secure them. Although it isn't that deep."

"How were you planning to do this without a partner?"

She lifted a shoulder. "I've done it before, but it usually takes me twice as long."

"I'll get the tanks," he muttered, getting to his feet.

Unzipping her backpack, she took out her compact waterproof camera, aimed it at him, and snapped a photo. "To mark the day we saved the bay. For posterity."

Beckett liked that idea. Someday he might look back on this simple task and realize it was a turning point. "Here, let me take one of you."

She posed with Brodie, smiling, relaxed, enjoying the moment.

He brought out the dive equipment from a storage bin, held up fins, gauged the size, then helped her with her tank as she helped with his.

"Diving buddies," he murmured, impressed by how thorough she checked the equipment and tested the mask.

They dived along the shelf in shallow patches of sand, stopping to watch the remaining kelp dance and sway in the currents. Sometimes they goofed around after tying the pods in place by smashing a few sea urchins on the rocks. But their goal beneath the water was to get as many kelp seedlings as possible stable so the babies had a chance to grow.

Their task took them closer and closer to shore until they had finally completed the grid. It was mid-afternoon when they surfaced—whooping and hollering—celebrating like kids.

"That didn't take as long as I thought," Kelly admitted as she hauled herself back aboard the boat where Brodie waited to lick her face.

"Easy now," she told the dog. "I have saltwater on me."

It didn't go unnoticed that his dog seemed taken with Kelly, Beckett realized as he climbed up behind her on the ladder. After shedding his tank and fins, he slid out of his wetsuit but left his swim trunks and T-shirt. He went to the helm, revved the engine, and motored toward the dock.

"I don't know about you, but I'm exhausted," she whooshed out after settling on the bench seat with her arm around the dog.

"Same here. Did you take enough pictures?"

"I think so. I'll put a package together tonight and send it to the biologist in charge of the lab. Dr. Warner may offer suggestions about how often I should check the kelp to make sure the photosynthesis progresses. The upcoming week should tell us a lot."

"Are you nervous about it?"

"Not really. We've done an excellent job with what we had to work with. I brought as much stuff as I could cram into my truck. It has to be good enough, right?"

"It is. With all the hard work we did, it'll be okay." He pulled the boat into an open slot next to the wharf, tossed a rope toward the pylon, and watched as Kelly secured it to the mooring.

She hopped onto the pier with Brodie at her heels. While the dog took off to pee, Beckett trailed behind. But when he jumped onto the wooden dock and joined her, she pivoted to plant a friendly kiss on his cheek for helping her today.

When he stepped closer, she saw the gleam in his eyes. The wheels kept turning as he gripped her by the shoulders, kissing her hard and hot, rough.

She'd figure out later why she found that so appealing. "Want that shower?"

"Oh, yeah. Your place is closer." He caught her hand and tugged her toward his truck. "Brodie, let's go. We have things to do."

Eleven

They made it to her house, but just barely. The front door hadn't even closed behind them when she slumped against the living room wall, knocking the ballcap she wore to the floor. She dropped her backpack, knotted her fists in his T-shirt, and yanked him into her.

He crushed his mouth over hers while his hands roamed down her body. Mouths fused, they stumbled toward the hallway, almost knocking over a lamp. He nipped her around the waist to keep her from falling, then hauled up her against him.

"Get me out of this," she pleaded, spinning around and letting him rip the zipper down on her wetsuit. She tugged off her Wellies, balancing on one foot. He got rid of his sandals while she wriggled out of the thermal wetsuit, leaving her in shorts and a tank top.

Beckett's fingers sneaked under her shirt, stroking smooth, silky skin along her bare back.

Need and desperation had her clawing at his shirt. When she spotted the prominent tattoo on his left shoulder, it brought her full stop. "Wait. What's this?"

"Later," he breathed out, covering her mouth again. Because he wanted to see all of her, he tugged off the tank top and tossed it in the air. No bra gave him access to those small, firm breasts.

By now, they'd made it to the bed. He simply picked her up, gave her a toss on the mattress then followed her down. They rolled, somehow squirming to work the rest of the clothing off and sending it flying.

Twisting.
Writhing.
Exploring.
Eager.

"Where's Brodie?" Kelly whooshed out.

"Probably peeing in the bushes."

"Will he take off?"

"Nope," he murmured as he sampled her neck. Slowing things down, he trailed his way down her body, leaving wet kisses in his wake. The heated storm felt like a furnace burning full throttle when she came lightning fast. He brought her up again and into a glorious freefall.

Her long sexy body quaked under his. She took things up a notch, like a wild thrill ride the second time around. She squeezed around him. They were falling, falling, falling into a dizzying satiny dive together, then up again higher for the euphoric finish. They sprinted through the rising tide of need—gliding out the other side through an ecstatic wave of pleasure.

Out of breath, he rested his brow on hers as her arms stretched around his back.

"Mmm," was all she could manage as she pressed her lips to his chin.

"I usually show a little bit more finesse than that. Not so much in a hurry."

"Do you hear me complaining?"

He chuckled and rolled to the side, his feet dangling off the full-size bed. He took one look at her mussed-up golden-brown tresses—no longer in a ponytail—cascading down her shoulders and found that foolishly satisfying. "That's the first time I've seen you with your hair down. I wondered what it would look like."

She let out a short laugh, more like a squeal, and propped her head on a closed fist. She ran her left hand over his tattoo before pressing her lips to his chest. "When I looked you up the first time and found out you were a SEAL, I read about what each symbol means. This anchor represents the Navy, of course."

"Of course," he repeated in that slow Virginia twang.

Her fingers kept walking along the ink. "The eagle shows how SEALS protect by air, the pistol by land, and the trident by water."

"Every SEAL gets the tattoo once they've completed training. Some make a statement with a big-ass one all over the back. That's not me. I decided smaller, over the heart, would do the same thing." He moved her hair out of the way and planted a kiss on her neck. "You're always surprising me."

"Let's hope I'm never that boring," she murmured as she nibbled her way across his taut muscled body. "What's this cute little sunflower here on your ribcage?"

"That's for Brigid. She loved sunflowers. My whole family got one." He refused to let bad memories kick in now and changed the subject. "Are you hungry?"

"I'm past hungry. I could eat a jar of peanut butter all by myself."

"Should I worry that you've got this thing for peanut butter?"

"Poor student here who learned to stretch her budget with PB&J fixed many creative ways, day or night. Ever had peanut butter on celery?"

He made a face. "We can do better than that. Let's order a pizza with everything on it, get it delivered," Beckett suggested.

"If I don't have to move from this spot, I'd show my appreciation in so many inventive ways. But I do think one of us should check on Brodie."

At the sound of his name, the dog woofed and leaped up, joining them on the bed.

"Oh," Kelly uttered, laughing. "Big dog. Small bed."

Beckett got up, naked, and strolled out to the living room to look for his cell phone. "We need to find you a dog."

She laid a hand on Brodie's head and scratched behind his ears. "You know, I think you might be onto something."

"Where the hell is my phone?" Beckett called out from the hallway. He spotted the front door wide open and crossed the room to close it.

"Side pocket of your boat bag, probably still in the truck."

"Oh, yeah. Thanks. Well, somebody's got to order the pizza."

"Use mine. It's—?" Where was it? "Probably in my backpack," she realized and swung her legs up and over Brodie to get to her feet. "But I could use my laptop to order online."

"Ah. That'll work," he declared, snagging his trunks and shirt off the floor, balancing on one foot to get dressed.

She grabbed a robe out of the closet and walked out to boot up her laptop. "Pizza's on me."

"You don't have to do that."

"Look, without your help, I wouldn't have finished this soon. I'd still be out there. Besides, I need to sign up for Longboard's delivery anyway. I'm not a complete tightwad. I do occasionally enjoy food delivery. Hand me my backpack, will you?"

He retrieved the bag by the door, then began to pick up her clothes off the floor. "I'm not sure, but I think we might've broken a record to get undressed."

"Records were made to be broken," she mumbled, clicking through to the restaurant's website. After making a few selections, she turned to Beckett. "Is it okay to combine sausage *and* pepperoni?"

"A girl after my heart. Yep. That's good. Put anything else you want on it, too."

She added mushrooms and spinach and then dug for her credit card to complete the order. "There. All done. It'll be here in twenty minutes."

"I just realized you don't have a TV," Beckett noted.

"No. If there's something on you want to watch, we can live-stream it from my laptop."

"Nah, that's okay. I just thought about unwinding with the baseball game on. We don't need it."

"Are you sure? What team?"

"Washington Nationals versus Pittsburg."

She traded browsers, hit a few keys on her laptop, clicked through several options for Major League Baseball, and brought up the game.

"How'd you do that so fast?"

"Sometimes I feel like I spend my entire life in front of a computer. I'm good at researching any topic. Which reminds me. I started looking into Brigid's—"

The doorbell rang.

Tail wagging, Brodie beat a path to the door.

"That's the pizza," Beckett said. "Brodie has a nose for the stuff."

After that, she didn't have the heart to bring up Brigid again. She sensed he didn't want to talk about it, so she ate her food without mentioning her own theory. She realized she'd need to pick a more opportune time if she wanted to discuss the case.

When they finished eating, they crashed on the couch with the laptop set up between them, the baseball game droning on in the background. During the sixth inning, though, they both fell asleep.

Sometime later, Kelly woke up in bed, not knowing how she got there. Still wearing her robe, she sat up, pushed her hair out of her face, yawned and stretched. She glanced around the room, looking for Beckett and Brodie. She listened but didn't hear anything.

Scooting out of bed, she could tell it was dark outside and had been for some time. "Geez, what time is it? How long did I sleep?"

She wandered into the kitchen and spotted a white piece of paper tacked to the pastel green fridge. Hurriedly scrawled, the note read: *Had to go to San Sebastian to hunt for a lost six-year-old boy who wandered off from his parents at the flea market. Sorry. You were sleeping so soundly that I carried you to bed. Don't know when I'll be back home. Will let you know.*

She found her phone on the counter. The time read twelve-fifty. Should she send him a text in the middle of the night? While she debated, she poured herself a glass of orange juice, drank it down, staring at her phone.

After deciding it wouldn't hurt to ask for an update, she keyed in: *Where are you?*

Right outside. I wasn't sure you'd be awake or even up.

She went to the front door, opened it, and saw Beckett standing there with Brodie. She couldn't say why, but her heart warmed.

"Get in here. The night's chilly. Did you find the boy?"

He grinned as his arms went around her waist. "We did. That makes Brodie two for two. He's on a hot streak."

"Did he get a treat?" Kelly wanted to know as Brodie bumped her leg.

"The boy's parents were so grateful they bought him an ice cream cone."

"Heroes should get ice cream, right? I like the idea of that. You both look exhausted, though."

"I'm used to going without sleep for extended periods of time. But I won't lie. I could use eight hours."

"Then let's get you to bed. I hope you haven't sapped all your strength," she said, wriggling her eyebrows. "You should get a reward, too."

He cocked a brow. "If you're suggesting what I think you're suggesting, I'm in. I'm never too tired for that."

Laughing, she took his hand. "Nothing slow about you. Let's go to bed. Good night, Brodie."

"Brodie, you stay out here and protect the perimeter," Beckett directed, winking at the dog.

The dog yawned, whined, but did as he was told, curling up by himself in the middle of the sofa.

Kelly couldn't sleep. She wasn't used to having a man in her bed. And this man took up more than half the full-size mattress, leaving her clinging to the edge like a monkey on a vine.

She got up, threw on her robe, and tiptoed across the room, shutting the door behind her as she headed for the living room. She found Brodie sprawled out on the couch.

"Great. So you're a space hog, too," she intoned as she picked up her laptop and carried it over to the kitchen table. After booting it up, she checked her emails and social media accounts, including skimming through science updates on her phone using Instagram.

While reading a few of the posts, her mind wandered back to that night when Brigid had gone missing. Instead of keeping her brain focused on marine biology updates, it drifted to missing persons.

She closed out of one browser and went to another. Her search results showed how many women had disappeared in the last five or six years within Santa Cruz County. Some within a few blocks of where Brigid last appeared on video footage.

Stunned at the geographical data, Kelly plugged in a few more essential factors. She kept digging until she narrowed down the list to seven college-age women who'd gone missing after a night on the town.

Kelly didn't believe in coincidences.

"You're good at this," Scott commented from the other side of the kitchen. Before Kelly could react, he added, "Use your research skills to find Brigid, to find the other bodies."

"There are more?"

"Yeah. You need to stop this guy. Imagine what would happen if Beckett got hold of him first. Keep watching that video. The clue is in the video."

"Don't go," Kelly whispered as she watched Scott float away. "Damn."

She glanced over at the dog to see Brodie sitting upright, almost smiling at her. She let out a sigh. "Could this place get any weirder?"

Brodie hopped off the sofa and trotted over to put his head in her lap.

She leaned forward to nuzzle his face. "That does it. I'm getting myself a dog. Got any brothers or sisters out there I don't know about?"

Twelve

In Beckett's mind, turning his backyard into a mini dog training facility had been nothing short of brilliant. Even though it meant sacrificing his lawn or doing without pretty plants and tidy landscaping, the setup gave him a perfect place to put Brodie through his paces—without distractions.

The bonus was he didn't need to cut the grass as often.

But his mother had showed up one day with a truckload of ornamental shrubs and a few trees, like the olive tree that still sat in a black plastic bucket on his patio. He had yet to transfer any of them into the ground, which was a bit ironic since he'd spent yesterday planting kelp in the ocean.

He scanned his backyard, proud of the work he'd done. He'd kept things simple and built most of the obstacle course himself since he knew a thing or two about running an obstacle course.

The A-frame he'd made out of plywood and went a long way in helping Brodie with agility. Same thing with the elevated dog walk and teeter-totter that helped the retriever balance at different heights. He'd created three jump stations out of plastic piping and bought a heavy-duty S-shaped tunnel at a big box store in San Sebastian.

It had taken months of training for Brodie to make any sort of progress at all. But lately, the pup had been improving his skills—other than a few lapses like jumping into women's laps.

Beckett had started Brodie's training at three months, the same day he'd brought him home from Cord's shelter. The two had made an instant connection at the kennel. And after the vet had recommended him, Beckett had no doubt he'd found his best four-legged friend.

"Not only is he the smartest dog in my kennels, but he's also the easiest-going pup here," Cord had boasted.

Beckett smiled at the memory.

He'd been around enough search and rescues to know that a reliable search dog should be able to work on any kind of terrain—rocks, woods, water, mountains, even frozen ground didn't matter. A dependable search dog should be as relaxed in urban areas around people as in the solitude of the rural countryside. They should be able to work rain or shine, in any type of weather, day or night. He'd done his best to provide Brodie with as many challenging situations as he could think to create, hoping they would both pass Debra's stringent exams.

Man and dog had started the day working on heeling off-leash and a series of stop commands. Something that wasn't Brodie's specialty. But after a workout, Beckett was convinced the retriever had improved in all the early morning backyard maneuvers that he'd thrown at him.

Except for one.

While he let Brodie run off some puppy energy as a reward, he tossed a tennis ball around and watched the dog jump in the air to fetch. He gave the dog a break before switching to the all-important scent training. It made sense to him. But he also felt nervous about it. Scent training last winter had been

Brodie's downfall. He liked to think that maybe the pup had been too young. At least, that's what he kept telling himself, hoping that Brodie would become certified this time around.

Coaching the golden retriever to keep still during an alert was another trickier part of training. Brodie had to learn to plop his butt on the ground and stay put without peeing, digging, or playing around.

Before the fetch game became exhausting, Beckett took the dog through different smells—different treats he'd placed around the yard.

In his heart, he believed, at the very least, Brodie had it in him to become a great tracker, an even better air-scent dog than Cyrus. Hadn't the pup proved his worth two times in a row on Friday and Saturday nights?

He'd learned a long time ago that a canine's scent ability was hundreds of times greater than that of humans. He'd seen those dogs in action overseas. Air-scent dogs could pick up a smell carried on the wind, then seek out its source or the point of greatest intensity.

Convinced Brodie had it in him to become an exceptional S-and-R dog, Beckett watched with pride as Brodie uncovered every treat.

But it was time for the big test, time to cap off the morning's workout by detecting human remains. Decomposition was tricky. It fell into that category of bones, blood, tissue, and body parts. Even detecting residue meant picking up on whether a body had been in a specific location, even if it was no longer there.

As a certified trainer, Debra had access to all kinds of medical waste materials used for decomposition training—extracted teeth, soiled gauze, subcutaneous fat from liposuctions, and human bones from college laboratories where donated cadavers provided blood and tissue samples. Some of it grossed Beckett out. But he could appreciate the value of its vital contribution to the cause, no matter how tiny the specimen.

For Brodie's test today, Beckett used an extracted tooth, a handful of human hair, and a small bone fragment the size of a dime. He'd hidden the items—bagged in plastic—in various spots all over the yard. The strands of hair were underneath one of the nursery pots at the back of the property with a lemon tree in it. The bone fragment was tucked away inside the patio chair cushion moved away from the deck. He'd shoved the extracted tooth between the firewood logs at the side of the house.

Standing in the middle of his yard, he realized how nervous he felt. Come on, Brodie, sniff out the dead guy, Beckett thought as he moved the dog into position. Instead of using that command, he tempered his directive using the euphemism they'd been calling the dead guy since Brodie was a puppy. "Come on, Brodie, go find Frankie. Find him, Brodie. Find Frankie."

Sniffing the air, the retriever trotted around the yard until he alerted, pawing at the dirt and showing interest in the patio chair before plopping his butt on the ground.

"Good, boy," Beckett said, running a hand over the dog's head as he pulled out the tiny piece of bone from its hiding place.

"Do it again, Brodie. Go find Frankie."

The retriever circled the yard, this time heading east toward the nursery pot. Again, Brodie alerted by pawing the ground before sitting in front of the fruit tree.

Beckett got down on one knee to ruffle the dog behind the ears. "Good job, boy. Good job. Now one more time. Go find Frankie."

Brodie wandered around the yard hunting, searching. The dog wasn't even close to the side of the house. Beckett let it play out, hoping Brodie would eventually pick up the scent.

After taking a prolonged sniff in the air, Brodie took off around the house, heading straight to the stack of wood and pawed the ground.

Beckett pulled out the baggie containing the extracted tooth. He pumped his fist in the air, then held out his hand with several treats. He bent down to Brodie's level and rested his head on the retriever's. "You did it, Brodie. Good job. Good dog. You're such a good boy."

"You have a nice setup here," Kelly remarked, strolling into the backyard. She'd been watching from the sidelines for twenty minutes, not wanting to distract Brodie. "And an even nicer dog. Looks like you have a winner."

"I don't want to get too cocky, but I believe he's ready for his big test tomorrow," Beckett noted, studying Kelly from head to toe. She wore a pair of jean shorts, a loose floral top, and sandals on her feet. She had her hair twisted into the ever-present ponytail and pulled through the ballcap that shaded her eyes.

"If it's okay with you, I'd like to go with you guys. I'll drop you off at Debra's place and drive around until you're ready for me to pick you up. How does that sound?" She really wanted to check out Santa Cruz and see the area where Brigid had disappeared for herself. But she didn't think sharing that with him right now would earn her any points.

"Sure. You don't want to stay and watch?"

"Nope. Too nerve-wracking. Plus, Brodie doesn't need another person there confusing him."

"We might've passed that stage," Beckett noted proudly. "Want something cold to drink? I drained my water bottle an hour ago. I could use a refill."

She patted her backpack. "I never go anywhere without my refillable stainless-steel bottle. But what I could use right now is a strong frappe. It's on me since you left this morning before we had a chance to finish our breakfast."

"Sorry about that. But I think the time was well spent. Brodie has made such great strides lately, and I wanted to build on it. I could use a Cappuccino. And Brodie could use a break."

She looped an arm through his. If she played her cards right, maybe she could work Brigid and the other missing women into the conversation.

Did every Callahan have trouble talking about Brigid? she wondered as she sat across Beckett, sipping her iced coffee. She'd danced around the topic until she finally blurted out, "Look, this might be painful to hear, but do you know there are other missing women in Santa Cruz in addition to Brigid? Like seven since she disappeared?"

His face went blank. "What? Are you sure?"

"Beckett, I've done nothing but study Brigid's case since Friday night. You might say that I'm hooked, maybe obsessed with finding out more. But I'm convinced she didn't walk to Shark Fin Cove. It's ridiculous to believe that. I don't think she drowned in the ocean either. I think she waited for someone outside that burger restaurant. Someone picked her up. Either someone she called or a stranger who snatched her out of the parking lot. The thing is her phone records would've indicated who she talked to after she left the bar. You said that you guys looked at her phone and nothing jumped out. Do you still have copies of the phone data?"

"Yes, we went through her phone records, and no, there was nothing that stood out. We tracked down every single number on that phone and talked to every individual. It was a dead end."

"Okay, could this have been a pre-arranged hookup? Could she have used a dating app that no one knew about, some secret app she might've been embarrassed about, an app where she avoided leaving the usual trail? The contact would've been directly from the app."

"My God, I never even considered that option."

"Look, I spent a lot of time in college. And there are a dozen ways to mask your activities, especially if you planned an evening out, kept the situation fluid, and let circumstances play to your advantage. The situation might change during the evening from one moment to the next. You may start at one bar but decide to go somewhere else at the spur of the moment. College kids are notorious for keeping their options open."

"But how on earth would we find who that was?"

"You'd have to go back through her laptop, find every available device she had at her disposal. Look for all the apps she downloaded. It might be as simple as a gaming app."

Beckett ran his hands through his hair. "Wow. I think the cops gave everything they had back to my parents. That stuff would be at their house, probably stored away in the garage. Wait a sec. That's why you want to go with us to Santa Cruz tomorrow, right? To take another look at the bar, the burger joint, and the cove."

"What can I say? I've fallen down the rabbit hole. There's also an online sleuth who lives there. I'd like to talk to her face to face. She runs a blog and seems fascinated by the Santa Cruz disappearances. She's even made a few posts about Brigid's night out and subsequent disappearance."

"Define fascinated. Is she one of those obsessed nutcases? Those crawled out of the woodwork after Brigid vanished."

She lifted a shoulder. "Who knows when you're dealing with someone over the Internet, hiding behind an avatar or a made-up profile. This person—whoever they are—seems to believe in a certain theory. I'd like to explore that in greater detail. To do that, I plan to set up a meeting." Her voice trailed off, leaving the theory vague.

"What?"

"I don't want you to think I'm getting all negative or anything, but—"

"We already figure Brigid is dead," Beckett stated. "No point in dancing around that. We resigned ourselves to that conclusion long ago and even had a family meeting about it. My parents went to court and had her declared legally dead last year."

"Doesn't that usually mean waiting seven years?"

"Depends on the extenuating circumstances and the person's inexplicable absence. In this case, the police firmly believe Brigid fell into the ocean and drowned. A detective testified to that before a judge. Then you have family and friends saying that Brigid would never have left without telling anyone. The judge agreed and declared her dead."

"I'm so sorry."

"It's not like we hadn't prepared ourselves. But you're suggesting that Brigid might've crossed paths with a serial killer?"

"I'm not suggesting it. I'm repeating what I found online about the next seven victims. Brigid might've been his first. I'm surprised you haven't run across these blog postings."

"After the hearing, I had to stop reacting to every blog or theory I saw. It's been almost six months since I last looked at all that stuff. I mean really looked. Those constant reminders crawl inside your brain and take control. All you think about is what *might've happened* until it drives you nuts. And without solid evidence, you'll never get the cops to change their minds."

She thought back to what Scott said about Beckett finding the guy responsible first and what he might do if he did. "I guess it would make a person a little crazy."

"Brigid's been gone almost six years. I'm not saying I'll stop looking. I know Birk will never quit. Not ever. But I'd like to find a way through life without thinking about Brigid all the time. At some point, I need to let it go and live. That's what I'm trying to do with Search and Rescue, with Terra Search & Recovery."

"I don't mind looking into it because this is new to me. I haven't lived it for the past five years."

"But you'd like to talk about it, right?"

"I could always contact this websleuth and talk about the case with her, leave you out of it entirely."

"You're that caught up in it?"

"I believe I am. Should I talk to Birk about my plan?"

"You realize Birk is the one who maintains the website, right? He's the one who follows every lead down to a nub."

She nodded. "I figured. I went through Brigid's website and read the posts."

"Dear God, the bug's taken control of you. When did this happen? You haven't been wrapped up in this the whole time, have you?"

A laugh escaped as she started to sip her coffee. "No. But it didn't take much for me to get hooked. Scott says the answer is in that CCTV footage. I've already watched it two dozen times."

"If you've been listening to Scott, you're grasping at straws. But hey, if you want to talk to Birk, I'll set it up." He lifted a hip, took out his cell phone from his back pocket, and texted his brother.

"You already know Birk is a prickly sort of guy. Don't expect too much from him."

"Why is he so bitter?"

"Life wears some of us down more than others. He's seen war and death. Then he gets stateside and finds out our baby sister has vanished without a trace. You turn to the cops for help but discover they're not crusaders like you thought. It makes a man bitter if you let it. Birk's let it eat at him."

"And he has this mysterious side investigation business," Kelly ventured.

"I wouldn't go mentioning that to Birk. He's touchy about what he does on the side."

"You didn't want any part of that?"

Beckett looked away, out the glass window to the sidewalk. "I wanted to find Brigid. That didn't happen. I decided to help other families find answers for them if I could. I found a way to do that. I help Birk out occasionally with the small stuff. I'm the computer geek who knows my way around an issue when it pops up."

"Sounds fascinating, one geek to another."

Beckett's cell phone dinged with a message. "Birk's available for lunch. I'll invite him to my place, and you can grill him there."

"I don't want to grill Birk. I just need to find out everything he knows."

"Good luck with that," Beckett murmured, getting to his feet.

"Where are you going?"

"Shopping. I need to buy stuff for lunch. I wouldn't feel right feeding anybody peanut butter sandwiches."

Thirteen

"Don't go bothering my parents with this shit," Birk shouted from across the kitchen. "I moved all of Brigid's stuff out of their garage and brought it to my house for a reason. There's nothing left to go through there. I don't need anyone, especially an amateur, butting in messing with things."

"Why did I think I'd get cooperation out of you two?" Kelly fired back, just as loud. "Have either of you gotten any farther into Brigid's disappearance? Is there progress I don't know about? Updates that refer to a cohesive, organized timeframe? A geographical map that tracks her movements? A complete picture of the night she went missing? Because if you haven't offered up any of those things, it sounds to me like you could use all the help you could get."

"What could it hurt allowing her access to Brigid's laptop?" Beckett tossed out.

"You would take her side since you're sleeping with her," Birk pointed out.

Kelly rolled her eyes. "Have you ever read the blog dedicated to the missing women in Santa Cruz?"

"Oh, brilliant," Birk spat out. "You're getting sucked in by one of those pretend sleuths. The blogger's name is Jade Weingarten, a hippie chick who thinks she's an online Sherlock Holmes. I've talked to Jade on multiple occasions. She's dug a trench, convinced herself there's a serial killer out there making women disappear. The only thing she has to go on is a *feeling*. She can't get the cops interested because she doesn't have a shred of proof."

Kelly threw up her hands. "That's what I'm trying to do is get the proof."

"Oh, please. What makes you think you'll have better luck than I had?" Birk reasoned.

"For one thing, I'm a better researcher than you are," Kelly expressed. "And I'm not emotionally attached. Sure, I can get emotional thinking about these missing women. Who wouldn't? But I'll keep my emotions and *feelings* out of the equation. Any observations and conclusions I make will be based on facts. In other words, I can keep an open mind about everything I find and come to a logical starting point."

Birk dug his hands into his pockets and began to pace. "All right, Miss Know-it-All. But when you come up with nothing after talking to the conspiracy theorist, I want an apology. And after sticking your nose in this, I want you to butt out for good."

"If I don't find anything new within two weeks, I'll not only apologize, but I'll also leave you alone forever. How does that sound?"

"You'll return everything intact?" Birk urged. "No holding anything back? Or making copies for your own files?"

"I promise I'll return everything to you personally." Kelly picked up her backpack and headed out of the kitchen.

"Where are you going?" Beckett asked.

"Since I'm locked into a tight timeframe now, I need to get started. And my first stop is to talk to this Jade Weingarten. You two have a nice lunch. I can find my way to Santa Cruz by myself."

She pivoted back to Birk. "And I want whatever you have delivered to my house tonight by six o'clock so that I can begin going through Brigid's stuff. Any questions?" When no one said anything, she added, "Good. Now we're all on the same page."

As soon as Kelly reached her truck, she sent Jade Weingarten an email through her blog site, introducing herself as a friend of Birk Callahan's.

But she didn't intend to wait around for a response. If Jade turned out to be a nutcase, she would proceed without her. And to do that, she needed to drive around Santa Cruz and get a feel for the area, see for herself where the other women went missing. She didn't need Jade or the Callahan brothers for that. There was ample information about each case online from three different bloggers fully engaged in the process.

After stopping by the house to grab her laptop and throw together a peanut butter sandwich, she headed down the Pacific Coast Highway to Santa Cruz.

Halfway there, her phone dinged with a message from Jade, offering to meet her at a coffee shop downtown.

Perfect, Kelly decided and texted back a reply, countering with a suggestion to meet across the street from the burger chain. *That* burger chain. Jade thought that location was even better.

Anxious about meeting a total stranger, Kelly reminded herself she'd picked a public place as she pulled to the intersection where Brigid had last appeared on video. At the light, she studied the layout—a burger joint on the right, a convenience store across the street, and a bookshop next door to that. A well-known national bank had a branch office located on the opposite side of the intersection.

Just as she thought, the numerous opportunities for CCTV footage were everywhere. So, why didn't anybody have a clue what happened to Brigid?

When the light turned green, she turned into the parking lot and spotted the woman almost immediately. She sent up a wave.

It was hard to miss the exotic-looking Jade Weingarten with her long dark hair and sultry brown eyes. And the thirty-something true-crime enthusiast didn't mind making a statement with her wardrobe choices. Jade wore a boho midi dress, turquoise trimmed in brown, with cowboy boots in beige-flowered leather. A string of eight colorful necklaces draped from her neck. Wide hooped earrings dangled from her ears. A pair of purple-colored sunglasses covered her eyes.

Kelly could see Birk's hippie chick reference. But where Birk thought it was weird, Kelly thought Jade's getup fit her personality to a tee from everything she'd read on her blog. Jade even dabbled in the paranormal. So far, the woman seemed to live up to her online persona.

Eager to make her acquaintance, Kelly got out of the pickup and extended her hand in greeting. "Thanks for meeting me. I really appreciate this. Not many people would agree to meet a stranger in person."

"I admit I read your email three times before it stuck. I couldn't believe Birk Callahan would recommend talking to me. He doesn't like me very much."

"I'm not sure Birk likes anyone. And for the record, he didn't exactly recommend it. In fact, he was not very cooperative at all." Kelly went into a detailed account outlining her conversation with Birk and his ultimate challenge. "He's given me two weeks to dig up something new."

"Now that I can believe," Jade said with a laugh. "The man issues ridiculous deadlines about a case almost six years old, and he thinks I'm crazy. Did he mention that I used to make my living as a blackjack dealer in Reno?"

Kelly snickered with laughter. "No, he didn't mention that. This might be a great time to bring up that I have zero experience dealing with kidnapping, abduction, or murder."

"Marine biologist. I looked you up, too. You're on the faculty at Redwood State University."

"Guilty. I made the mistake of spending twenty minutes looking for details on Brigid's case and fell down the rabbit hole. Your blog was one of the bright spots I found, though."

"Thanks for that. It's easy enough to get caught up in a murder or a disappearance, especially when the answers elude even law enforcement. We're not so obsessed with the things we can explain but rather the stuff we can't. That's what makes it a deep, dark puzzle that messes with your head."

"Well put. As I explained earlier, I'd like to sit down and pick your brain about Brigid. I'm asking you to get me up to speed on her personality from an outsider's perspective. I think you're the best place to start. What was she like? What were her flaws? How did she get along with the people in her inner circle? Who was she dating? I could ask her brothers, but it might not get me the real Brigid. They seem to keep her up there on that lofty pedestal, which I don't think is real."

Jade nodded in understanding. "I like you. You see, I don't think the family knew the real Brigid. It happens more often than not. Her family was three thousand miles away. And let me tell you, from what

I know, the girl took full advantage of her newfound freedom with no one looking over her shoulder."

"I've been there. It's unrealistic to think that Brigid didn't want to sow a few wild oats without anyone telling her what to do."

"Exactly. We've all been away from home for the first time. You do things you wouldn't normally do. I'm glad you're here and happy to give you my opinion, for what it's worth."

"Great. I think you're onto something with the serial killer angle, which is another reason I'm here."

"Then we're on the same page. Tell you what, why don't we take this meeting back to my house? I live around the corner. I'll make us a fresh pot of coffee, we can exchange ideas, and you can start your questions from the beginning."

As Kelly followed Jade's little silver Honda convertible down a tree-lined street, she wondered what the two had in common. A scientist and an amateur sleuth who ran a blogsite shouldn't have felt like a compatible kinship. Yet, Kelly felt drawn to the woman. And they'd barely discussed Brigid's case.

When the Honda swung into the driveway of an adorable Craftsman bungalow, Kelly found an open slot on the street. After gathering up her bag, she could only stare at the peacock blue house with white trim and the tortoise-shell cat perched in the front window looking at her with huge green eyes.

"Don't mind Cosmo," Jade began as she led the way into a plant-filled foyer. "That's his favorite spot. He likes to sun himself and watch the foot traffic on the sidewalk. Don't ask me why. Most of the time, he's too much of a lazybones to move from his happy place."

"He won't dart out the door?"

"Cosmo? No way. He's an indoor cat who likes to observe life from the windowsill. Plus, he doesn't like to get too far from his food dish, as you can tell."

Kelly chuckled and looked around the room. "You have the cutest house."

"It's not mine. I rent from the sweetest little old lady. She's been my landlord for five years now. I was lucky to get this place so close to the arts district. I'll put on that coffee. Do you like peanut butter cookies? I made a batch this morning. They're my favorite."

Kelly sputtered with laughter. "Who doesn't love peanut butter on everything? I think we're looking at a long friendship here."

"My thoughts exactly."

The two women bonded over a steady stream of cookies and strong, Italian-roast coffee.

Kelly found Jade not only likable but thoroughly knowledgeable about Brigid's case. "It's like you took the time to research and dig deep."

"I tried to talk to everyone who knew her. Everyone. That took years to do."

"Why do you suppose Birk doesn't believe the serial killer theory?"

"My honest take is that he and his brother have convinced themselves that Brigid was involved in a hit and run that happened out of camera range. And the driver or maybe a passenger disposed of the body."

"A hit and run? A car accident? Beckett never said a word to me like that. Did Birk?"

"He brought it up the first time we met. And for a while there, I thought it might be true. Although it's possible, I don't think that's what happened. There's nothing to back it up. Have you met Brigid's parents yet?"

"No. Why?"

"Because Craig and Betty Callahan don't believe it either. I know because I ran into them last Christmas at the mall while doing my last-minute shopping. They told me they never miss reading my blog. Betty or Craig calls me probably once a month. They're convinced, like me, that Brigid was the first victim of a serial killer. And they encouraged me to keep digging."

"Isn't that interesting that the sons don't share that opinion? If it means anything at all, the serial killer theory is the best one. I think she intended to meet someone that night, someone she'd met on an app, and that someone was the killer."

"You should know that I don't have access to everything in Brigid's file. Instead, I made my own notes. Which begs the question, how would we come up with who she met? And if we did, how would we ever get the police to change their minds? Once they're locked in on a theory, it's hard to get them to budge. I'll give you an example. A couple of years ago, I talked to the lead detective on the case. I approached him at a police convention in San Francisco. I explained that I'd tried to walk from the burger joint to Shark Fin Cove and lasted about forty-five minutes before giving up. You know what that man said to me?"

"What?"

"He said you're not young, twenty, lost, and motivated to keep moving in the dark. He didn't like that I challenged him about it. Was there a roundtable discussion among the cops about what a college student would do and how she would react in that situation? Because it certainly seemed to me like the police were projecting what they thought a twenty-year-old would do without a shred of proof."

"I'm convinced she was waiting for someone to pick her up. I'm even convinced she left the bar that night—not because she argued with a friend—but to meet up with someone. It's ridiculous to believe Brigid walked to the cove. I intended to try doing it today."

"Oh, please try. See how long you last and get back to me."

"I will. Full disclosure here. I got Birk to let me go through Brigid's laptop."

"I'm very impressed. I don't see sweet-talking Birk into anything he doesn't want to do. How did you manage that?"

"Beckett had a hand in convincing him. Now that I've had time to look back on the discussion, Beckett didn't look happy about my standing up to his brother. Maybe I've ruined another relationship."

"You know what they say. Better to find out now than later."

"It's strange how Brigid's disappearance brought me to Santa Cruz. And here I am talking to you."

"Why is that strange?"

"I didn't plan on any of this, certainly not meeting Beckett or getting involved with anyone this summer. Right about now, I should be outlining my research paper. Instead, I'm talking about something totally out of my field, like a possible murder, at the very least an abduction, or something entirely weird."

"You're making a new friend."

"I could always use a friend. Have you ever seen a ghost?"

Jade lifted a brow. "You're into the paranormal? You didn't mention that in your email. We do have a lot in common."

"I guess you could say I'm a recent convert. Although you don't grow up around Lake Tahoe without hearing a few ghost stories."

"I grew up in Oregon. Eugene is my hometown. The mausoleum and graveyard there are backdrops for hundreds of ghostly sightings over the years. We heard about them even as kids. But I experienced my first and very personal story when my mom died."

"I'm so sorry. When did she die?"

"I was eleven when she developed breast cancer. She died when I was fourteen, leaving my little sister and me to go live with my mom's sister in Reno. But before we left, my mother came to me one night and told me everything would be okay. It was so real that I thought she'd come back to us. And get this, my sister saw her, too. So this wasn't *my* imagination or me projecting or whatever you want to call it. I'm convinced it really happened."

"Is that the only time you talked to your mom?"

"No. It became a regular occurrence once we got to Reno, especially whenever I had a difficult issue confronting me." Jade tilted her head to stare at Kelly. "You've seen one too?"

"I've talked to him. His name is Scott, and he's been dead for years. Apparently, this guy's a fixture in Pelican Pointe. Everyone seems to have a Scott story. Even Birk gave me his take."

"Birk has seen him, too."

"Apparently everyone who lives there has. Scott says the answer to finding Brigid is in that CCTV footage you have on your blog."

"Really? Interesting. Do you want the specifics on the other women while you're here?"

"Of course. If we could find just one, it would be a victory."

Jade went over to a china cabinet and scooped up several manila file folders. She slid the stack across the table and booted up her laptop. "Brigid Callahan went missing on the first chilly Friday night in October five and a half years ago. By spring of the following year, two other women had disappeared under similar circumstances. Eighteen-year-old Jennifer Langley, a freshman at the same university, went missing the first week of April from the same general area where Brigid was last seen. Jennifer had spent the early evening at a party given by her sister-in-law two blocks from my house. She never made it back to her dorm room. The people at the party say she wasn't drunk or intoxicated when she left. Then, four months later, in August, a nineteen-year-old at the art institute named Samja Whatley disappeared after an evening out with her parents, visiting from out of town. Samja had eaten dinner down the street from that burger place."

"No kidding?"

"You see the similarity, right? When Samja didn't return home to her apartment, her roommates became concerned and called the police the following day. Samja is the only African American so far on the list. But keep reading. Later, we add Hispanic and Indigenous women to the victim list."

Kelly went through Jade's very organized files. "There's twenty-four-year-old Chelsea Lindenhall in January. She tells her roommates she's going to the gym around seven in the evening but never makes it there. And no one has seen her since."

"The police found Chelsea's car in a grocery store parking lot a week later. No sign of Chelsea." Jade tapped the next folder. "Then, at the end of May, seventeen-year-old Catalina DeGuerin, a student at the community college, goes out to pick up chips and dips for her mom, who is hosting a Memorial Day party, and disappears without a trace."

"That occurs a mile from the burger joint. Weird. Now we're well into the third year of disappearances when Monica Tisdale, twenty, goes out with friends to a bar before the school year starts, leaves the bar by herself at around midnight, and doesn't make it back home."

"Similar to Brigid's case in so many ways. For one, the location is across the street from Clever Pete's at a dive called The Tipsy Cow. It's still in business. And get this, Monica was drinking on a fake ID."

"Like Brigid."

"Yep."

"Maybe the killer has ties to creating fake IDs."

"Possibly. I think you're missing one from two years ago. Lannie Overstreet who was seen leaving classes, then crossing the bridge at UC Santa Cruz to the parking lot. She never makes it onto the bus. The CCTV footage backs that up. When Lannie doesn't check in at home, her parents file a missing person report. No one has seen her since."

"I've got goosebumps over this one. I know that bridge. I almost got mugged there."

Jade raised a brow. "Are you sure it was a mugging? Could it have been an attempted kidnapping? When did this happen?"

"Two years ago, after a lecture. I walked across the bridge to catch the shuttle back to my hotel. If it hadn't been for—" Scott thought Kelly. But instead of saying his name, she went on, "a good Samaritan intervened, and the mugger ran off."

"You're lucky. Lannie Overstreet disappeared two years ago. Look at the date."

"October 16th. That's roughly seven weeks before I was at the same spot in December."

Jade shuddered. "Talk about spooky. You could've been his next victim. Now, fast forward to a few months ago, last February. Another Indigenous woman disappears. This time around, the killer snatches someone closer to your age group. Robin Galle was thirty, a graduate from Redwood State and a teacher."

"Oh, my God. That's uncanny. I teach at Redwood State, and I've never heard of this case."

"See? That right there is proof these cases aren't getting much attention. It's the reason people like me do this. It's the reason we get upset with law enforcement. It's why we're out there beating the drum, shaking every tree for answers. We need someone to take up the cause and admit these cases are linked to a single killer."

"Is it okay to make copies of these files? I'll need to go to a copy store to get it done."

"No need. My printer thinks it's a copier. Feel free to make as many copies of anything you want to take with you and study later."

"I'd like to use these cases to make a convincing case with Beckett and Birk. And I know just the way to get through to them."

"How?"

"Same way I get through to my hard-headed students—a PowerPoint presentation with photos and plenty of specifics."

"You go girl. If you need my help, you have only to pick up the phone and ask."

"Thanks, Jade. If not for you, I'd be on my own in this."

"You aren't alone. I'll even go with you to Shark Fin Cove."

Kelly glanced at the clock. "I didn't realize it's so late. I need to walk the route out there."

Jade shook her head. "I'm telling you, you're wasting your time."

"No, I won't. I'll video the entire process to show Beckett when I get back."

"Good thinking. I'll work the camera phone."

Kelly didn't get far along the ten-mile route to Shark Fin Cove before giving up trying to navigate the heavily congested traffic nightmare. She didn't even make it to the remote part of the road before signaling Jade she was ready to quit.

As cars whizzed by them in the northbound lanes, she held up the map on her phone. "There are seven closer beach destinations Brigid could've gone to that night. No one in their right mind would walk all that way out in the middle of nowhere."

"You have to see it for yourself to realize it's impractical," Jade emphasized as she waited to merge back into traffic. "For the police to hang their entire theory on it is just plain silly."

"Is it always like this? The gridlock seems worse than when I was here last. And that was two years ago."

"Mostly, it's nonstop. Where to now?"

"I have another idea. It's a long shot. But at this point, what do we have to lose?"

Before sunset, Kelly and Jade strolled into The Tipsy Cow—a country and western theme bar—and asked to speak to the manager.

A sexy-looking jock type, tanned, toned, and towering in size, greeted them from a side office. "What can I do for your ladies?"

"We're looking into the Monica Tisdale disappearance," Kelly began. "Were you working here back then?"

"Nope. But I've heard of the case. Who hasn't? Updates every year on the anniversary of her disappearance and the grieving mom begging for the public's help."

"People seem to remember when an attractive blond, a college student out drinking on a fake ID, goes missing without a trace," Jade pointed out for effect.

Kelly pointed to several security cameras. "Were these cameras in place back then?"

"They've been here since the bar opened six years ago. Our security company insists on storing the surveillance just in case there's a criminal complaint down the road."

"Just what we wanted to hear," Kelly replied. "What would we have to do to get you to dig out the ones from October of that year?"

"Are you nuts? That would take weeks. Plus, the footage isn't available to me or any other employee at the bar."

"Then who would we need to contact about getting our hands on certain dates from several years back?"

"Our security company is Ward Warriors, owned by a guy named Tony Ward. Tony handles everything from our software updates to credit card fraud. His brother Allen is the bar owner's lawyer." The hunky manager led them into his office, rummaged through a drawer, and pulled out two business cards. "One card is for the security company. The other is for our attorney. You can contact them directly and see what they say. Don't be surprised if they try to dissuade you."

Kelly frowned. "Why? This isn't the first time anyone has requested the CCTV footage, is it?"

"We don't want to get sued. It's that simple. I wouldn't be surprised if both places tell you that footage no longer exists."

Kelly traded looks with Jade. "There are other ways of getting footage, more challenging from five years ago than two. But it's certainly worth a try."

"An appeal to the public online," Jade uttered in agreement. "I'm on it. Hopefully, when Monica went missing, this place was packed. Since I'm local, I'll take care of it on my end with my next blog post, appealing for cell phone footage from that night."

The manager cleared his throat. "If it's any consolation, right after I started working here after Monica went missing, the bar got fined for serving college kids drinking on fake IDs. Our bartenders are much older these days and more dedicated to following rules and procedures."

"Good to know. Shouldn't we get something to eat while we're here," Jade suggested with a shrug. "Unless you're anxious to get back to Pelican Pointe."

"Might as well. I'm not in the mood to go back home and eat by myself. Besides, I'm still picking your brain."

The bar manager grinned. "I'll get you set up. How about free appetizers?"

"Who says no to free anything?" Jade remarked as they walked back into the bar.

"Not me. Even if it's bar food." Kelly nudged Jade as they followed the manager to a pub table. "I'd like your opinion about the other Internet sleuths, the ones who post about Brigid's case but aren't local to Santa Cruz. Tell me everything you know about them."

"I've got a list," Jade cracked. "They're good, but I'm better."

Kelly laughed. "I thought you might say that. Let's order quesadillas and guacamole with a margarita."

"I knew I liked you for a reason. Will you be okay to drive later?"

"If I keep it to one drink, I'll be fine." When her phone dinged with a message from Beckett, it warmed her heart. "Look at this. Beckett's worried about me."

"He's the softer version of Birk for sure."

"Well, I like him," Kelly kidded as she keyed in a return message. "I think I might just keep him."

Kelly ended up having two margaritas and stuffing herself with Mexican food. When she arrived back home around ten-thirty, she was shocked to see Beckett waiting for her in his truck.

"I brought over Brigid's stuff and didn't want to leave it on the front porch."

"That's so sweet. Thank you. I appreciate you backing me up with your brother. Earlier. Although you didn't look that happy about it. But you stood up for me, and that's the important thing."

"How'd everything go with Jade?"

"We hit it off. No matter what Birk thinks about her, she's very knowledgeable about your sister's case. We've already made progress."

Beckett lifted a brow. "How so?"

"Why don't you come in, and I'll go over everything."

"If I come in, I won't want to leave tonight. And I have Brodie's big test in the morning. It's his last chance, Kelly."

She laid a hand on his cheek. "I'll help you unload Brigid's stuff, then you should head home and get some sleep. It'll give me time to go through her laptop and create a preliminary presentation. I want you and Birk on board with this. Both of you. For that to happen, I need to lay out everything in a detailed format."

"Like a timeline? We already did that. It's probably in one of these boxes."

"No, much more than a timeline. This time tomorrow night, after Brodie gets his certification, we'll sit down and go over everything. How does that sound?"

"It sounds like you've gotten pulled into Brigid's case in a big way."

"So have others. You're not alone in wanting to solve it."

He pressed his lips to her hand. "I don't want it to take over your life."

"It won't."

"As long as you understand that there's very little hope of anything changing from law enforcement's perspective."

"We'll see about that."

"You sound like I did two years ago."

"Take Brodie home and get a good night's sleep. Stop worrying about me."

"That's difficult to do when I'm crazy about you."

Kelly nuzzled his jawline. "Nice to hear because I'm crazy right back. Would you mind if I borrowed your boat tomorrow to check on the progress of my research?"

"It's all yours. On second thought, maybe I could come in for half an hour."

She threw her head back with a laugh. "Oh, you are so tempting in my weakened, intoxicated state of mind. I don't mind being the strong one tonight. Get Brodie home and text me updates. We'll celebrate after his big test."

Fourteen

Monday morning began as it often did this time of year along the coast, with a gray cloud cover that blossomed into a curtain of dappled sunshine by midmorning.

While Beckett and Brodie headed to Santa Cruz, Kelly checked on her kelp beds. She waded through the marsh and found the stalks had already rooted. Each had grown a whopping eighteen inches to two feet in just a few days. Delighted with the results, she did a happy dance through the shallow water, then realized she didn't want to disturb the other plants.

From there, she tiptoed out of the marshland onto solid footing. But she spent the next thirty minutes taking the time to appreciate how the landscape might already be changing.

The next stop was the pier and Beckett's boat. Smuggler's Bay was calm as glass. She checked wind directions and speed and decided the breeze came from the south.

Anxious to check on the sea stars, she tossed her equipment onto the deck of the cabin cruiser and got comfortable at the helm. After familiarizing herself with the controls, she felt confident enough to start the engine. She reminded herself that she was only going a mere forty yards to the mouth of the bay, maybe not even that far. But it wasn't her boat. She needed to be extra careful.

Bouncing along the water's surface, she felt the wind pick up and shift to a westerly direction. She lifted her face into the sun, enjoying the sea breeze, and the outdoors. Once she reached the spot where they'd dropped the sea stars into the water, she circled, turning the boat to the east, and cut the engine. She pulled on diving gear, grabbed her underwater camera, and went to work.

Much to her relief, the rocky reef and its sediment had exploded with orange and yellowish sea stars. They seemed to be thriving, walking across the sea shelf in slow, deliberate motion, munching on anything in their path. Days into her experiment, the hungry starfish had already dined on an entire patch of purple sea urchins. She took a dozen photographs for confirmation to email back to the lab.

She stayed beneath the water longer than she should have. Her tank was almost empty by the time she surfaced and hauled herself out of the water. She slid off the diving tank and zipped out of her wetsuit, stripping down to the shorts and top she wore underneath. She went straight to her notebooks, jotting down notations in her logbook, feeling a sense of accomplishment.

But the euphoric mood didn't last long. Glancing toward shore, she caught sight of a scowling Birk waiting for her on the dock.

She decided to take her time heading in. Standing at the helm, she put the boat into gear and made a slow turn in the water before pulling into a slot, then tossing Birk the rope to tie onto the pylon. Before disembarking, she called out, "Beckett gave me permission to use the boat."

Birk fastened the boat down and helped her climb onto the dock. "I'm not here about that. Have you had a chance to dig into Brigid's laptop yet?"

"Not yet. I needed to check on my project first." She took a closer look at Birk's face and realized how tense he seemed. "Why?"

"Two things. First, I'm sorry I yelled at you yesterday. I know you're only trying to help."

"Okay. Thanks for that. What's the second thing?"

"There's something I've never shared with Beckett about Brigid's night out."

Kelly's jaw dropped. "Why? No, better still, *what* haven't you shared?"

"Brigid was involved with an older man, married with kids, who had no intentions of leaving his wife. It was a messy, no-win affair. There's no other way to describe it."

"Ah. One of her professors, maybe?"

"No. I would've thought Jade had mentioned it."

Disappointed in the new friend she'd made last night, Kelly frowned. "She didn't. Who was it?"

"Ezra Guthrie Jr."

"Whoa. The son of the hedge fund guy? How did she meet him? He must've been forty back then."

"Thirty-six. They met when Guthrie guest-lectured one of her business classes."

"You talked to him?"

"Three times. Junior referred to their affair as 'friends with benefits.' Before you zero in on Junior. Don't. On the night Brigid went missing, he was at his beach house in Santa Barbara with his wife and kids, hosting a dinner party, corroborated by several independent witnesses and his smartphone data."

"And you didn't want to share this with your brother because…?"

"Beckett and Brigid were close despite their age differences. He supported her in just about everything she wanted to do, was even sending her money every month for incidentals at school in case her budget ran short. If he found out she was dating a married man, I was afraid he'd think less of her."

"Then why tell me?"

"Because you're good at research. You would've eventually found out on your own. This way, I'm saving you some time and effort."

"I don't want to fight with you at every turn, Birk. But I think you should tell Beckett. I don't want to keep secrets like that because it's a big one to hoard."

"I was afraid you'd say that."

"I hate to add to your stress, but is there any chance Brigid was seeing someone else besides the married guy? Because I believe that she left the bar to meet up with that person." Kelly held up her hands. "Don't look at me like that. I'm not that long out of school, okay? I know college kids. I know high school kids. Parents swear up and down they know their kids. They don't. I've had male and female friends who juggled dating three people at once. If you want to call it dating. They juggled hookups like a game and had burner phones to communicate with each person. So don't tell me it isn't possible."

"In my line of work, I've seen it all. I won't bother arguing the point. I never thought Brigid would date a sleazebag like Junior. So when it comes to her personal life, anything is possible. She was living away from home, no longer under parental control, and trying to act like how she thought an adult would act. But I never uncovered a second involvement. And I'm a very thorough investigator."

"I don't doubt that for a minute. But did you look for one, really dig, after you discovered Ezra Junior? Or did you say to yourself, 'okay, I've found out Brigid's secret,' and move on? It's a valid reaction. I mean, why would you think she was involved with anyone else other than the obvious?"

Birk's brow creased with deep lines. "Damn. You have a point. I didn't look too hard into her relationships after that. That's no excuse because she's my sister. I pride myself on finding out everything there is to know about a victim."

"You were too close to the case. So what if you didn't go after dirt on your own sister? What brother would want to do that? I'm not a professional, but anyone could see that Brigid's disappearance hurt both you and Beckett tremendously. It's affected everything in your life for the past five years. And not knowing what happened that night is eating you up. Having just gone through a scare with my parents, I know it would kill me not to have answers."

She looped an arm through his. "Buy me a frappe, and we'll sit down like two civilized adults and discuss how and when to tell Beckett. Then we'll decide the best approach to uncovering Brigid's other secrets—because I'd bet money she had them."

Birk's lips curved.

"Is that a smile?" Kelly said, nudging him in the ribs. "I got a smile out of Birk Callahan. Wow." She let go of his arm and did a happy dance before crossing the street to The Perky Pelican.

"You're not just nerdy. You're weird and pushy."

"Nerdy?" She tilted her head to study his face. "I'll take that as a compliment. Weird? Sure. Pushy? I guess I am. I didn't make it through grad school by default. I had to learn to stand up for myself. When I thought I was right about something, I'd go to great lengths to prove my theory and stick to my hypothesis until I got my point across. It's the essence of academia. Make a splash by being assertive in the department."

Paula was behind the counter. They gave her their coffee order and took a seat at one of the tables.

Sipping her coffee, Kelly leaned back in her chair. "Getting back to Brigid. I don't for one second believe she walked to Shark Fin Cove. I tried it on foot and lasted less than fifteen minutes. You reach a point where you're away from the hustle and bustle of traffic. But that takes a long time to get there. You're out in the middle of nowhere, surrounded by farmland, no streetlights, nothing but darkness. No woman by herself would head in that direction unless she got turned around, which is possible, but I'm not buying it. What do you think happened to your sister that night? Jade mentioned that you thought she might've been involved in a hit and run and that the driver panicked and disposed of her body."

"At the time, it was as likely as any other explanation. Now, I'm convinced someone abducted Brigid."

"Then why wouldn't you believe that a serial killer is responsible?"

"Probability. I deal in facts, not speculation."

"I'm sorry, Birk. But so far, I haven't seen a lot of hard facts about Brigid's case either way. Granted, I'm playing catch up. Allowing a serial killer to operate for almost six years unchecked while he racks up victim after victim should be a priority for anyone, including an investigator like yourself. Let's say you're right. Let's say Brigid wasn't his first victim. Let's say Brigid's disappearance is not part of the other missing women. There are still seven victims unaccounted for *after* she went missing. Coincidence? I don't think so. Call it a gut feeling or whatever, but I'm a single woman very glad at the moment that I'm not living in Santa Cruz. Of course, I'm probably too old for this guy. He seems to prefer women between the ages of seventeen and twenty-five."

"Jade has certainly influenced your opinion."

"That's a bit insulting, Birk. I made up my mind on my own from reading about the other women. Jade simply reinforced what I'd decided for myself. As a scientist, I deal in facts. I don't believe in coincidences. All I'm asking from you is to give me a chance to delve into everything, then let the results stand on their own merit."

"And you'll abide by the same results?"

"Absolutely. If I determine that these disappearances aren't linked, I'll say so. If I find out that Brigid's case is in no way connected, I'll admit I was wrong. So are you okay with me digging into Brigid's social life?"

"Sure. I already did that, but another set of eyes wouldn't hurt."

Her phone dinged with a message. She held it up so Birk could read the content. "Looks like Terra Search & Recovery has its own search dog. Brodie passed."

Birk's mouth spread into a smile again. "I'll say one thing about Beckett. He never gave up on that dog. Not once."

"We should have a party for them," Kelly said. "A celebration. What do you think?"

"It's a good idea. We should recognize the personal aspect of it. Beckett bonded with Brodie from the beginning better than I did. We should mark it as a huge step forward for the company to have its own S-and-R dog, a huge accomplishment. It means not relying on Debra to provide us with one of her dogs whenever there's a search and rescue situation. Although it took longer to train Brodie than we thought."

"Sometimes things take longer. What's that old saying? 'Good things come to those who wait.' Because of Brodie, I'm thinking of getting a dog."

"You should. There's a shelter full to the brim with dogs ready for homes."

"My landlord might have something to say about that. What about you?"

"I travel way too much. A lot of the time, I only get an hour's notice before having to leave. That's not fair to a dog. Don't you do a lot of fieldwork?"

"This summer. Sure. But a dog could come along with me."

"What breed are you looking for?"

"Maybe something smallish. I just want to save one from being alone. I figure I'm alone. The dog is alone. We might as well form a unit."

Birk stared over at her and flashed a grin. "You're willing to take on an energetic dog like Brodie?"

"Brodie's not so bad. But maybe something slightly smaller. Look, this is all wishful thinking on my part. I'm a renter, living in a house that isn't mine. My landlord will be the deciding factor. And I'm sure he won't be happy about me bringing in a dog to his nice, fresh redo. The house still smells like paint. Then there's my apartment back in Hayward. Management will up my rent at the slightest sign I brought home a dog. Or a cat, for that matter."

"Then you'd better be good at housetraining him. Ever done that before?"

"It's been a while, but I think I know how it works—plenty of poop pads and a crate, lots of walks outside."

"Be sure to ask Beckett how his experience with Brodie went. That was before the dog became a superstar. Let's just say Brodie didn't make anything easy, least of all housetraining him."

"So, how should we celebrate?"

"Burgers. Brodie loves burgers."

She got to her feet. "You set it up. If you need anything, call me. I'll be home, going through Brigid's laptop."

Two hours later, Beckett and the 'superstar' strutted up to Kelly's door in a triumphant march of validation. "He did it. You should've seen him. Brodie blew Debra's socks off!"

Kelly ushered them in and dropped to one knee to wrap Brodie up in a hug. "Nothing like vindication, eh, boy?"

"I'm cooking tonight. Burgers for everybody, including Brodie."

She snickered with laughter. "So this is how Birk sets up a celebration. He gets you to cook."

"Trust me. You don't want to eat anything from Birk's kitchen that he makes himself. Or his grill. The man's a walking disaster. He can't even scramble a decent egg."

"Thanks for the warning."

Beckett spied Brigid's laptop spread out on the kitchen table. "Any progress?"

"Some. I know I said we'd go into it today, but I'd like to push that out farther. I'm just getting started after Birk and I met for coffee this morning. We sat down and had a good conversation."

Surprised, Beckett turned her in his arms and pressed his lips to hers. "Then it's a good day all around."

"Mmm. You both deserve a treat. But you're distracting me from my research. Go away until tonight."

"Maybe I can help you go through Brigid's stuff. I left it to Birk to do all that before. Since you're reopening every box, I should probably refamiliarize myself with everything here." He sat down at the table.

She accepted the help and realized it would fall to her to tell him about the married lover. But how?

He noticed her hedging. "What's up? You did find something, didn't you?"

Her shoulders dropped. She let out a little sigh. "Beckett, when I mentioned that Brigid might've met up with her killer that night using a social app, you didn't seem all that surprised. Why is that?"

"My sister was entitled to a social life. For God's sake, she was no longer a little kid. She told me that enough times. Sure, I thought she went a little wild between seventeen and twenty. How do you stop that from happening?"

"How do you know that? Weren't you overseas at the time?"

"My dad told me. He even asked me to talk to her when I came home on leave. She was home during summer break. So at a Fourth of July picnic, I took her aside for a long talk. She got verbally defensive about me trying to tell her what to do. I knew then she wouldn't listen, not to me or anyone. She went wild out here in California, didn't she?"

Kelly frowned. "Wait a sec. You already know about Guthrie, don't you?"

Beckett's lips curved. "Yep. For almost four years now. Birk thinks he kept it from me. And as soon as you said you guys talked over coffee, I knew Junior must've been the little nugget Birk let slip."

She narrowed her eyes. "Why didn't you just tell Birk you knew?"

"What was the point? When you were Brigid's age, did you appreciate anyone butting into your personal life, trying to tell you how to live? Probably not. By the time I was twenty, I'd spent two years in the Navy. And believe me, I wouldn't want anyone knowing the stupid things I've done. When you're that age, you feel invincible. Ask Birk if he ever let anyone tell him what to do outside the chain of command. The Callahans are a stubborn bunch, especially Birk. He shouldn't have expected a different reaction out of Brigid."

Kelly nodded. "Yeah, I can relate to that. Why would Brigid want anyone telling her what to do? But if you ask me, it's a recipe for disaster."

"Exactly. Her older brother—even if I am her favorite brother—wasn't about to tell her how to live. She reacted the way I thought she'd respond. She stormed off, got on her phone, and acted like a petulant child. Then several hours later, after she'd had time to cool off, she started talking to me again. We were fine. Adulthood is more than a number."

"The talk didn't do any good, though."

"Nope. And three months later, she was gone."

"But if you knew she was living on the wild side, why didn't you dig harder into her social life?"

"I'm telling you, we did. But after Guthrie Junior, we hit a brick wall. We didn't find any evidence she'd been seeing anyone else. And her roommates couldn't come up with a name. They told us that Brigid spent a lot of time on her phone. That's it. What college kid doesn't spend every minute on their phone. It wasn't helpful. But we didn't find any unusual text messages of a sexual nature to anyone else."

"Weird," Kelly muttered. "I wonder…"

"What?"

"If she had a second phone."

"You're kidding?"

"That would explain how she communicated with the married guy and others she didn't want anyone else to know about." When she noticed he was staring, she added, "Are you prepared to learn things about Brigid you didn't know?"

His jaw tightened. "I wouldn't say prepared. I can't imagine why Brigid would have a burner phone. It's not like she was a drug dealer or something."

"Whatever we find in her personal life, Brigid didn't deserve to go missing. Remember that."

Brodie came up and rested his head on Kelly's knee. She nuzzled his face and scrubbed behind his ears. "You look bone tired. You've had a busy day, haven't you?"

"Could I leave him here with you while running a few errands? I need to buy stuff for the burgers tonight."

"Sure. What time is this celebration?"

"I think I can get everything ready foodwise by six."

"You do what you need to do. I'll keep Brodie entertained. Maybe later we'll go for a walk down to the pier. I'll bring Brodie over around five-thirty and help set things up. How does that sound?"

"Great. See you two then. I gotta get moving."

Beckett left without the dog making a fuss, which surprised them both. While she got back to work, looking through Brigid's laptop, Brodie curled up at her feet to take a nap.

She picked up where she'd left off—reading through emails. Kelly skimmed the boring stuff and focused on Brigid's emails around the time of her disappearance. The college student had discarded a great many others. But right now, she centered her attention on anything that looked like it might connect to the night out with friends. After reading the email thread from everyone involved, she moved on to the week leading up to that October night. But nothing stood out. It seemed like ordinary conversations from a twenty-year-old in her second year of college.

She found an email where Brigid discussed switching majors with one of her professors. She wanted to ditch business school for a career in communications. The idea of making her living standing in front of the camera seemed to come out of nowhere. Brigid toyed with that idea for a few weeks until it became clear that changing majors would add time and tuition to getting a degree. She'd dropped the idea and settled on sticking with business, where she wouldn't lose credits.

Kelly leaned back in her chair, realizing she was slowly getting to see this young woman in a whole new light.

She kept at the emails until Brodie needed to go outside.

"Let's stretch our legs and clear our heads with a long walk on the beach," Kelly suggested, hooking Brodie's leash to his collar. "And if you're a good boy, we'll hunt down ice cream."

Fifteen

That afternoon when Kelly and Brodie arrived at Beckett's, he was already in the backyard firing up the grill.

"What have you got there?" Beckett called out, noting that she'd braided her hair into one long plait that hung down the back. Her pale blue dress fluttered around her knees, showing off her long legs. She wore some kind of dangly medallion thing around her neck that exposed her silky skin. Her strappy sandals flaunted her long, narrow feet with toenails painted bright white. She strolled in with his dog, just enough sway in her hips to look sexy and confident.

She held up a dozen brightly colored Japanese lanterns she'd bought. "I know. Silly, right? But I thought they looked festive. Brodie and I found them at Murphy's Market, marked down in the party section, seventy-five percent off. They have these little LED lights in them. How could I pass up a bargain like that?"

She looked around for a place to hang them and spotted the mile-high stack of hamburger patties. "Wow. How many people are coming to this thing?"

"The guest list sort of multiplied. Birk invited our parents and Debra, who invited most of the Sand-R team, then word got out around town. I'm anticipating a big turnout."

"On a Monday night? I thought it would be like ten people." She got busy stringing the first of her paper lanterns across the covered patio, then took the rest and stretched them along the tree line and back fence. She tested the lights and stood back to assess how they looked.

"There. What do you think?"

"I think you look amazing. The lights are a bonus."

She grinned and threw her arms around his back. "You clean up nice, too."

"You clean up better."

People began to show up with side dishes of all kinds. From potato salad to baked beans to desserts, everybody brought something and added it to the folding table, set up underneath a canopy.

Kelly didn't recognize a single face. But it didn't seem to matter. They all came up to her one by one and introduced themselves.

Craig and Betty Callahan arrived with Birk. The sixty-year-old couple marched right up and shook her hand. They were graying, their dark hair tipping silver at the edges. But these two showed resilience and radiance in a way that reminded her of her own parents. She could tell they liked each other.

The petite Betty had a firm handshake. "We're so glad to meet you. Birk told us what you're doing for Brigid."

"He did, did he? Well, as you know, I'm not an investigator. But I'm willing to help in any way I can. Did your sons mention they helped me find my parents? I know firsthand what great work they do, so this is my way of paying it forward if I can."

Betty laid a hand on Kelly's arm. "At this stage, we appreciate anything anyone can do."

"As long as you don't expect too much."

Craig, a lanky man like his sons, found that funny. "After such a long time, we know better than to expect anything at all. Don't we, Betty?"

"But we haven't given up," the woman emphasized, waving to her younger son at the grill.

"That's sad."

"It is, but it's the sad truth," Craig remarked. "That's why we keep in touch with Jade Weingarten. At least once a month, she writes a blog post that helps keep Brigid's name in the public eye. She posts things contrary to what the cops believe. The police may not like her, but we do."

"Jade caught my attention, too," Kelly confessed. "And I think her theory has merit."

"Will you send us updates?" Betty requested. "If you find anything at all on Brigid's laptop that the police might've overlooked or not dug into deep enough."

Kelly saw the hope on their faces and wanted to give them a solution more now than ever. But she had to lay out the reality. "The chances of that are slim."

"We know the chances aren't very good," Craig stated. "Every day that goes by without movement on the case means that answers get more elusive. We're not expecting a miracle. By now, that's what it would take to solve this case, a miracle."

Kelly laid a hand on Betty's shoulder. "So you're down to relying on a marine biologist and a former blackjack dealer to solve the case. Think about that for a minute. What are the odds?"

Betty's lips curved. She leaned closer to Kelly's ear. "I'll do you one better. It takes seasoned detectives to conclude that my daughter walked ten miles in the dark by herself to a remote beach and fell into the water drunk."

"What she said," Craig echoed with a nod. "Most ridiculous thing of all is that dumbass theory."

Birk shoved a beer toward his dad and handed his mother a glass of white wine. "You two looked like you could use a drink."

Craig gave his son a nudge. "Doesn't Kelly deserve one, too?"

"I've only got two hands," Birk grumbled. "Besides, she's the reason everybody came. Nobody passes up a chance to meet the newcomer. She needs her hands free."

"Poppycock. Chatting with all these people is thirsty work," Betty pointed out, handing off the glass of Chablis to Kelly. "You stay put to meet-and-greet. I know where to find my own wine."

As Betty headed toward the refreshment table, the reception line grew longer. The lineup streamed past Kelly. People dropped their names, names she would probably never remember. Although a few stood out.

She met Ryder McLachlan and his wife, Julianne Dickinson. Julianne—principal at Pelican Pointe Elementary—cornered her about teaching a summer camp for nerds. "I know you're here for the summer working on a project. But would it be possible to talk you into teaching a science class at our summer camp in June? It lasts four weeks. It's for some of our fifth and sixth graders who've shown a propensity toward science. We want them to stay sharp over the summer. And it might be an opportunity to get them interested in marine biology. No one's ever too young to become interested in science. What better place to study the ocean than right here within our own shores? And with a noted marine biologist and science professor to boot."

"Oh, I don't know about that. I'm not that well-known." Kelly thought back to her last semester. Her brain focused on those uninterested and slightly unruly freshmen she'd had for an hour every day that stared back at her with a blank look on their faces. "I'm not really that great at inspiring kids."

"Who says? Get them interested early and keep their attention. I bet you're an inspiration and just don't know it. Our students could help you with your research. They'd be willing to perform any menial task that might keep them interested in science until school begins in the fall."

"I wish I'd had someone like that to see me through the lazy, hazy days of summer vacation back in Tahoe. I hated not being in school."

"There you go. My point exactly. At least think about it," Julianne said, glancing at the line behind her. She offered Kelly a business card. "Call me. Maybe we could have a girls' night out and go over the specifics."

"Cassidy Kennison, the new chef at the B&B, mentioned a girls' night out. We should get together some night."

"That's a great idea. Friday night works for me."

"This coming Friday? Sure. I'll get in touch with Cassidy and set it up."

"I'll round up a few women I know who need a night out. We'll make it a fun thing."

After that, Kelly met the florist, Drea Jennings, her husband, Zach Dennison, the other third of Troy's construction crew, and the owners of the drug store, Ross and Jill Campbell. By the time Beckett had taken the burgers off the grill, her brain blurred with names and faces.

It was an impromptu event like nothing she'd ever experienced where an entire town seemed interested in meeting her. She wasn't sure why.

She took her plate and found a spot on the lawn near where Beckett held court. It was the first time she realized he had his own fan club. Several people gathered around—including Knox Williams and his mom—hanging on his every word as he retold how Brodie found the missing Santa Cruz girl.

Hero Brodie plopped down next to her and yawned as if bored with the event. The dog worked his charm, eyeing her plate with soulful big brown eyes and licking his chops.

"You're not fooling me," Kelly noted. "You want my burger, don't you?"

The dog woofed in reply.

Kelly broke her burger in half, letting the pup eat out of her hand. "I'm giving in only because you're the guest of honor. I can't let you go hungry, now can I? If I didn't know better, I'd say you were grinning at me."

Brodie whined and nuzzled her hand.

"I think my dog is in love," Beckett said, sitting next to her on the grass.

"It's mutual. The more time I spend around Brodie, the more I want a dog." She held up her phone. "I even have the landlord's number queued up."

"Cord and Keegan were supposed to be here tonight. But an emergency surgery on a cat kept Cord at the clinic. And Keegan had one of the seals go into labor."

"Keegan runs the marine mammal rescue, right? It's on my to-do list of things to see while I'm here. I wouldn't mind seeing a seal give birth."

He shook his head. "You are a geek. Blood doesn't bother you?"

"Let's just say I've dissected my share of sharks in my time and anything else that lives in the ocean."

"And it doesn't bother you?"

"Well, no. I guess I have a strong stomach for things like that, always have." She glanced around the yard. "How do you think the party's going so far? I met your mom and dad."

"They're a kick, aren't they?"

She stretched out her legs and leaned back on her hands. "Your parents are rocks. Their strength amazes me after everything they've gone through. They like the work Jade's been doing. I pointed out they're down to putting their trust in a blackjack dealer and me. That's desperation if you ask me. I hope I don't disappoint them."

"You couldn't. They realize it's a longshot."

"It shouldn't be. If there's data somewhere that points the police in a different direction—"

"But have you found anything yet?"

She shook her head. "Nope. Not so much as a secondary email account or a hidden profile. But I'm just getting started."

"I almost hope you find something that backs up how she met up with someone that night. If not for Brigid's sake, for my parents. It's been hell watching them not know what happened."

Before she could reply, her phone dinged with a text. "It's from Jade. She wants to get together tomorrow here. Is it okay if I let her look through Brigid's laptop?"

"Sure. The more, the merrier."

To Kelly, he didn't sound thrilled at the prospect. "Look, I trust Jade not to release anything she finds on her blog that could be embarrassing to Brigid."

"You think that's what I'm worried about? It's not. Brigid's gone. No matter what secret she kept to herself, it needs to be uncovered, especially if it got her killed."

"We need to dig to find out what it was."

"I just want this to end. This relentless pursuit is overwhelming at times. Today was a good day. It's a joyous feeling whenever we find a kid like Knox or Elena alive. But no matter what happens in our lives, it always circles back to Brigid. Sometimes I wonder if we'll always be feeling this void for the rest of our lives."

Brodie started barking when Debra rounded the corner of the house with her animals in tow—an Australian shepherd and a border collie.

"Sorry we're late," Deb shouted to Beckett. "But we hit rush hour."

"It's okay. I'll put on fresh burgers," he said, starting to stand up.

Deb waved away the offer. "No need. I see there's plenty here to eat. My dogs and I won't starve."

"Want more wine?" Beckett asked Kelly.

"Nah, I think I'll head home. I have a lot of data to enter from my time in the field today. Thanks for letting me use your boat."

"Any time."

"On top of playing catch up, I'd like to continue going through Brigid's laptop, so I'll be ready for Jade." She tilted her head and ran a finger down his cheek. "But you could always drop by later after your guests leave."

"That sounds like a plan."

Kelly got to her feet but crouched down to pet the dogs and gave Brodie some extra love. "Play nice with the other boys and girls."

Brodie licked her face.

Birk made his way across the lawn. "You leaving already?"

"Fraid so. Work. I'll find your parents before I go, though."

"They're inside with Zach and Ryder talking about hiring them to renovate their kitchen. Mom's getting an estimate while Dad's got this sick look on his face wondering if he'll have to sell a kidney to pay for it."

"Home improvement loan," Kelly countered. "That's how my mom got her dream kitchen. Of course, they'll be paying for it until they're eighty, but until then, Mom gets to enjoy one beautiful room where she drinks her coffee."

Beckett cocked a brow. "And your dad?"

"Oh, he gets the peace and quiet of not having to listen to Mom bitch about how the kitchen needs a redo."

Kelly discovered there were downsides to rummaging through someone else's personal life. She kept feeling guilty whenever she encountered a steamy email or text belonging to Brigid from the married lover. After reading several, she realized Junior never planned to leave his wife despite the promises he made to Brigid.

She didn't waste too much time delving further but copied them into a different file folder to refer to later. After narrowing the focus to Brigid's daily emails, she began to go through the most recent ones right before the disappearance, cataloging each one into separate folders. Once she got those organized, she moved from the laptop to hard copies of Brigid's phone records. The massive list covered six months before her disappearance.

Kelly began to read through the data, highlighting the most recent text messages from that last week, then from that last day. She cross-referenced phone numbers, jotted down notes next to the most frequent texts or calls, and vowed to put names to each number.

She opened her laptop to create a spreadsheet, then organized each entry by area code to research those numbers, hoping the Internet would produce a link back to the owners. Most of the time, she got a name. But that still left a lot of numbers that didn't.

She copied the ones she couldn't identify and added them into a separate column.

As she was about to call it a night and power down the laptops, Kelly realized she had forgotten to check Brigid's spam and trash folders. She opened Brigid's email account again and discovered over a thousand junk messages there. So much for the tech giants that promise they would delete emails after thirty days. Five years later, the trash folder still sat there full of discarded emails. It contained a whopping fifteen hundred.

She skimmed through the spam file first, then made a sweep through the trash. On the twenty-fifth page, that's when she saw it—the welcome email from the app called SecretSingles, a popular online hookup slash dating site geared to college kids.

Eight months before she'd gone missing, Brigid had used her phone to sign up, create an online profile with a password, and called herself CandaceSC.

The welcome email had all the pertinent information she needed to access the account.

Kelly's pulse quickened as she reached for her iPhone. Before she could enter Brigid's world, she'd need to download the app onto her own device. It took a few minutes to complete the process. When the app popped up, it appeared the company marketed its product to young adults who wanted anonymous yet adventurous mystery hookups, fulfilling the promise of a one-time fantasy date.

The idea of that gave Kelly chills. "Oh, my God, this is a predator's hunting ground."

After keying in the specific information and password, the app opened to Candace's home page. A photo of the pretty twenty-year-old college student stared back at her, the provocative pose in see-through lingerie unmistakable in its intent. It had been there all this time.

When she heard footsteps on the porch, she got to her feet and darted to the door. Before Beckett could say a word, she blurted out, "I found it. I found a lead. I know the app Brigid used the night she disappeared. All we have to do is unmask the last profile she contacted."

"Show me everything."

She took him through Brigid's profile and the basics of SecretSingles. "The app itself isn't very sophisticated other than maintaining secretive chat rooms where you get to know the person you're meeting."

"Get-to-know in theory," Beckett stressed. "Anyone could lie their ass off. And probably do."

"It's a predator's dream come true."

He rubbed his forehead to try and soothe away the ache that hurt so bad it made his eyeballs bulge. "Why would she—? How could she be that stupid?"

"You said it yourself. When you're twenty, you feel invincible like nothing bad could ever happen."

"Would you have signed up on a website like this?"

"No, it's not my kind of thing. But it was a different time. Kids do stupid, trendy things nowadays."

"Don't try to justify it."

"Let me know when you're over this anger spurt because we have more important questions than why Brigid signed up. I'd say she heard about this app from one of her friends. Didn't you tell me that Birk talked to her roommates?"

"He did. Well, we both did. At different times. Jeez, probably together, we spoke to them a total of a dozen times over the years."

"One of them is obviously holding something back." She caught the tired look on his face, took his chin, and tilted it up to her level. "It's been a long day for you and Brodie. Let's get some sleep and hit this hard and heavy tomorrow. We'll get Jade and Birk on this. The four of us will come up with a strategy. Sound like a plan?"

"Yeah."

"Then let me help you to bed. Need something for that headache?"

"Just you. I need you tonight, Kelly."

She kissed the top of his head. "I'm not going anywhere."

Sixteen

By six the next morning, Beckett hadn't slept much. He'd always been an early riser. But the day felt different somehow. A light had finally burst on the scene out of the darkness, and he couldn't ignore the implication.

After starting a pot of coffee, he texted Birk, reminding him to make time for Jade's visit, emphasizing that the meeting with Jade was a priority. *Update with Jade at eleven at my place. Don't blow it off—new stuff to discuss.*

The first rays of sun began to stream through the window when Birk sent a reply. In his usual brevity, it read: *I'll be there.*

He tried to focus on making breakfast for Kelly setting out eggs and orange juice. But his heart wasn't in it. He thought she was still asleep anyway as he opened the back door to let Brodie out.

"Stay close," he directed. "There's no fence out there. I don't want to have to send out a search party for the newest member of the canine search-and-rescue team."

When the coffeemaker beeped at the end of the cycle, he poured himself a cup and didn't bother with cream or sugar. He needed the straight caffeine bump and leaned on the counter to gulp that first hit.

He heard footsteps in the hallway and saw a tousle-haired Kelly rounding the corner into the kitchen. Her hair had come out of its braid. She wore a short plaid robe that shouldn't have been sexy.

"I guess I don't have to ask how you slept?"

"Sorry. I didn't mean to wake you."

"No problem. I like getting up at the crack of dawn to watch you drink coffee."

"Am I seeing your grouchy side?"

"You've already seen it." She took the mug he was holding and chugged the warm, strong black liquid. "There. That will prevent you from seeing it again."

He chuckled and got himself another cup from the cabinet and filled it with more coffee.

When Kelly heard Brodie at the back door, she let him into the kitchen, rubbing him behind his ears. "Where've you been?"

The dog did a happy dance before nuzzling her legs.

"How do I find a sweet dog like Brodie?"

"You get lucky. Like I said before, you ask Cord for the easiest-going resident dog he has living at the shelter. Maybe the dog that's been there the longest. It might not be a golden retriever."

"I just want a sweet dog," Kelly muttered as she hugged Brodie. "Has he eaten? I bought him a dog bowl for when he's here and some dry dog food. I wasn't sure what kind to get. But Brodie seemed to like the dog pictured on the big yellow bag."

"That's the same brand I buy him. I saw the dog bowl and water dish set up in the corner. It's amazing how you think of things like that." He thought of Kimberly and couldn't imagine the reporter going to the trouble. He dumped a healthy serving into what was now Brodie's dog dish and filled up his water bowl.

"Want breakfast?" he offered. "I can scramble us some eggs."

She made a face. "I feel like cereal, honey-roasted oats, I think." She got down a bowl and the cereal box out of the cupboard, then went to the fridge and grabbed the milk. "If you want eggs, though, I could fry them up. I'm not a bad cook. Margie says that's your usual breakfast order—three over-easy eggs with crispy hash browns and a side of bacon. I don't have hash browns or bacon, though."

"Margie told you that?"

"Yeah. When I stopped in to get ice cream cones for Brodie and me yesterday. I guess Margie thought the subject of breakfast might come up. Who knows? Anyway, I'm happy to fix them before I sit down to eat."

"Okay. I want to see how you fry eggs."

She lifted a brow. "Is that a challenge?"

"No. I just want to see your method."

She got out a skillet and some butter, turned the heat on the stove to a low setting, then waited for the butter to melt. She cracked three eggs into the pan, letting them simmer for a few minutes. When they were ready to turn—with a skillful flick of the spatula—she flipped the eggs without breaking the yoke. "Over-easy, right?"

He eyed her movements, the sway of her hips as she put everything into the effort. "Perfect. I'm not talking about the eggs," he said as he moved her hair aside and pressed kisses along her neck.

She moved the skillet to another burner and turned in his arms. "You're not eating these eggs cold after I hovered over a hot stove."

He took her mouth, a slow kiss that gave rise to another kind of hunger. "If you say so."

"I do. I'll make toast." But she didn't move.

Beckett's phone rang, interrupting the moment. "Damn." He slid the device off the counter and looked at the screen. "It's Debra. I better take this. It could be a search. Hello?"

She watched him walk into the living room to take the call, then slid the eggs onto a plate. After making four slices of toast, she sat down to eat her cereal.

When he came back in, he plopped into a chair.

"Do you need to go?"

"No. But Brodie and I are on standby. Two kids riding ATVs went missing overnight near Soquel State Forest. If Debra needs reinforcements, we'll be heading out around noon."

"Should we move up the meeting with Jade?"

"Good idea. You contact Jade, see if she can make it earlier, and I'll get in touch with Birk, move it up an hour."

Later that morning, Jade soaked up the new information like a sponge. "CandaceSC on SecretSingles was right there the entire time. Unbelievable."

"I don't see how we missed this," Birk acknowledged as the four of them gathered around Beckett's kitchen table. "I consider myself a good investigator. But this makes me wonder what else I could've missed."

Jade laid a hand on his shoulder. "It doesn't matter. The important thing is Kelly uncovered it now. It's a game-changer. For the first time in five years, we know why Brigid left the bar that night to meet this mystery date."

Kelly shook her head. "Now wait a sec. It's still a theory until we locate the exact profile she contacted that night. The troubling thing is that one of her friends must've been holding back this key piece to the puzzle. They had to know she used this app and had a 'date' that night. Beckett says you guys talked to Brigid's friends multiple times. And not one mentioned SecretSingles."

"We hounded her friends for years after the fact until they stopped talking to us," Birk replied.

"Then I have a question. In your opinion, which one is more likely to have lied straight to your face?" Kelly asked.

Beckett traded looks with Birk.

"Phoebe Carpenter," the brothers uttered at the same time.

Beckett nodded. "Brigid's roommate for eighteen months. Phoebe wouldn't look me in the eye the first time I talked to her. Then the second time around, she was all over the place but made sure to stay vague. Very vague."

"Whenever I talked to her, she kept her answers to a minimum," Birk added. "Short yes or no pops, right up to the last time I interviewed her a year ago."

Kelly glanced at Jade. "Maybe it's time for some girl talk. Do we have a current address for Phoebe?"

Jade dug through her notes before pulling out an index card paper clipped to Phoebe's contact sheet. "Last known address is in San Sebastian, where Phoebe worked as an apartment manager. We could go see her this afternoon."

"If she's still working there. Let's plan on finding out. Is there any way to get Brigid's cell phone pings from the police? It would be helpful to see the data mapped in hard copies."

"I don't think you should expect that kind of sharing from the cops," Jade reasoned.

Birk cleared his throat. "That's why I made my own copies, the information I gathered from the carrier on my own dime. Don't ask."

Jade narrowed her eyes on Birk. "Wow. Straight-laced Birch Callahan used his expertise to get around the system. I'm impressed."

Birk gave her a slight smile. "I'm not that straight-laced. You have no idea what I'm capable of when I'm motivated."

"Oh, I very much think I do," Jade responded. "Based on my vast experience at reading people, the quiet types are always the ones I worry about." She held up a hand. "Don't go knocking the blackjack dealer. I know what I know."

"I wouldn't dare," Birk ventured. "Dealers are keen observers of human nature. They pick up on various tells."

Jade angled a brow, confused by the comment. "Yes, we do."

Kelly noted the electricity between the two. But she was there to keep the focus on Brigid. "So, if I want a look at that data, it's in the boxes you provided me?"

"Everything is in there, probably in one of the newer cartons."

"Before I forget," Kelly began, "Did anyone respond to your blog post appeal about footage on Monica Tisdale? I checked the comments, but there wasn't anything earth-shattering. Maybe if they had information, they sent it to your blog through a private message."

"I wish. So far, nothing's turned up. I wish people understood how important tiplines are. Law enforcement relies on them for a reason."

Beckett got to his feet and began to pace. "I need to know something. Does anyone here think that it's possible Brigid might still be alive?"

Kelly sucked in a breath and was the first one to speak. "No. I'm sorry. I don't."

Jade shook her head. "Ditto for me. I wish I had a reason to think differently."

Beckett and Birk eyed each other, but Birk was the one who voiced the sentiment. "If Brigid were alive, she couldn't stay away from her family this long, not for five and a half years. She wouldn't do that to Mom and Dad."

"Yeah," Beckett said softly. "I just had to hear it reinforced." He laid a hand over his heart. "There's a tiny part of me that holds the hope. Then there's the rest that knows it's not possible. I just want to know where she is and bring her home for Mom and Dad."

"I want to know what happened to her," Birk disclosed. "I want the person who did this, who made her disappear, who put her family through agony. I won't rest until I find him."

"We all want the same thing," Kelly reiterated. "In all my work, this seems as important as anything I've ever done."

"Exactly how I feel," Jade added. "Since starting my blog, I feel like I have a purpose." She turned to Kelly. "I'll help you go through the phone data."

"Okay. But first, we call that apartment complex and see if Phoebe Carpenter is still there."

Birk's phone rang first, then Beckett's.

"It's Debra," Beckett said to Kelly.

Birk held up his text. "The first search team that went out six hours ago still hasn't found the two kids or their ATVs. Deb needs us there to take over at Fern Canyon. She says we won't need the boat."

Beckett took Kelly by the shoulders, kissed her long and hard in front of the others. When he let go, he pressed an extra kiss to her forehead. "This search could take a while."

"I'll see you when I see you," Kelly said with a grin. "Take care of yourself, both of you, take care."

Beckett pointed a finger at both women. "Take my advice, and don't take any guff off Phoebe. Even when Brigid was around, she's been known to stretch the truth."

Birk agreed. "She's a self-proclaimed b-i-t-c-h according to her social media profiles. Don't look at me like that. Phoebe uses the same profile name with that word in the title. I swear. She's Miz Bitch in one and Bitch Queen in another. The list goes on. Jade knows. We've talked about this before."

Jade nodded in confirmation. "She's a piece of work. Phoebe once avoided jury duty by lying to a municipal court judge about not having a babysitter for her daughter. You guessed it. Phoebe doesn't even have a kid."

"Wow. Maybe Phoebe was on SecretSingles, too."

"Check it out," Beckett said as he rounded up Brodie. "We need to hit the road, like ten minutes ago."

It didn't take much of a hunt to locate Phoebe's online history. Everything from MySpace as a teenager to her present-day twenty-five-year-old self. In addition to SecretSingles, Kelly found Phoebe's profile on several dating apps—nine at last count.

"Busy girl," Jade muttered, leaning over Kelly's shoulder at the laptop. "I called the apartment complex. She's no longer working there. But using a people locator site, I tracked down her current employer. She went to work as a massage therapist at one of the spas and resorts near the beach in Santa Cruz called Sea Cliffs."

"Hmm. I haven't had a day at the spa in three years. How about you?"

Jade grinned. "I like the way you think."

Kelly scanned her phone for the number at Sea Cliffs Resort. "We need to find out what days Phoebe's working and make an appointment."

"Good thinking. She can't refuse to talk to us if we're a customer."

When the concierge picked up, she told Kelly that the hotel didn't take outside appointments. To get a massage, one had to be a guest.

"Make a room reservation for me," Jade whispered. "It'll be good research for the blog."

Kelly put a hand over her phone. "Are you sure? What if you book a room only to find out Phoebe's not there that day?"

"Then I'll show up at her house. I also found her address online. She lives half a mile from me in Santa Cruz."

"Interesting. Maybe Phoebe's come full circle over time. It has been five and a half years." Kelly disconnected the call without making a reservation for Jade.

"Hey, why'd you do that?"

"Because I have a better idea. And it's almost fool proof."

"We're showing up at her house, aren't we?"

"It's better if you don't go alone."

"Sounds like a plan. But I'll drive."

"Why? What do you have against my twelve-year-old truck?"

"Not a thing. But my Honda is much better on gas mileage than your, um—"

"Clunker," Kelly supplied and sent her a sidelong glance. "Something tells me my old pickup just got dissed."

"For your information, I planned on saying *Chevy*," Jade emphasized.

"It's just as well. I rode over here with Beckett," Kelly explained. After locking up Beckett's house, she got into Jade's spiffy convertible, settling into the passenger seat. "The old clunker is back at my place."

"Want to talk about this thing with you and Beckett? How long did you say you've been in town?"

Kelly sputtered with laughter. "Not long. We met twenty minutes after I got here."

"Wow. That might be a record. Nothing slow about you, is there?" Jade pointed out as she picked up speed and headed toward the highway. "You know, I almost moved to Pelican Pointe once."

"Why didn't you?"

"It's complicated."

"Oh, come on. You can do better than that."

"I guess I wasn't ready for small-town living back then. But now that I've seen it up close, I'm rethinking my decision. It's beautiful here and certainly more peaceful than Santa Cruz."

With Jade's foot on the gas, the little Honda breezed past the countryside, giving up a picture-perfect coastline view of the cliffs.

Kelly breathed in the sea air. "I love it here. It's a lot better than living in Hayward, considering the traffic on 880 is regularly bumper to bumper. Since we're being so honest, are you sure it isn't because Birk Callahan lives here?"

Jade's face fell. "Am I that obvious?"

"No. But women pick up on these things better than men do. How long have you felt this way about him?"

Jade blew out a breath. "Since that first time I asked for a meeting. I still remember Birk getting so mad at me for butting into his investigation. He yelled at me right there on the sidewalk cafe. I know how pathetic that sounds like I have a schoolgirl crush on a man who hates me. And I haven't had a schoolgirl crush since sixth grade."

"I didn't see Birk's dislike on display today. Instead, I saw a man with such inner anger that he's driven to help others. He uses what happened to Brigid to get up every day and do something for other people. Both brothers have that inner fire. A word of caution, though. Don't get fooled into thinking Birk's anything different than what he is. Birk is a complicated man. I know because Beckett is the same. They've seen and done things that you and I can only imagine. That tends to stick with a person."

"I know. I looked up Birk before I ever considered meeting with him. And that was after talking long-distance with Craig and Betty back when they lived in Virginia. You forget that I've been looking into this case almost from the beginning. It's the reason I'd like to help solve it, if for no other reason than to give the entire family a chunk of peace, maybe just a little corner of it anyway."

"I get it. Without Brigid's disappearance hovering like a cloud over everything, by solving it, you'd know if Birk is the man you think he is."

Jade took her eyes off the road long enough to look at Kelly. "Oh, my God. That's how you feel about Beckett, isn't it?"

"Beckett's indicated to me that he's ready to move past it. I don't think Birk fits neatly into that category. Not yet anyway. You need to know if Birk is that walking ticking timebomb that can't be domesticated," Kelly provided. "He might have a flip side he doesn't want the world to see."

"Birk certainly has a mysterious side. See? You get it. Is his fiery persona a result of Brigid's disappearance, or has he already fallen into an abyss that no one can help him crawl out of? I need to know, Kelly."

"I know you do. What is it you think you see in Birk?"

"I think deep down he's not fooling anybody. Birch Callahan has a big heart. And I keep telling myself it's that deep down big heart that I'm attracted to. Have you seen him on a search-and-rescue? I have. He's amazing with the dogs."

"How is it you've been around him like that?" The answer hit Kelly then. "How many times have you slept together?"

"Off and on for about two years. It started the night I volunteered to help search for one of my elderly neighbors who'd wandered off. He spotted me standing there waiting for my instructions. We'd already butted heads once or twice over Brigid's case because he didn't agree with anything I'd written on my blog. But there was an attraction I can't explain. I don't think he could either."

"You never said a word."

"What was I supposed to do, brag about how I'd slept with the brother of a victim? It wasn't my finest hour. Besides, to him, it's nothing more than casual sex. He usually doesn't even spend the night."

"That sounds like Birk. You know, he told me he couldn't have his own dog because he travels too much. That's why Debra assigns him Pepsi."

"I know that's what he says. But I think he wants one. I once caught him holding Cosmo up to his chest, whispering to him. It was the cutest thing. That's why I think the man has a soft side that he doesn't want the world to see."

"You know what? After we finish talking to Phoebe, I'd like to find this Soquel State Forest and see Beckett and Brodie do their thing firsthand."

"Then let's do it." Ready to make that happen, Jade stepped on the gas.

Seventeen

The upscale loft building where Phoebe Carpenter called home was only five blocks from the old Clever Pete's downtown site and around the corner from Jade's house.

They found Phoebe as uncooperative as she had been five years earlier. A tall, model-thin woman with reddish-brown hair wearing a pale pink bathrobe tried to shut the door in their faces.

But Jade wasn't having it. She wedged her foot in between the doorframe and the door. "Look, we know about SecretSingles, the dating app. We know Brigid was on there. And so were you. We know you argued with Brigid that night before she left the nightclub. You knew she intended to meet someone from that dating app that night but never told the police. Why not? Why keep a detail like that to yourself?"

"Because you knew the person she was meeting, didn't you?" Kelly charged, her voice echoing down the corridor to Phoebe's neighbors. "How about if we tell the world her roommate has known all along who made her disappear?"

The door cracked open, then wider. Phoebe motioned them through the doorway. "Fine. Come on in. At least you're not Brigid's overbearing brothers come to bug me again. Those two are jerks. They believe their sister was a saint. Trust me, she was the farthest thing from it."

"It's past time to tell us what you know," Kelly stressed, scanning the spacious loft area.

"Who are you people?"

"Online sleuths," Kelly blurted out before Jade could answer. "I'm the novice. Jade is the blogger who keeps this case going. We're independent of the family. Anything you tell us will not leave this room."

"Yeah. Right," Phoebe muttered.

Jade took a seat on the sofa without an invitation. "Just tell us what you know."

"If you didn't kill her, then you have nothing to fear," Kelly assured the woman.

Phoebe visibly bristled and tightened the robe around her waist. "I did not kill Brigid. Okay? Most of those nutjobs on SecretSingles were weird. But Brigid liked that about them. The weirder, the better."

"Weird how?" Kelly asked.

Phoebe sent her an incredulous look. "Jeez, are you two hags so old you don't remember kinky sex?"

Kelly cut her eyes to Jade. "My idea of kinky is having sex on the beach under the stars. You?"

"Same here. I don't think Phoebe is talking about that, though. Why don't you sit down and spell it out for us old hags?" Jade urged.

"These weirdos liked to dress up in stupid costumes," Phoebe explained, plopping down in a side chair. "What kind of grown men do that sort of thing? They belonged to some type of role-playing club, like cosplaying the middle ages or ancient Rome. Brigid found it exciting and funny. I found it stupid and ridiculous, even to some degree dangerous. The first time I went out with one of them, the guy pulled what looked like a knife and held it to my throat. It turns out it was a short saber with a curved edge."

"Sounds like a scimitar," Kelly prompted. "Or maybe a shamshir. Perhaps a kilij."

Jade narrowed her eyes. "A what?"

"It's a short, curved sword, known by several names that originated in the Middle East. It was prominent in combat when soldiers used to ride horses and fight hand to hand. Hollywood uses them in battle scenes of that era all the time."

"Ah," Jade nodded and turned back to Phoebe. "So this SecretSingles guy held that to your throat?"

"Yes. One of the scariest things that ever happened to me. This guy was dressed up in this long flowing silk robe, pretending to look Middle Eastern," Phoebe added.

"Like Lawrence of Arabia," Kelly surmised.

"Who? I don't know who that is. But he wanted to make me think that he could speak Arabic from start to finish."

Kelly leaned forward. "But he wasn't Middle Eastern?"

"No. Just pretending. Like an actor playing a part. These guys dressed up in weird outfits and behaved like it was all fun and games."

"It sounds like you went out several times," Jade corrected.

"No!" Phoebe shouted. "You're not listening. Not me. Once was enough. I didn't want those guys near me. But Brigid thought it was great fun. She probably went out with this one guy a dozen times. Not me. I let that one asshole do whatever he wanted to do and got out of there. Fast. When I got back to the apartment, I told Brigid I never wanted to go through that again. And I never did. The whole thing wasn't for me."

"But you never deleted your profile," Jade pointed out.

Phoebe blinked back tears. "Brigid wouldn't hear of it. She wanted me to hand off the guys I didn't want. She didn't reply to the weirdest-looking ones—and there were a lot—Star Wars characters, men dressed up as Spock, a Wookie, that sort of thing. But she did seem to gravitate to this one guy in particular who looked like Brad Pitt in that movie *Troy*. You know, the one with the long blond hair—not kidding here. Brigid said every time they hooked up, he wore a helmet thing over his face. I remember she mentioned that it looked as if he had access to the drama department because the stuff was mostly props. Anyway, the guy looked stupid and ridiculous to me. It's a shame Brigid didn't share my opinion."

"Wait a sec. How do you know what this man looked like?"

"Are you kidding? Brigid took pictures."

Kelly exchanged looks with Jade. "What? Where are the photos?"

"On her phone, I guess. Brigid took photos every time they connected."

"We don't have her physical phone. And I didn't find any photos on her laptop," Kelly noted. "Did this guy know she took pictures of him?"

"I don't think so. Sometimes she was very sneaky about it, though, filming the encounter to watch later."

"Did you ever watch it with Brigid?"

"Sometimes. But you couldn't make out the guy's face."

"Because of the helmet?"

"Yeah. And because her phone was several feet away during the event. And it was usually dark, very dark. Do you think that's what happened the night she disappeared? He caught her filming him?"

"I don't know," Kelly said, pushing her hair back from her face. She began to pace the loft. "This is almost unbelievable. Brigid scheduled a hookup with this kooky Roman soldier lookalike and took off into the night to meet him. Who does that?"

"I knew you wouldn't believe me," Phoebe declared. "But that one night, he gave her specific instructions to wait at the side of the road by the burger place until he got there."

Kelly frowned. "Was that the usual method to this madness? Did she often meet him at midnight out in the middle of nowhere?"

"No. This felt different. Look, I tried to talk her out of going. I did everything I could. But Brigid could be intractable when she wanted to do something. No one was going to tell her what to do."

Jade shifted on the couch. "I don't understand why you didn't share this with Beckett or Birk? Five years ago, it could've made all the difference in locating her. Now, we're stuck not knowing where to look? She could be anywhere along that stretch of beach north of Santa Cruz."

Kelly decided to take another approach. She got up and laid a hand on Phoebe's shoulder. "The blame train left the station a long time ago. We're not here to pass judgment. Where would Brigid normally meet this guy?"

"I don't know exactly. But the night I met the weirdo with the sword, it was a warehouse downtown that looked deserted."

"A vacant warehouse?"

Phoebe shook her head. "No, not vacant. You walked into this main room, and you could see stage sets cordoned off to the left and right of the entrance. Each used heavy-duty curtains to partition the different scenes. It was just too surreal for me."

"You mean like a movie set?" Jade asked.

"Exactly. When I was there, I remember I saw a gladiator theme room next door to what looked like a Biblical motif. Those are the only two I remember. I know it sounds crazy, but that's what Brigid was into because she'd been thinking about becoming an actress. She didn't want her family finding out until she could make connections and start getting a few auditions that led to real acting jobs."

"I read emails where Brigid claimed she wanted to change her major to communications. But she did mention she liked the idea of being in front of a camera." Kelly looked at Jade. "This side of her might explain her fascination with different role-playing characters. Did you ever see Brigid dress up?"

"All the time. But sex wasn't always involved in every encounter."

"Really?" Kelly noticed Phoebe fidgeting with the belt on her robe. "What else are you not telling us?"

The massage therapist let out a sigh. "I'm sorry to have to say this, but Brigid changed. She wasn't the same person I met my first year at school. She wasn't the girl I knew anymore. She was no longer shy and reserved. Brigid loved watching herself on video. If you think I could ever tell her family how much she changed in two years, you just don't know me. It wasn't up to me to tell them Brigid wanted to be an actress."

Jade bit her lip. "No, it wasn't." She angled toward Kelly. "I did discover back when I started this case that Brigid's first choice for college was UCLA because she wanted to be near Hollywood and the glamour of Los Angeles. She applied there but got turned down. She settled for going to UC Santa Cruz. Her major then was political science at the time. But she got disillusioned with that during her freshman year."

"Brigid got disillusioned with a lot of stuff," Phoebe confirmed. "But you may not know that once Brigid lost interest in political science and business courses, she stopped going to class. She had this burning desire to become an actress. From that point on, everything about her life was over the top. Everything. When she found out Sandra Bullock and Shirley MacLaine were also from Virginia, she watched every movie those two ever made, over and over again. She set out to explore her zany, adventurous side. Those were her words, not mine."

"Enter the world of secret dating and cosplaying," Kelly concluded.

"Unfortunately."

Jade got to her feet. "Thanks for talking to us."

"If you think of anything else, call me," Kelly encouraged, handing Phoebe a business card.

"You're a marine biologist?"

"I told you we weren't cops. We're just two ordinary women trying to find out what happened to Brigid, trying to help the family find some peace of mind."

"If I think of anything, I'll let you know," Phoebe promised.

They left it like that. But back in the car, Kelly turned to Jade. "Do you think Phoebe's telling us the truth?"

"For the most part. You?"

"Yeah. Except for calling us old hags, I kind of liked her. She wasn't what I thought. The one thing I'm having trouble believing, though, is that Phoebe hooked up one time and one time only. Not that it's an important detail about Brigid."

"I was skeptical about it too. That is kind of a stretch. I do think we're looking at several members of the drama department. Who else would have that kind of access to costumes and props?"

"Local theater people would."

"Wow. You're right. I forgot Santa Cruz has an active community theater. What's our next stop?"

"For me, it's getting my hands on those photos Brigid took. Maybe they're stored on iCloud."

"Or a jump drive somewhere."

Kelly huffed out a sigh. "Nothing is ever easy, is it?"

"Not with this case. It seems just when you think you're making headway, you get shoved in another direction. Do you plan to tell Beckett everything Phoebe told us about his sister?"

"Would you tell Birk?"

"Not me. I'd leave that up to you. I don't want to get my head snapped off."

"Lucky me. Getting hungry?"

"Starving."

"There's a sandwich shop around the corner. We should get an order to-go and take Beckett and Birk some food."

"Is that allowed?"

"Feeding the search teams? I wouldn't think Debra would mind. Maybe we should get a sack of sandwiches. That way, it won't be too obvious. The teams have to come back to base camp sometime, right?"

"Yeah. I guess they do. Do you know what Beckett likes? What kind of sandwich?"

"Not really, other than ham and cheese with lots of mayo. We'll vary the order, though. How picky can two hungry men be when they haven't eaten since breakfast?"

"Good point. But I know Birk favors meatball sandwiches."

"Then we'll order a couple of those along with something simple—the ham and cheese, some with mustard, some with mayo. We'll plan to be there waiting for them when they come out of the forest?" When she noticed the skepticism on Jade's face, she added, "Trust me, it won't be that obvious. We're already nearby, practically at the entrance to Soquel State Park. Birk will never suspect anything out of the ordinary. What's better than showing up with food? It shows you're empathetic enough to feed the volunteers."

Jade wasn't convinced. "Birk isn't the type of man you trick. He's suspicious by nature."

"I can't argue with either statement. But stop worrying. We're less than twenty minutes from where they are. It's natural to bring them something to eat."

"You're like trying to stop a freight train barreling down the track. It's very annoying."

"It won't get awkward. I promise. I better GPS the directions."

On the eastern slope of the Santa Cruz Mountains, nestled among patches of Sitka spruce, a dozen search and rescue teams spread out in Soquel State Forest looking for two fourteen-year-old boys.

While Birk and his dog Pepsi scoured the Prairie Creek area, Beckett and Brodie agreed to take the route through Fern Canyon. The picturesque wall of leafy ferns vining down the sides of the valley was a popular spot for tourists. But Beckett refused to believe that two ATV enthusiasts like Todd Loomis and David Hightower had lingered very long at this breathtaking scenic spot.

"Not fourteen-year-old boys," Beckett muttered to Brodie. "Too young to appreciate the sweeping vistas, they're more likely to have headed for that lollipop trail up ahead where they could pick up speed, enjoy the bumpy ride, and circle back to do it again."

He could make out faint ATV tracks in the shallow, cobbled stream, adding weight to that theory. A promising sign, Beckett noted as he and Brodie trekked further up the path until they reached the other side of the canyon wall. With his nose to the ground, Brodie sniffed his way through the creek.

With another mile to go before they reached the top of the trailhead, they made a right toward the Old Logging Road, poking along the outer rim with a carpet of soft pine needles under their feet.

Beckett heard the waterfall before it came into view. But as soon as he rounded the bend, he spotted a mountain lion with her cubs lapping up the water from the pool below. Staying downwind of the pack, he pulled on Brodie's leash to backtrack, retracing their steps to reach the top of the trailhead from the west side instead of the east.

The first stretch leveled out, making for an easy angled ascent. Midway up, at about seventy-five feet in elevation, the path became rocky and muddy.

Beckett spotted recent ATV tracks leading to a rock ledge. He got a bad feeling when Brodie climbed up the outcrop, a flat set of boulders that extended to an overhang.

It wasn't a surprise when Brodie plopped his butt near the edge and let out a bark.

"Good dog," Beckett muttered, reaching in his pocket to reward Brodie with a chunky treat before looking over the side of the bluff. He spotted two ATVs flipped over at the bottom of a canyon, maybe thirty feet down from the boulders.

"I'll be damned. They must've missed the turn and skidded right over the embankment. Good dog, Brodie. Good boy," he repeated, reinforcing Brodie's sighting with another treat.

He looked around for a way to climb down into the pit. "Todd, David, are you down there?" he bellowed.

"Help us," one of the boys called out, his voice hoarse and weak from yelling. "I broke my leg in the fall. Todd hit his head. He's been in and out all morning. Our canteen's out of water. And I can't reach my quad for the spare."

"Hang on. Help's coming," Beckett shouted, picking up his two-way to call in his location. "This is Search-and-Rescue Six. We've located them a mile past Fern Canyon, down thirty feet, possibly more, wedged in a tight ravine. David reports a broken leg. Todd has a head injury. We'll need all hands to get them out unless you want to send air support. Over."

Birk was the first to respond. "This is Search-and-Rescue Four. Do you have a visual? Can you reach them? Over."

"Visual on David. Not Todd. I can descend into the pit to check their condition. But once I'm down, I might not be able to climb back up. Advise on that. I would say that's a negative on pulling them out without rope and a basket. Will definitely need help extracting both injured boys, especially if one is unconscious. Over."

"This is Search-and-Rescue One. I'm alerting County Air Rescue now," Debra interjected, making the call. "Paramedics enroute. Will advise as to their ETA. Over."

"Search-and-Rescue Six. Affirmative. Brodie and I will keep the boys in sight until air support arrives. Over and out," Beckett said. As he angled toward the ledge, he heard crying and sniffling coming from below. "David, it's gonna be okay. Can you give me a better picture of Todd's condition? Is he breathing?"

"Yeah. But he's slipped in and out since it happened. I saw a black bear this morning and had to shoo him away. I thought for sure we were goners."

Beckett didn't want to mention how the mother mountain lion could have easily looped back around to the pit. They had enough to worry about without adding a cougar into the mix, so he kept making small talk.

"How did this happen? Did you miss the bend in the road?"

"It was getting dark, but we didn't want to go back to camp. We kept heading farther and farther away instead of turning around. By the time we decided to head back, we had forgotten how winding the path was. We were racing, trying to beat each other down the hill. In the dark, we sailed right over the cliff."

The catch in David's voice told Beckett the boy had reached his breaking point.

Beckett heard sirens in the distance. "Hear that? That's probably the EMTs entering the park now. You just need to hold on for a few more minutes. Can you do that?"

"Yeah, I guess so."

Beckett heard the sound of a helicopter approaching from the south. His pulse picked up as he tried to block out memories from another time, another place. Doing his best to focus on the current situation and not the past, he glanced over at Brodie and realized his dog showed signs of anxiety at the noise from the blades.

"Come here, boy. We'll take care of each other. I won't let anything happen to you," Beckett vowed, holding tight to the dog. "We'll make it out of here and back home. I promise."

Beckett was surprised to see Kelly waiting for him back at base camp. Jade had parked her car next to his pickup. Both women were sitting at one of the picnic tables. Birk had already taken a seat next to Jade and had devoured half of a giant sub sandwich.

Kelly held up a paper sack in one hand and a large drink in the other. "We thought you could use some food."

"Thanks. I could eat two of everything in that bag."

"We brought plenty. And there's a meatball sandwich for Brodie, too."

Exhausted, Beckett dropped down next to Kelly on the bench. "Of course, there is. You wouldn't forget him. Any ham and cheese in there for me?"

Kelly chuckled. "How did I know you'd go for the ham and cheese first. I did bring backup."

"Start with the meatball," Birk advised, swigging part of his Coke. "That's what I did. And I'm thinking of starting on the ham and cheese."

Jade slid the second sandwich in front of Birk. "No need to be shy about eating. You guys were out here for the better part of the day working up an appetite."

Birk's mouth curved in a rare smile. "Have you ever taken a ride in a private jet?"

"Who? Me? No. Why?"

"Because I need to fly to San Diego. You could give me a ride to the airport. Or better still, you could come with me. We could call it a getaway. You'd need to pack an overnight bag."

Jade blinked in surprise. She glanced over at Kelly and smiled. "I think I'd like that. How long are we talking about, one day or two? Because I need to get the neighbor lady next door to feed Cosmo."

Instead of answering Jade's question, Birk had already started thinking ahead. "Since we need to make several stops, we should probably get going. Beckett, are you okay to hold down the fort while I'm gone?"

"Depends on how long you plan to be in San Diego," Beckett said between bites. "Jade's not the only one wanting to know."

"Probably two days at the most. I'm taking the plane down there."

Beckett nodded. "I got that. Fly into Palomar Airport instead of Lindbergh Field, will you? Palomar's safer. Last time I landed at Lindbergh, I almost got taken out by a commercial jet while trying to dodge one of the parking garages."

"I remember that. Good idea." Birk polished off his sandwich and nudged Jade. "Thanks for the grub. I can't believe you remembered I liked meatballs."

Jade lifted a shoulder. "No big deal. The sub shop was running a special."

"We should probably get going," Birk repeated. "I'll call ahead and have them hold a car for us."

"Have fun," Kelly called out after Jade. "Go wild in San Diego."

Kelly waited for the couple to drive off in the Honda before turning to Beckett. "Why didn't you tell me those two were involved?"

"Is that what they are?" He lifted a shoulder. "They're on and off. What's to tell?"

"You're kidding, right? Birk practically went nuts when I mentioned Jade's name. He called her a crazy hippie. And today, you could feel the sexual tension popping between those two from across the table. What gives?"

"You could? I didn't notice a thing."

She punched his shoulder in a playful gesture. "You did so."

"Maybe. Technically, Birk called Jade a hippie chick and a pretend sleuth. What disclosure was I supposed to toss out at that critical moment? Oh, by the way, Birk's also got a thing for the hippie chick. That's his business, not mine or yours. Did Jade mention their relationship?"

Hesitant to answer since he seemed to want to protect his brother, Kelly did the same thing. "Let's just say Jade played it as cool as Birk and leave it at that."

"I'm ready to pack it in, too," Beckett said, glancing in Debra's direction. "Let's get out of here."

But before they could load up, Debra waved Beckett down. "Any idea how Brodie has been so lucky lately? It's unbelievable the way your dog has responded of late."

"You mean phenomenal," Kelly corrected. "Brodie's risen to the occasion each time he's been called upon to do his job."

Debra narrowed her eyes on Kelly. "I was talking to Beckett."

Beckett shifted his feet. "All I know is that I trained him hard the last month or so. I'm not sure what you're suggesting, though. You're the one dishing out the placements of each team. I can't help it if Brodie found the kids within our assigned grid. I'm sorry the kids weren't in yours or Birk's."

"That's not what I meant to say at all," Debra backtracked. "Whatever you're doing, keep at it. Brodie's on a roll. He's my number one go-to S-and-R dog right now. And you know what that means, right? Don't ever turn off your phone. In addition to your water searches, be prepared to drop what you're doing at a moment's notice. Brodie is now officially the top dog at the County Search and Rescue."

Kelly beamed, bending at the waist to fluff Brodie's fur. "Hear that, Brodie? You're the Rock Star of Santa Cruz."

Eighteen

Over the next two days, Kelly and Beckett spent their downtime together focusing on the reforestation project. The kelp grew faster than expected as the sea stars did their job and kept the purple sea urchins in check. A fact that still amazed both of them.

She sat on the deck of the *Brigid,* steadying her laptop, documenting the progress of the day as Beckett motored the boat back to the dock. After updating her spreadsheets, she closed the lid and stared over at the newest addition to her household—a two-year-old lively female German Shepherd Alaskan Husky mix dubbed Journey.

Eight months ago, Cord Bennett and his wife Keegan had stepped in at the last moment to save Journey from death row at a dumpy shelter in Las Vegas. They'd driven round-trip, more than a thousand miles, to bring her back to Cord's kennels, where she'd been ever since. Despite their best efforts, no one expressed interest in adopting such a large breed dog.

Kelly couldn't understand why.

Journey had a beautiful, unusual coat. The combination of reddish-brown, fawn, and white markings made her stand out from all the rest. But not enough to get her adopted.

After a long conversation with her landlords—Logan Donnelly and his wife Kinsey—the couple had encouraged Kelly to adopt not just any shelter dog but specifically the one that had been there the longest. That dog turned out to be Journey.

It was a bonus that Kelly had fallen in love.

"You're staring at her again," Beckett charged as he rounded the deck, tying off the moorings in the harbor.

"That's because I still can't believe she's mine. I'm beginning to think this town of yours is almost magical in its approach to life in general. What landlord approves adopting a dog without adjusting my short-term lease or charging me more per month?"

Beckett chuckled. "I doubt Logan puts money ahead of anything. He's solid that way. An unusual guy. His wife is like that too."

"That must mean he has a lot of it. That's what I'm saying, though. That type of thinking is unheard of in Hayward."

"You're not in Hayward."

But she would be at the end of summer, thought Kelly. "My apartment lease is up in August. When I get back there, I'm thinking of looking for a house to rent with a yard."

At the notion of her leaving, Beckett's heart dropped. But he managed to play it cool and keep his mouth shut as she continued to talk.

"Journey needs a place to run around. It breaks my heart when I think about how much time she spent in a cage. Cord did the best he could with all the dogs he has, but still—"

"Why don't we take the dogs over to that island I mentioned and let them run around, build a fire, have that cookout I promised? Journey seems to have her sea legs. She's fine on the water. It won't take that long to get there. We'll eat supper outdoors and gaze at the stars tonight."

The dog wandered over to her new owner and laid her head in Kelly's lap. Not to be outdone, Brodie nuzzled his way in for a head scratch.

"That's a great idea," Kelly said as she managed to satisfy both dogs craving her attention. She kissed and snuggled noses, scratched ears, and watched as Journey dropped beside her for a belly rub. "But we'll need to go shopping for groceries. And more dog food. I might have underestimated Journey's appetite."

"You'll get it down," Beckett assured her. "Brodie can go through a fifty-pound bag in about three weeks. And you've seen him eat his share of table food, which I don't recommend, but it is what it is. How long's it been since you've had a dog?"

"Not since Lilly Pad died when I graduated high school. So...twelve years."

"Lilly Pad? That's such a girlie name."

"True. But then she was a little thing, a Yorkie terrier mix. The name just sort of fit. My dad brought Lilly Pad home for my eighth birthday after a co-worker's dog had puppies. We were inseparable."

"A Yorkie to a German Shepherd Husky mix is quite the transition."

"I know." Journey licked Kelly's face. "But we'll make it work, won't we, Journey? If I have to take a second job to afford a bigger place to live, I'll figure it out. Who knows? Maybe the six-figure research job will open up."

Kelly didn't give her situation another thought. She planned to enjoy the evening on the spit of island with Beckett, Brodie, and her new best friend.

As the boat bounced along in the water, Beckett rounded the bend to a slice of land, mostly rock and dirt with a smattering of scrub. "This is as close as I dare get without running us aground."

"Look how small it is. Even up close, it's tiny," Kelly remarked as she hugged Journey. "But it has places to explore, girl. Good thing we both have adventurous hearts." She turned back to stare at Beckett. "Maybe we all do."

"There's something to be said for the explorer in all of us. If we hurry, we'll have the meal out of the way and be able to watch the sunset." Beckett brought the boat around again to lower the anchor so they wouldn't drift in the tide.

They toted their groceries, a cooler, and picnic supplies through the shallow water while the dogs swam to shore. Brodie and Journey took off to investigate what the island had to offer while Beckett and Kelly set up camp, lugged their chairs to the firepit, then gathered wood.

Even though they had to purchase the littleneck clams from Murphy's Market instead of digging for them, it didn't matter. By the time Beckett began his meal prep, Kelly was starving. She watched as he sauteed garlic and butter in a large skillet over an open flame, then dumped the clams into the hot pan. He added a generous amount of white wine from a box before covering it with a lid.

"Who knew Navy SEALS cooked like pros?" Kelly cracked. "You should start a food truck."

"Not for me. But we know how to survive under all kinds of conditions. This is paradise compared to some places I've seen."

Kelly glanced around at the sparse selection of trees and shrubs. The more prolific were the silky oaks and sycamores. But even they were considered seedlings at barely six feet tall. "Someone needs to reforest the plant life here, especially the Himalayan cedar and lemon-scented gum trees."

Beckett looked over at the stumps. "How can you tell what they were?"

"I took a course in forestry. Then again, my parents work in a national forest."

"These have been cut down for firewood probably by campers. I'm not sure anyone's ever talked about replacing them."

"Well, that's a shame. I'd love to spend a season here just to reforest the land. We should've brought more stuff and some camping gear. We could've spent the night here and dived on the old shipwreck in the morning."

"There's not much left of that ship, not much to see. A writer lives in town who wrote a book about it. But in this case, he embellished the legend. The hull is all that's left. But the idea fascinates tourists enough to keep Simon busy all summer. Hence, a lot of people come to this island and hack away at the trees."

"Like that massive Ficus macrophylla over there. Just look at the size of the trunk. That tree is probably sixty, seventy years old. It should be taken care of, not chopped up for firewood. Wonder if anyone's ever mentioned that to Jordan and Nick?" Kelly wandered over to the supplies and filled a plastic cup with some of the wine. "I might bring it up when I see them again because the trees and shrubs should be replanted at least once every two years to keep up the vegetation. Otherwise, people will keep chopping down everything they see until there's nothing left. It wouldn't take much money to replant a patch of smaller native trees. The town could put on a fundraiser."

Beckett snatched her around the waist. "I love it when you get on your soapbox."

She threw her arms around his neck. "I could argue that depleting the natural resources is never a win."

He closed his mouth over hers in a slow, simmering melt that left her wanting more than food. When the shells on the clams began to pop open, he let her go. "You did say you were hungry?"

"Mmm. Yeah. I did say that."

He dumped the steamed clams into a metal bowl while Kelly unboxed a carton of Margie's potato salad made from baby reds. She forked over a bite, then held a sample up to Beckett's mouth. "Taste this. Either I'm ravenous, or this is the most delicious stuff I've ever had."

"To hear Margie tell it, her process is top-secret. She refuses to share the recipe with anyone, including her staff. Try the clams with some of that leftover garlic butter."

Kelly swiped the clam through the butter, then took a bite and closed her eyes. "Delicious. Now, this is what I call a picnic."

They devoured everything within reach and emptied the box of wine.

As they leaned back on a log, their legs outstretched, she nudged Beckett and pointed to Journey and Brodie chasing a lizard. "Look at those two. It's like they've been together for years."

Beckett tilted his head skyward and pointed to a barely visible moon. "Daytime moon. Clear skies mean we'll have a first-row seat to see the stars tonight."

"Did you know that the moon outperforms the sun when it comes to gamma rays?"

"Is that right?"

"Gamma rays have small wavelengths, but they produce the most abundant energy."

"Like supernovas exploding."

She grinned. "Exactly. Gamma rays burn hotter than anything else in the electromagnetic field. If you look through a powerful telescope, they're responsible for neutron stars, the radiation making them look like pulsating lights. Those wavelengths make the moon appear less bright—four hundred thousand times less bright."

"Making the moon barely visible in the daylight."

"Especially when the sun is out. The moon can't compete by merely reflecting the sunlight, so to the naked eye, it dims and fades away."

"You are the most fascinating female I've ever known. I'd love to attend one of your lectures sometime."

"Oh, I don't know about that. My lectures are usually boring. Kids have been known to sleep through them. I even had one student come up to me and say that was the best sleep he'd had since he started college."

"Smartass. Did he pass the class?"

"That's just it, as it turns out, he was my best student."

"You're way too hard on yourself."

"I don't think so. I'm just not a very good teacher." In an effort to change the subject, she shifted slightly against the log. "Wonder how things are going between Jade and Birk?"

"You never told me what, if anything, you or Jade got out of Phoebe," Beckett prompted.

"You're not going to like it."

"Why? I told you she'd bad-mouth Brigid."

"That's not exactly what Phoebe did." Kelly went into as much detail as she could about the videos Brigid taped and the different exotic outfits supposedly worn in the films. "Did your sister ever mention she wanted to become an actress? Did she ever say she liked the idea of improv and wanted to explore its creative process?"

"You're not talking about stand-up, are you? You're talking about sex with a stranger. I don't believe that. I wouldn't rely on Phoebe's word about anything."

"See? That's where I think you're wrong. It's the wrong approach. What if it might be a lead, Beckett? Maybe Brigid talked to or knew someone inside the University's drama department. It was right there on campus, accessible to all students. If she dressed up, where did she get the costumes? Costumes aren't cheap unless she borrowed the clothes from the drama department. I don't see a poor student like Brigid shelling out money to play dress-up. Even thrift stores don't give away their vintage clothing. But if she borrowed a few, who's to say the perpetrator didn't do the same thing? Maybe he's the one who put the idea about acting in her head. That could be who provided costumes. Maybe that's how the two met."

For the first time, Beckett dropped his defensive demeanor. "Okay, I see your point. Then we should talk to whoever was in charge of the drama department five, six years ago. Why the hell didn't Phoebe mention this sooner?"

Kelly let out a sigh. "Sometimes, you and Birk come off as a tad overbearing. Where your sister's concerned, I don't blame you. You want answers. I get that. But that's why it's better to let Jade follow the lead here. She's twenty minutes away from campus. Let her make initial contact, and then we'll follow up. I know this isn't happening at breakneck speed, but at this stage, at least it's happening."

"I know you're going out of your way to help. The slow process is the reason I'm tired of the whole thing. Just admitting that, verbalizing it, makes me feel guilty."

"I know it does. But you and Birk have done everything there is to do. You can't change law enforcement's theory unless there's something new, something big that will change their minds. Jade and I know this. Let us take the burden off you and Birk for once. If we fail, if we come up with nothing, then pick it back up again when you feel not so beaten down."

He was mulling that over when his cell phone lit up with several text messages. "Oh jeez. It's the Sheriff's Department, Debra, *and* Birk. The County needs my help locating a drowning victim who went into the Sacramento River three hours ago. Birk and Jade are on their way back now, but fog conditions delay their takeoff in San Diego."

"That's okay. I'll go with you." She glanced over at the dogs. The two canines had finally run out of steam and had snuggled next to each other for a nap. "I'll flip you for who wakes them up."

Beckett chuckled as he leaned over and planted a kiss on her cheek. "Thanks. If this is a sign of things to come, I'll get handed the stuff you don't want to do, right?"

"They're sleeping so peacefully. Aren't they adorable together?"

"Adorable," Beckett muttered, getting to his feet. "Come on, Brodie. Rise and shine. Wake up your girlfriend. It's time to go to work."

Much of the eleven hundred square miles stretching along the Sacramento River twisted past fertile fields laden with crops and rich farmland. Miles of tomato plantations, nut tree farms, and bottomlands filled with growing asparagus reminded people that in these parts, agriculture remained king.

Woodlands of willow and oak overlooked inlets dotted with houseboats where people lived year-round. The Sacramento River, as it met up with the San Joaquin, attracted skiers, boaters, and kayakers from the nearby small towns like Bay Point, Pittsburg, and Antioch.

In other more remote parts of the river, though, signs went up warning against the dangerous currents. These rural sections prohibited swimming, wading, or diving because waters were especially hazardous when the snowpack melted in spring, high in the Sierra, affecting the undertow. The rising water levels made the current run faster and the water colder.

But many often ignored the warnings and tempted fate. Teenagers were the worst. They often snuck out to meet up, taking rowboats or dinghies out to the tiny islands in the middle of the river to party—their version of going to the beach.

Drownings were a regular occurrence. Bodies usually surfaced sooner or later. But upset and grieving families often didn't want to wait days or weeks to recover a loved one.

If the County called off a search because of nightfall, a third-party outfit like Terra Search and Rescue might step in to continue looking in the dark. A decision appreciated by the grateful family of missing fourteen-year-old Meara Harding.

When Meara, the daughter of a pistachio farmer, decided to ditch her last period classes to go swimming with her friends, she figured she'd be home by supper. But a swift current took her under, then swept her downstream.

Beckett had to determine how far.

He'd let Kelly drive, even though they were towing the boat. He'd used the ninety-minute drive-time from Pelican Pointe to calculate the best place to start.

"How does that work?" Kelly inquired.

He held up his phone and pointed to the app he'd developed. "I got the wind data online along with the tide table reports from this afternoon. Considering I've been to this location multiple times, I know the river's winding shoreline firsthand, which is why the topography is already loaded into my database. I key in the wind and tidal data to tell me how far the body might have traveled. I know the river bottom has all kinds of junk in it from previous sonar readings. Knowing that should help eliminate certain objects right away."

Kelly swallowed hard. "As impressed as I am by all that, it means we're looking at recovery."

"We could hope for a miracle. This early in the process, I never rule it out. But the likelihood the girl's alive is slim. The parents already know that."

"Every time you go out on one of these situations, do you upload the topography from whatever area and keep it in your app?"

"It makes things a lot easier when I'm called back out to the same spot over and over again."

"Is it okay to bring Journey with us on the boat? I want to help you with the river search, but I don't want to leave her alone in the car."

"Sure. Journey's shown she's fine on the water."

As Kelly drove into the delta, she tried to familiarize herself with the area. "It's been a while since I've been here. How do you want me to approach the river? From the east or the west?"

"What you want to do up here at the four-way stop is keep going straight. The road takes you right to the boat launch. You're doing fine."

By the time they unhooked the boat and launched the cruiser into the river's dark waters, the onlookers had thinned out. Even most media outlets had called it a night, leaving Meara's family and friends to huddle near the estuary where she had gone swimming.

After scrambling to get the dogs on board, Beckett headed eastward toward Stockton.

Standing beside him at the helm, Kelly studied the sonar screen. "Why didn't I notice this equipment before now? Your state-of-the-art scanner not only produces an extremely detailed high-definition 3-D image complete with the latest technology, but it keeps logs for reviewing later. How cool is that?"

"I always try to upgrade it whenever there's a new version."

"Awesome. Want me to steer while you keep your eyes on the river bottom? You probably know more about what to look for than I do."

"Sure."

They changed positions. Their first pass produced nothing other than a few false readings. The second pass was no better. But Beckett wasn't about to give up.

"Did you account for the temperature of the water?" Kelly wanted to know.

He nodded, keeping his eyes on the screen. "By now, the water feels like fifty-five degrees minimum. Going for a late-night swim in May is a bad idea." He narrowed his eyes on the screen. "I don't understand why we're not picking up her body."

"Isn't this near the same slough where you found the two teenagers?"

"Threemile Slough is on the other side almost due north of this spot off the Sacramento River. We'll branch off into the San Joaquin River in a few minutes. Why?"

"Because look how the current picks up and becomes vicious near the mouth of the inlet. What if the riptide tossed the girl around and threw her up against the banks? What if she's stuck in debris? What if I veer a little more to the south and head toward that small peninsula that juts out?"

"As long as you don't run aground, I'm okay with that."

Searching waters no one else wanted to explore at this time of night was tricky. But Kelly was careful as she slowed her speed. She steered toward the sharp curve that channeled into another canal. They passed an RV park.

While Beckett continued mapping the narrow pass and checking the banks, his eyes never left the digital screen.

When she rounded the tip of the isthmus and came out on the eastern shoreline, Beckett sat up straighter. "Stop. Kill the engines. I think that's Meara. I think we've got her, maybe forty yards from us. She's tangled up in those vines. Hit the searchlights."

Kelly flipped on the outside forward lights, then shut down the motor. She leaned in and peered over Beckett's shoulder. "Wait a sec. Did I just see her move?"

"Those are the waves. I think." But he increased the image size, sharpened the focus, and zeroed in closer. "Jeez. Maybe not." He reached for the radio. "This is Beckett Callahan. Terra Search and Rescue. We've found what we think is Meara on the far eastern shore of the San Joaquin where it breaks toward Jersey Point—"

"Beckett, wait. I'm almost positive I saw an arm move."

"Hold on. Over." He adjusted the outside lights, focusing on the body and the riverbank. He reassessed. "It's possible Meara's alive. I'm going in. Don't say anything to the family yet, though. Is that clear? Over."

The voice over the radio crackled in response. "Affirmative. We're on our way. But be advised there's heavy debris littering the river bottom. Broken glass. Splintered wood. An array of trash. Sharp metals. That sort of thing. Over."

"Understood. But if the girl's alive, every minute counts. Over and out."

She followed him around to the deck. "You should at least put on a wetsuit."

"No time," he replied as he kicked off his trainers and jumped into the water.

Before Kelly could grab Brodie's collar, the dog followed him into the river.

Beckett swam over to the barely conscious Meara, who seemed to be trying to wriggle out of the tangled web of vines to no avail. He fought the twisted branches until he reached her, pulling her up the rugged bank and out of the water.

The dog made his way through the brambles onshore as Beckett checked for a pulse. After picking up a faint rhythm, he realized her breathing was too shallow. He cleared her airway, beginning chest compressions and mouth to mouth.

After several minutes of CPR, the young teen's eyelids fluttered open as a motorboat pulled up to the bank and shined a light up the embankment. Someone shouted, "Air Medical is on its way. Transport is ten minutes out. Keep up the CPR."

"She's coming around," Beckett affirmed, maintaining compressions.

Meara's head rolled to one side. She tried to cough. Instead, she tossed up a torrent of dirty river water.

Later, he sat on one of the bunks below deck, letting Kelly treat his minor wounds.

"Who knows how long Meara was there, clinging to those branches?" Kelly noted as she applied hydrogen peroxide to the deep cuts and scratches along the length of Beckett's arms. "You could've at least given me a full minute warning before jumping overboard. Next time, I'd like a heads up, if you don't mind."

"Yes, ma'am."

She pressed kisses to the top of his head, ran her hands through his hair. She spread little kisses to his ear, cheek, and finally, his mouth. "I've never met anyone like you before. You do what you do at sometimes great risk to yourself. You're used to taking risks. It takes some getting used to that. What you did tonight was amazing. Watching you dive into the water like that to save a child was the bravest thing I've ever seen."

She angled closer, nuzzling her body to his. "Doesn't this bucket have a shower?"

His brow quirked upward. "It does. What did you have in mind?"

"Although Brodie smells as bad as you do, it's not him I'm thinking of tossing in the shower." She put an arm around his waist and drew him down a short hallway into the tiny bathroom he called the head. She leaned over, turned on the showerhead, and yanked up his shirt. "It's time to get you out of these smelly clothes. Ever had sex in this particular head?"

He sent her a wicked grin and boosted her up. "Come to think of it, I don't believe I have. Time to correct that little detail now."

Nineteen

"So, how was San Diego?" Kelly asked Jade over the phone the next day.

"It was fantastic. Birk seemed different. That is until I brought up our conversation with Phoebe. That's when the fireworks went off. And I'm not talking about the good kind."

"Same with Beckett. But then I explained the drama department might be a lead no one had ever pursued."

"Wow, girl, you handled it better than I did. You think on your feet. I like that. Birk yelled at me for about fifteen minutes before he settled down. We managed to enjoy the rest of our time together. But I explained that his reaction was the very reason Phoebe wouldn't open up to him in the first place."

"The confrontational approach might not work with me either," Kelly stated.

"Or me. So now it's all on the table. We either find new evidence, or this opportunity will slip away again. God knows for how long. I'm heading over to the University this afternoon. It's lousy timing, though. The semester is over. Everyone's cleared out until August. I'll be lucky to find a custodian to let me into the building."

"We just need one or two names from five years back, someone in charge of costumes or someone with access to wardrobe backstage, even a list of who acted in their productions during that timeframe would help."

"I might be able to find that out from a past production online. But what if this guy is an alumnus with past connections to the department? That will be more difficult to pin down. The point is, I'll do my best. Did you get a chance to look at those pings from Brigid's phone?"

Kelly glanced over at the stack of boxes she hadn't searched. "Beckett volunteered to help with that and keep his cool while doing it."

"Good luck with that."

"Let's get together tonight with Birk and go over what we know. My place or Beckett's. The thing is, I went ahead and adopted a shelter dog. I don't want to throw too many new places at her at once."

"Aww. What's her name? What kind of dog did you get?"

"Come see for yourself tonight. Her name's Journey. She's big, but she has the gentlest soul."

"Journey? Such a perfect name for someone with a backstory."

"I like how you get that. She's a bit daring and strong-willed. But I believe that's how she survived up to now. I thought the name fit."

"Oh, it does. Want me to bring anything?"

Journey trotted over to rub against Kelly's legs. "Nah. We'll figure it out as we go, it might be as simple as ordering pizzas, or maybe I'll be inspired to cook. Who knows?"

"Whatever it is, make it simple. The goal is to discuss Brigid's case with two stubborn men. But if you want to make peanut butter cookies, I wouldn't object to that for dessert."

"I'll see what I can come up with." Kelly heard Beckett's truck pull up outside. "Look, I need to go. Talk to you tonight. Stay safe. And if you need my help with anything at UC, let me know."

Beckett opened the door carrying two huge bags of dog food. Brodie darted into the kitchen to say hello to Journey.

"Look at that. Brodie missed his girlfriend."

"I see that," Kelly noted, angling her head for a kiss. "And did you miss yours?"

He bent to peck her on the cheek. "I did. Heavy stuff here. Where do you want to store it?"

"I cleared out a section of cupboards with doors under the row of cabinets. I figure Journey won't be able to open a cabinet door, right?"

"Don't bet on it. Brodie figured out where I keep his food within three days."

"I'll put my Journey up against clever and smart any day, but let's hope she doesn't go hunting for her food." Kelly dragged her laptop so Beckett could view the screen. "I guess you saw the news story out of Sacramento. It starts, 'Ex-Navy SEAL from Terra Search and Rescue saves teenager after County shuts down the search for the night.' Beckett Callahan has made a career locating bodies and drowning victims. But last night, a little before midnight, he was able to find Meara Harding alive, clinging to the banks of the San Joaquin River near the Levee…' The article goes on to say how grateful the family is that you found their daughter and didn't give up looking for her. You were the difference between finding Meara alive rather than dead."

"I'm just glad it turned out the way it did," Beckett remarked, shoving the bags of dog food into the cabinet. He pivoted toward Journey, the dog staring right at him as he closed the doors. "She's already onto the hiding place. Dig out the next bowl of chow and she won't even have to go searching for it."

Kelly hooted with laughter and attempted to distract Journey by heading into the living room. "Boxes of stuff to hit. Remember?"

Joining her next to the cartons, Beckett ran a hand through his hair. "Oh, man. I just don't feel it today. After the events of last night, I'm not up for going through this stuff. Don't be mad."

Kelly laid a hand on his arm. "I'm not. Don't worry about it. I probably need to see this stuff firsthand and read through it myself for it to have an impact. You don't need to hang around."

He shifted his feet in a guilty stance. "I've got some stuff to do, some errands to run. Can Brodie stay with you?"

"Of course."

"Want me to pick up anything for tonight?"

"While you're out? Sure. I thought about pizza."

"What about one of those family-sized pans of lasagna Fischer Robbins makes up ahead of time? We could pop one in the oven, warm it up, put out some green stuff to go with it."

"Perfect. Grab some more of that local wine, too. Jade mentioned she wanted to try it. And could you pick up a dessert, like a peanut butter cheesecake or something?"

"You're kidding, right? Peanut butter? Does it have to be that?"

"Never mind. I'll take care of dessert."

"Okay. See you around four."

"Should I ask where you're going or give you some space to do your thing?"

He smiled and kissed her hair. "I just need some alone time. The boat needs some maintenance. Birk and I plan to have a couple of beers, spiff up the interior, maybe squeegee out the shower. No big secret."

Kelly watched him go without further comment. But the explanation didn't feel right to her. She didn't have time to dwell on his weird behavior. Instead, she took the lid off the first carton and dug through its contents, hunting for the phone records and the pings. She ultimately found the two files stored away in separate file boxes. One set of documents had been stuffed into a large brown envelope while the other gathered dust in a shoebox.

Odd, Kelly decided that since the brothers had reviewed everything multiple times, the phone records were unorganized.

She marked each entry from the night Brigid disappeared with a highlighter and then transferred the information to a database for referencing later. She gathered the data on the pings and created a geographical map using one of her software applications commonly used for underwater landforms.

Using the Internet, she decided to look for any crimes near the burger joint on that evening. She discounted the petty things like stolen bicycles and break-ins, refining her search. She stared at the screen when a double homicide popped up. After jotting down the details, she stretched her back and stared at the dogs.

"I do all the work, and you guys get to nap. How fair is that? I need a break to clear my head. Cookies would help. There's peanut butter in it for you if you're both good. How does that sound?"

Brodie was the first to get to his feet, seeming to comprehend that the question involved food. Journey followed the retriever's lead and nuzzled Kelly.

"That's a yes, then," Kelly determined and headed to the kitchen to prehcat the oven.

Birk was already aboard the *Brigid* scrubbing the deck with a mop when Beckett arrived at the pier.

"Was San Diego a successful trip?" Beckett asked, picking up a hose to rinse off the cleaner Birk had used to wash the durable PVC surface. "Did Jade suspect anything?"

"No. She went shopping a couple of hours after we got to the hotel. Everything went according to plan."

"So, to her, it was simply a romantic impromptu getaway?" When all he got was a grunt from Birk, Beckett snapped, "Are you gonna put that stupid mop down and talk to me? How did negotiations go? When is the extraction? How many people this time?"

"It's happening Friday. And the number hasn't changed. It's still eight total. It's my understanding that we fly to Baja. Someone will meet us at the airport and take us to Colima by boat, the neutral spot I negotiated for the exchange. Wolfson approved the plan himself."

"I'm not that concerned about Wolfson. He'll be in his throne room back in San Jose, monitoring everything safely from his mansion away from the line of fire. It's our asses on the line again with minimal backup."

"I've worked with the boat captain before and our contact in Colima. Both men come highly recommended. But as usual, we should always prepare for a few surprises."

"We're bringing plenty of firepower in case things go south, right?"

"A shitload that will be transferred to the boat by tonight."

"Jeez. How do I tell Kelly I'll be out of town come Friday? I'm not sure how I feel about having to come up with a story."

"Welcome to the world of relationships and lying about what we do. Jade mentioned a girls' night out. That should keep Jade and Kelly busy Friday night. It's one of the reasons I moved up the exchange."

"What about a fishing trip?"

"Tricky. You'd probably have to come back with one or two. We both would. Roosterfish is always a popular catch in May, though. I checked. Just in case. The other kinds of fish aren't quite as active in the Sea of Cortez this time of year."

"Talk about doing your research. I don't even know what kind of fish that is. But Kelly will know. Trust me."

Birk reached in his pocket for his phone and held up a picture. "Blue-grayish stripe with a funny-looking dorsal fin. They're hard to catch, too. It makes for a better story when we get back."

"Send me that photo," Beckett directed. "I doubt it fools Kelly, but it's worth a try. How do I explain an emergency fishing trip for roosterfish?"

"It's simple. A buddy of ours who runs a fishing charter had a couple of cancellations at the last minute. He offered us the charter for free if we could get there on short notice. I figure we're men. We fish. We can go fishing on somebody else's dime, right?"

"And Jade bought this?"

"I thought we'd spring it on them together at the meeting tonight over dinner. Make it seem more real."

"I planned to pick up lasagna. On second thought, maybe we need to upgrade this to something a little fancier."

"Like wine and dine them at Perry Altman's place? I beg to differ. You take them to The Pointe, and they'll know something is up, that we're trying to butter them up for what's coming. It's so obvious. But if you casually mention it over a regular meal, it fits right in with a spur-of-the-moment offer to go fishing."

"I bow to the master. You've done this before. I suppose Jade mentioned Phoebe?"

"She did. My gut told me all along that woman was holding something back. Brigid never said a word to you about becoming an actress?"

"Not a word. What on earth was she thinking meeting up with strangers like that?"

"Hey, times have changed. Remember that R&R to Crete we took? Those two sisters? We didn't even know their names. The point I'm trying to make is that you can't have it both ways. I was angry at first. Ask Jade how it almost ruined our time together. But I'd be hypocritical to think Brigid was immune to sowing her wild oats. We were far from saints when we were twenty."

"How can you compare the two? Going out to meet a stranger got her killed, Birk."

"Our world travels could've gotten us killed at any moment," Birk fired back. "In case you haven't noticed, it's a dangerous world everywhere."

"We were trained to look for danger. Brigid was a naïve kid."

"Oh, crap," Birk said, checking his watch. "I told Jade I'd pick her up. I need to leave now," he said, handing his brother the mop. "She's spending the night tonight."

"Wanna bet? Not after she finds out you're ditching her to head down to Mexico first thing tomorrow morning to fish."

Beckett ordered the family-size lasagna from Longboard's and picked it up on his way to Kelly's house.

With an Italian aroma wafting around him, the dogs met him at the door sensing food. The house already smelled like sugar and peanut butter. "You didn't need to bake anything. Fischer had a vanilla bean cheesecake that I picked up."

"Oh. Thanks. I received a text from Jade. She and Birk will be here any minute. I already have the oven warming. I'll just slip in the lasagna, set the timer, and start throwing together a salad. I'm anxious to hear what happened at the drama department."

"Did you find the phone data you needed?" Beckett asked, handing off the food.

"I did. But maybe I should wait to go into what I found until Birk and Jade arrive."

"No. Go ahead. What is it? Now I'm curious."

"It's just that Birk could be right about Brigid's disappearance not having anything to do with the other missing women."

"What? When did you come to that conclusion?"

"A couple of hours ago. Were you aware that the night Brigid went missing, there was a double homicide nearby, like four blocks away from the burger chain? What if she saw something she wasn't supposed to see? Or maybe she was at the wrong place at the wrong time."

Beckett rubbed the back of his neck. "I don't know, Kelly. That seems even more far-fetched than the serial killer angle."

"Hang with me for a sec, okay. The double homicide involved a middle-aged couple. The cops immediately zeroed in on their daughter. And about six months later, arrested her for the double murder."

"Arrested who?" Birk asked as he came through the door, carrying several bottles of wine.

"Kelly was just getting to that," Beckett announced. "She thinks it might be related to Brigid's disappearance."

"Let's get dinner out of the way, and I'll explain everything in greater detail," Kelly said, looking over at Jade. "Hey. You look nice tonight."

"Thanks. Is this the new pup? Aww. She's adorable," Jade said, running her fingers through Journey's thick reddish-brown coat while the dog sniffed her. "She probably smells Cosmo."

"What did you find out from the university?"

Jade stood up and followed Birk into the kitchen. "I ran into a roadblock from the get-go. No one there could remember who was in charge of the wardrobe department six years ago. But I got a list of names to contact who might know. It will take a great deal of phone banking. The other problem is that I discovered it's not exactly a tightly run ship, no matter the timeframe. The older woman I spoke to said people come and go at will. Students often allow their friends to borrow clothes for parties. They don't always bring the outfits back. It's been a common practice that goes all the way back to the 1970s."

"That's disappointing," Kelly remarked as she set out three kinds of dressing for the salad.

"Tell me about it. Who got arrested and for what?"

"Double homicide very near the burger place on the night Brigid went missing. The victims were Kenneth Aldridge and his wife, Marilyn. Their daughter is Bethany Aldridge. She has several DUIs with reckless endangerment and a long history of petty theft, shoplifting, and marijuana possession. The cops say that she killed her parents with a .22 caliber handgun belonging to her father between midnight and one-thirty that morning. They think Bethany used her key to get inside the house and shot them while they slept. Her motive was their million-dollar life insurance. Bethany maintained her innocence right up until she was found guilty and sentenced to life in prison."

Birk lifted a shoulder. "So, how does this relate to Brigid?"

Kelly cut her eyes to Jade before she pivoted back to Birk. "You once said you thought Brigid might've been a hit and run victim. With Bethany's reckless driving record, her string of DUIs, her proximity to where Brigid was last seen, and the Aldridge house, Bethany could've hit Brigid while leaving the crime scene, panicked, then disposed of your sister's body at Shark Fin Cove."

"Do you really think that's what happened?" Beckett stated.

"No. But I told both of you I'd look at this with a fresh set of eyes. I believe in full disclosure. It's up to you to accept the Bethany Aldridge version. Jade and I could set up an interview with her at the prison. Confront her with the theory and see what happens."

"You'd do that?" Beckett asked.

"You bet I would. You should also know that I believe whatever happened that night was captured on CCTV. Is the video lost forever that shows what occurred? Yeah. Probably. But I've looked at that street view two dozen times. There were at least five cameras aimed at that spot. At least. I know CCTV footage from that busy intersection had to exist at some point. As far as I know, it was never looked at, never examined. I didn't unearth it in those boxes. There's nothing in the notes about CCTV."

Beckett let out an audible sigh and traded looks with his brother. "If only we'd reacted sooner, gotten out here sooner, canvassed the businesses sooner."

Birk leaned against the counter and shook his head. "We did the best we could with what we had. The cops kept telling us we were getting in the way. So we backed off, thinking they'd investigate and find her. Don't go down the guilt road. You need to get off that and stay off. We tried the best we could. We might've let Brigid down, but we honestly did everything to try and find her."

Kelly ran a hand down Beckett's arm. "I think it's time you both stop beating yourselves up. You've spent years trying to find out what happened. I'm not suggesting you stop trying to dig for the truth. I'm saying, give yourselves a break. There's nothing either of you could've done that night even if you'd been three miles from that burger joint. Whatever happened, happened fast."

"Well put," Jade remarked. "And I've been on this case for five years."

When the timer dinged on the lasagna, Kelly angled toward the oven. "Now, sit down, and let's eat a nice, hot meal. I'll tell you what I did with the pings."

"You mapped everything?" Beckett noted midway through his salad.

"And transferred Brigid's phone records from that last week into a database. As I see it, Jade and I could start with the incoming and outgoing calls when Brigid was in the bar, go from there."

"I like that idea," Jade said. "It's more relevant than the contact list from the drama department."

"We'll see," Kelly muttered as she pushed her salad bowl aside and took her first bite of Fischer's lasagna. "This is good stuff." She glanced over at Jade. "I have peanut butter cookies for dessert or vanilla bean cheesecake."

"Can I have both?" Jade cracked. "Crumble the cookies on top of the cheesecake."

Birk chuckled. "I like a woman with a healthy appetite. But where do you put all that?

"How else? I have a rigorous workout routine."

Kelly tittered with laughter. "Yeah, her workout consists of walking to the coffee shop around the corner, toting Cosmo in her backpack."

"Hey, have you seen the size of that cat? Cosmo weighs at least eighteen pounds. You try carting him uphill to the coffee shop and back."

Kelly got up to get dessert plates and slice the cheesecake. "Who wants it served Jade-style?"

"I'll give it a try," Birk offered, nudging his brother.

Beckett cleared his throat to get Kelly's attention. "Before I forget, I'll need you to watch Brodie tomorrow and part of Saturday."

"Sure. No problem. What's up?"

Birk picked up the thread. "Beckett and I have this great opportunity to go deep-sea fishing for roosterfish down in Baja. It's a free charter. We'll be back sometime Saturday afternoon."

"A free charter? When did all this happen?" Kelly wondered.

Beckett stuck to the cover story. "This Navy buddy of ours had cancellations. The boat's available for free. Why pass up a chance like this?"

"I didn't even know you two fished," Kelly pointed out.

Jade nodded, exchanging glances with Kelly. "Imagine an overnight trip to catch roosterfish. Who could pass that up? That's a new one for me. What about you, Kelly?"

"Oh, no, not at all. Most of my boyfriends go searching for the hard-to-reel-in roosterfish at some point in our relationship. It's usually after two months of dating, though. But with the way the world is today, things move a lot faster, especially since everyone knows roosterfish peak in May."

Jade snickered and held up her wineglass. "Good thing Kelly and I made plans to go out Friday night."

"I promise I'll make it up to you when we get back," Beckett promised.

Kelly sent him a sweet grin. "No problem. Just be sure and take a photo of that roosterfish for me, will you? I've never seen the real thing."

Beckett rolled his eyes and sneered at Birk. "Taking photos is on my big brother. Everybody knows he's a much better angler than I am."

"Better shot, too," Birk boasted. "But that's for another dinner story."

Twenty

The following morning in the dark, Kelly roused from sleep in time to watch Beckett put on his pants.

"I didn't mean to wake you. I didn't mean to make so much noise, but I need to stop at my house to grab all my gear."

"Fishing equipment, right?" she murmured as she shoved her hair out of her face and lifted her head to squint at the clock. "Is that the right time? Does that say four-thirty?"

"Sorry," Beckett repeated, placing a kiss on her hair. "Go back to sleep."

"Where are you staying again? Did you leave me that contact information?"

"Um. I'm not sure yet. Birk has all that information. I'll text it to you. Later."

"Later," Kelly echoed, latching onto his shirt, pulling him closer, fisting the material in her hands. "Whatever you're doing with your brother, I don't care. I know you can't tell me. That's okay. Just be careful. Okay? Don't get hurt. For God's sake, stay safe."

He ran a finger down her cheek. "When have I ever had a woman like you waiting for me? The answer is never. Don't worry about me. I can take care of myself. I'll be back."

Her eyes misted over. When a tear trickled down her cheek, she fought to stay composed. "You better. I don't mind being the first to say it. I love you, Beckett. I love you. Do you hear me?"

"I love you, too. I gotta go. It messes up the timing if I'm late to the airport."

"Don't mess up. Stay safe."

"I will. Take the boat out. Check on your kelp beds, your sea stars. Make sure they're getting the job done. Keep busy until I get back."

She watched Beckett walk out of the room and closed her eyes. The waterworks came then. This time, she didn't try to stop the tears.

Twenty-One

After Beckett left, Kelly couldn't get back to sleep. She scooped up her phone, checked her emails, and scrolled through her social media accounts.

Wide awake, the dogs joined her on the bed. She realized Brodie and Journey were just as antsy. If they couldn't settle down, no one was going back to sleep.

Like a zombie, she got up and got dressed, grabbing a pair of jeans and a sweater off the chair. She pulled on a pair of boots and stumbled down the hallway, the dogs trailing behind. She let them out the back door, hoping a potty break would help calm them down.

As she watched them scamper onto the grass, she warned Brodie, "Please, don't let Journey wander off. Keep an eye on her."

Brodie whined and went to a corner of the lawn to do his business. Like a dutiful friend, Journey followed.

Kelly made coffee and plopped down to wait for it to brew. But her stomach churned with an uneasy feeling. She'd known Beckett wasn't going fishing. Now, she worried about the real reason for his trip.

"What kind of stuff do ex-Navy SEALS do?" she wondered aloud, searching online for an answer.

She wasn't surprised when the Internet failed to provide a solution.

"This is crazy," Kelly admitted. "I'll take the boat out and go through my day like a normal person. I'll pretend Beckett's gone fishing. Yeah. That's what I'll do."

She let the dogs back in, fed them, and filled a Thermos with coffee. She ignored the hunger pains building in her stomach and made a peanut butter sandwich for later. She stuffed treats for the dogs into a tote bag, snatched some bottled water out of the cabinet, and added two cans of warm soda to the haul.

After attaching leashes to the dogs, she opened the front door and ran smack into a worried Jade. "What are you doing here?"

"Did Beckett tell you what this trip is all about?"

"No. But it's not fishing. I know that much. What did Birk say?"

"Not a thing, closed-mouthed as ever. But I told him I knew he wasn't going fishing. Do they think we're stupid? Roosterfishing?"

"Not exactly the most creative story, is it?"

Jade looked at Kelly's canvas bag. "Where are you going? Shopping at this hour? It's not even daylight yet."

"To the boat. I can't sit around here all day and worry. I need to keep busy."

"Sounds like a plan. Mind if I tag along?"

"You don't even have to ask. Let's spend the morning on the water, watch the sun come up. I'll check on my project, take some notes, and update my database. Maybe I'll dive, see for myself that the sea stars devoured the sea urchins. Then we'll head back here for lunch and start going over Brigid's phone calls from that night."

"I wouldn't mind seeing your project for myself," Jade concluded.

Bolstered with each other's company, the two women made it through the morning.

Even though Kelly kept checking her phone, there were no texts from Beckett. When they got back to the house, they warmed up leftovers from the night before and polished off the cheesecake and the rest of the cookies.

Mid-afternoon, a text message from Julianne Dickinson popped up confirming their meeting time at The Shipwreck.

Kelly sighed and turned to Jade. "I'm not in the mood to spend hours at a bar. What should I tell her? The chef at the B&B already promised Jordan a night out. Julianne and Cassidy are counting on me to show up. But I don't feel like making small talk when Beckett is on a pretend fishing trip doing God knows what."

"I hear you, but what's the alternative? Sit around here and watch *An Officer and a Gentleman* for the millionth time? No thanks. And I can't stuff my face with another batch of cookies or cheesecake. I'm sugar logged. I'd rather numb my worry with a dirty martini, or a strong golden rum disguised as a mojito."

Kelly let out a laugh. "I could live with that. I'm so glad you showed up when you did. Don't go back to Santa Cruz tonight, okay? Stay here. We'll have a good old-fashioned sleepover."

"You don't have to talk me into it. I stuffed my overnight bag in the trunk. Sue me if I couldn't stand the thought of spending tonight by myself."

"Worrying," Kelly finished as she keyed in a reply to Julianne, then sent a reminder to Cassidy Kennison to meet them at the bar between six-thirty and seven, whichever worked best for her.

"Misery loves company," Jade concluded. "Now, let's start calling back these phone numbers. You take incoming. I'll do the outgoing."

"Hell, yeah. If our men go traipsing off to do whatever without telling us the truth, maybe we can solve Brigid's disappearance without them."

Having Jade in the house made the time pass quickly for Kelly. Around five-thirty, they abandoned their phone project to shower, primp, and fuss with their hair.

"It's a good thing I started getting ready early," Kelly lamented. "I never know what to do with my hair. That's why I always end up twisting it into a ponytail."

"I'll fix it," Jade offered. "You should wear it down tonight. I brought my curling iron."

"You travel with a curling iron? That's the problem for me. I packed nothing for the summer except a few tops, wet suits, jeans, and shorts."

"Nothing wrong with a basic wardrobe. But I've always found that the hair doesn't take care of itself."

"Yours is always so shiny and wavy and manageable."

"Will get yours tamed. Do you trust me?"

"I suppose. Don't make me look silly."

"Would I do that? Watch the master work her magic," Jade boasted, getting rid of Kelly's dead ends by snipping them off, then applying a sleek and shine conditioner from her bag. She used the hot iron she'd brought to twist Kelly's long tresses into waves, giving her face a softer look.

When Jade finished, she stepped back and handed Kelly a mirror. "What do you think?"

"Wow. I don't even recognize myself. You're a genius."

"Sure I am. I saw the marine biologist with a Ph.D. out there on the water this morning. You're the genius, growing kelp, regenerating sea stars. I'm just good with makeup and hair."

"We all have things we excel at," Kelly replied. "I don't think I've looked this good since my aunt did my hair the night of my senior prom." She twirled in front of the mirror a second time and smiled. "Scratch that. On second thought, this is ten times better than Aunt Hope's old-fashioned 'do. She made me look like Nellie Oleson."

Jade doubled over in laughter. "You mean the mean girl on *Little House on the Prairie*?"

"That's the one."

"You don't look anything like that."

"If you'd done that to my hair tonight, it might have ended our friendship. Oh, jeez, look at the time. We need to go. And I'm driving this time."

Kelly and Jade found Julianne, Jordan, and Cassidy in the back of the pub, holding a table for them as people hovered.

"Thank goodness you got here when you did," Jordan began, "I thought we'd have to fight someone for this place to sit. People grabbed a few chairs already without asking."

"We'll take them back," Kelly proposed before introducing Jade. "I'll get the drinks going."

"No, you sit," Jade directed. "I already know what we want to drink. But hold my chair. I don't want to have to fight for it, but I'm in the mood for a good row if it comes to that."

Kelly watched as Jade took off, zig-zagging her way to the bar. "How long have you been waiting?"

"Not long. How's the new puppy?" Julianne asked.

"Journey's such a sweetheart. I can't thank Cord and Keegan enough for saving her life and allowing me the chance to give her a good home."

"There's Keegan now," Jordon pointed out, waving wildly to get Keegan's attention. "You can tell her yourself."

Kelly shook hands with Keegan. "It's an honor to finally meet you. I've read everything your grandfather, Porter Fanning, ever wrote on marine life. I interned on his research vessel, *Moonlight Mile*, my junior year of high school. It was an experience that stuck with me through college and was my motivation to tough it out in grad school."

"What a nice thing to say," Keegan said, taking a seat next to Kelly. "My grandfather was an extraordinary man. I bet he recognized your remarkable talent that summer. Just look at what you've done with our own Sandpiper Marsh and Smuggler's Bay. I can see the kelp bouncing back from my upstairs window. It's an incredible turnaround. I've taken a few photos to document the progress you've made. I want the Coastal Blue Trust to know about your work."

Kelly's heart raced. "Really? That would be fantastic. Dr. Fanning certainly inspired me for those three months to make the ocean a better place. I guess it stuck."

"It did more than stick. What you're doing for our slice of coastline is more than I could ever hope for." Keegan traded looks with the school principal. "No wonder Julianne wants you to head up our Summer Science Camp. You'd be fantastic at it. Have you ever thought of teaching at that level, catching kids early, and getting them interested in ocean conservation? Do you have any idea the impact you'd make on the local children?"

"You should do it," Jade encouraged, balancing a tray with multiple drinks on it. "I took the liberty of ordering refills since the crowd is two-deep, and the bartender seems overwhelmed. Anyone interested in a mojito?"

Over cocktails, the women talked as best they could with the noise around them until the band took the stage. After that, the loud music made chatting impossible.

The noisy vibe got to Kelly almost from the start. It wasn't the band's fault. She just wasn't in the mood to party. She kept checking her phone, then looking over at Jade to see if Birk had sent a text. Not hearing from Beckett was almost as bad as the raucous crowd.

But Kelly didn't want to be the first one to leave. Lucky for her, Jordan was the one who called it a night.

"I need to get back to the B&B."

"Are you okay to drive?" Kelly asked.

"I'm fine. I only had two glasses of Chardonnay."

When Jordan stood up, Kelly tapped Jade on the shoulder. "Look, I'm out of here, too."

"Why? Aren't you having fun?"

Kelly ticked off the reasons. "I'm walking Jordan to her car. The music is giving me a headache. And I need to check on the dogs. Pick one. But the truth is I shouldn't leave Journey and Brodie alone for more than two hours. I don't want them to feel abandoned. Plus, I need fresh air and time to think."

"I'll go with you."

"No, you don't have to do that. Stay if you want. You seemed to be having more fun anyway. But when you get ready to leave, text me, and I'll swing by to pick you up." When Kelly saw the look on Jade's face, she added, "Indulge me. I don't want a repeat of Brigid. I don't want you walking out of here alone."

"Fine. But I can take care of myself."

"Famous last words, my friend. Just call me when you're ready for that sleepover. I'll still be up."

Kelly had left the porch light on along with every single light in the house for the dogs. She could hear Journey bark on the other side of the door before she unlocked it.

The dogs acted like she'd been gone for a week instead of a couple of hours. She bent on one knee and fluffed some fur. They showed their gratitude with slobbering licks and kisses. "Guys, I'm not going anywhere. I'm home to stay. It's okay to spread the love out over the next few hours."

To prove it, she took off her jacket and tossed it on the sofa, used the remote to turn on the TV, and let it drone on in the background for white noise.

"Let's refresh your water bowls. And maybe get you a cookie for being so good. You were good, right?" She looked around the rooms for any shoe chewing, toilet paper disasters, puddles, or worse. Not finding anything, she beamed at Brodie, then Journey. "Nice job, guys. You need a big reward. Treats in the kitchen, then outside to potty before settling down for the night."

She hung out on the patio, waiting for the dogs to pee, checking her emails, messages, and even her social media accounts—nothing from Beckett popped up.

Back inside, she opened her laptop and began scanning the database she'd created with Brigid's phone data.

When the front door burst open, the dogs had a bark fest. They calmed down when they saw it was only Jade. "You're worried about me walking home when you forgot to lock your front door."

"The dogs will keep me safe. What are you doing here? Did you walk from the bar?"

"No. Keegan gave me a ride. She lives practically across the street from you. It was no fun there without you."

"Aww. Thanks."

Jade studied the screen and tried to read the email. "Who are you writing?"

"I'm emailing one of my friends, asking him to do a cell phone dump in the area where Brigid was last seen. The window being two hours before she left the bar to two hours after she arrived in front of the burger joint—roughly eleven o'clock to two. That should cover the timeframe. I don't know why I didn't think of this sooner."

Jade frowned and took a seat on the couch. "You never mentioned that you knew anyone who could get around a court order?"

"I'm a researcher. I've had to rely on a hacker—his name is Isaac Packard—more times than I care to admit."

"Well, I'm impressed. If only we had Brigid's Android. It would make things so much easier."

Kelly narrowed her eyes at Jade. "Hold on a minute. Are you saying Brigid had an Android cell phone?"

"Yeah. Why?"

"Are you sure it wasn't an iPhone?"

"Absolutely. Why?"

"Because Brigid also had a Google account, a Google email. I should've figured this out before tonight. I slogged through thousands of stuff in her trash and spam folders. Why didn't I do a total digital scan and track the phone?"

"Like a digital ghost trail, you mean?"

"Yeah. Have you ever wondered how Google knows exactly which ads to tailor to your specifications? Or how Google knows your exact buying habits? Everything you order? It's because anytime you do anything from your phone online, they're constantly tracking your Smartphone, especially if you never turn it off."

"Wow. Google doesn't do that with an iPhone?"

"Of course they do. But Apple makes it easier to turn off the notifications and my location when you initially set up your phone. Look don't get too excited about this. It's a long shot at best. I'm not saying it's a done deal. But if Brigid kept her Android GPS turned on, in other words, her Google directions, Google would keep a log of her phone movements."

"You're kidding? I'm still not sure I get it. Didn't Birk and Beckett try all that? Isn't that the same thing as a ping?"

"Nope, not at all. Google tracks everything you do and keeps a log. Pings are more ballpark. The tracking log is exact."

"But we already know the pings led us to Shark Fin Cove. How will GPS movements tell us anything different than that?"

"For one thing, it's GPS, Jade. The Global Positioning System transmits radio signals that are picked up by satellite from anywhere on Earth—from Point A to Point B—the data will be infinitely more precise than a ping."

"This sounds promising."

"Yeah. Well, like I said, don't get your hopes up. Not yet anyway. I won't know for certain until I delve further into Brigid's Google account and grab the digital data, if there is any."

"But we don't have her phone."

"I don't need it, Jade. Her Google log is key."

Kelly remained hopeful as she did a deeper dive into Brigid's account, comparing a series of activities to others, narrowing down the scope. "See here. One of the entries shows that Brigid keyed in how to get back to her apartment. Why would she do that if she intended to meet up with someone? That's weird to me, maybe even contradictory to that theory."

"Maybe she did meet up with someone, but it went south, and she needed to get out of there fast. Maybe she tried to run."

"That must be it. Why would she need to know the directions back to her apartment unless she was somehow disoriented, in an unfamiliar area of Santa Cruz she'd never been before and didn't know how to get back home." Kelly zeroed in on another entry. "But look, this is even weirder. She doesn't head back home. Brigid is heading in the opposite direction of her apartment."

"She must've been lost," Jade concluded and made a face. "That could validate law enforcement's theory."

"Not necessarily. Remember, the prevailing theory is she's drunk, wandering around on the road to Shark Fin Cove, and falls into the ocean. The body is swept away and never recovered. Yet, she's sober enough to ask for directions back to her apartment."

"But we both don't buy that theory. Figure in Birk and Beckett, her parents, and we've formed our own wall against that whole thing. How do we prove it's not true?"

"I'm sticking with someone in those incoming phone records who could have intentionally led Brigid off the beaten path."

"The serial killer?"

"That's what I'm thinking. But following her digital footprint through the log will take some time to map. I never said I was an expert at this."

"We've come farther in a week together than I ever did by myself. That's huge, Kelly."

"True. But I'm beat. Starting the day at four-thirty didn't help. My brain is tired. My eyes are blurry. And I don't want to miss a critical piece of the log. You look just as tired as I am. There's a twin bed in the room I took for an office. I'm never in there. I do more work at the kitchen table."

Kelly was about to reach over and turn off the TV when Jade's mouth dropped open. "What's wrong?"

"Turn up the volume," Jade said in a voice that had grown cold. "It's breaking news out of Mexico."

Kelly adjusted the sound.

After two weeks held in a jungle compound against their will, an American executive and his staff of seven—abducted from their hotel while on a company retreat—were freed by private security guards after a tense exchange in Colima with the hostage-takers.

Kelly nudged Jade. "Oh, my God. Tell me that's not Beckett and Birk."

"I wish I could. But with the Callahan brothers, anything is possible."

"That's what I was afraid you'd say."

"Does this mean we're dating men who still work for the government?"

"At the very least, it means we're dating superheroes."

Twenty-Two

Beckett watched the sun climb over the mountains to the east as he leaned back in the co-pilot's seat and let Birk land the Citation. It was a bumpy touchdown on the airstrip where they'd left more than thirty-six hours earlier and where Wolfson stored his jet.

"I need sleep," Birk announced once he'd taxied the plane and stopped in front of the hangar.

"Be grateful the State Department handled transporting Wolfson's employees back to San Jose. If I had to listen to that one whiny guy for another second, I might've popped him myself."

"Can you say entitled?"

"More like a privileged asshole which is why I'm glad the State Department took them off our hands. Right now, I just want twelve hours of uninterrupted sack time."

"How do you propose we get that once Jade and Kelly find out we're back?"

"I'll take my chances. I'm not lying to Kelly again."

"They didn't buy it anyway," Birk pointed out. "How many text messages did you get from Kelly?"

"None. You?"

"None. That kind of radio silence probably doesn't bode well."

"Jade will forgive you. She always does."

"I should've told her the truth."

"Too late now. At least we don't need to pony up stupid photos of a stupid fish."

"That's the upside. Look, let's just level with them and beg for sleep."

"Good plan. Like your fish story went over so well. Let's just get back to Pelican Pointe and deal with what comes. I'm too tired to put up much of a fight anyway."

They unloaded their gear from the baggage hold and transported it to Beckett's pickup.

Beckett took the wheel to drive back to Pelican Pointe. "Use my phone to text Kelly for me, will you? Did you text Jade?"

"I thought I'd surprise her. You could drop me off at her house if you want. If you take a right up here, it's a straight shot to downtown Santa Cruz."

"Do you really think that's such a good idea? Maybe you should text her first."

"Where's the surprise in that?"

"Do what you want. But text Kelly for me, or I'll pull over and do it myself."

"What do you want me to say?"

"What do you think? That I'm back and that I'll see her in forty-five minutes or so."

Birk keyed in the message and got a reply within seconds. "She's glad you're safe. She says she loves you. Wow. You used the L-word? Really? It's been like two weeks, Beck. What are you thinking?"

Beckett gave him a shrug. "What can I say? I do love her. Might as well go all-in for once."

Birk rolled his eyes and read Kelly's next text. "Oh man, Jade spent the weekend with Kelly."

"Sounds like we have two women who get along with each other. What's wrong with that?"

"It sounds close to expectations and commitment."

"Man up, bro. You've known for two years how you feel about Jade. Time to put up or shut up. You better send her a text."

"Just speed up, will you? You're driving like an old man. I'd like to get home before I turn forty."

"Can you believe him?" Jade ranted as she paced the length of the kitchen. "Beckett sends you a text as soon as he lands. Does Birch think to do that to me? No."

As she shouted, her phone dinged.

"See?" Kelly began. "Birk's just a few minutes behind the curveball. What does he say?"

"Jeez. I don't think this is really from Birk."

"Why? What does it say?"

"He says he missed me. I think someone kidnapped Birk and kept him in Mexico. Someone else has his phone."

Kelly sputtered with laughter. "Jade, Birk's just been through an intense ordeal. His true feelings might be surfacing."

"After two years, it's about damn time."

"Has it been that long since the two of you first hooked up?"

"Okay. Maybe three and a half years. But we've seen each other steadily for two. And once about six months ago, I mentioned that I was thinking of moving to Pelican Pointe. You should have seen the terror that came into his eyes. It was downright embarrassing. I wanted to take back the words as soon as I said them."

"He's a commitment-phobe. Most men are. I'm not looking to marry Beckett." She dropped into a chair at the table and covered her face with her hands.

"Oh, my God, we said the L-word to each other right before he left. That seems like a week ago."

"Uh-huh. Who's in a pickle now? I'll make the coffee. You look like you need it now more than ever."

"I should fix scrambled eggs. And bacon. We should make breakfast for them, have it waiting."

"What they need now is sleep," Jade commented as she measured out coffee and hit the brew cycle. "But you're right. A good breakfast would go a long way to helping them chill after such an ordeal."

It was Kelly who got up to pace. "What about telling Beckett and Birk what we discovered? How do we handle that? You said yourself they need sleep. Shouldn't we ease them into the data we uncovered before hitting them over the head with everything?"

"You're not even finished yet. Why dump this in their laps before they've had time to recharge?"

"So we keep it to ourselves? Is that what you're saying?"

"Just until we finish researching the phone data. I don't see any reason to mention anything at this point until we see the cell phone dump."

"Okay. I can live with that. Let's make a huge breakfast, feed them, and get them to bed. Then we pick up where we left off."

"Sounds like a plan. I make great pancakes. Birk loves pancakes."

"Then we'll stuff them with pancakes and get to work."

Breakfast was a relaxed reunion. The four cracked jokes over stacks of pancakes, laughing it up without mentioning Mexico. That lasted until Kelly started clearing the table when Beckett pushed back to help.

"Don't get up," Kelly emphasized. "Fishing takes a lot out of a person. Fishing being the euphemism for whatever happened in Colima." She held up a hand. "I don't want details. But next time, it might be better to simply say something like, 'I need to go out of town for Wolfson.'"

"I can do that," Beckett said. "What about you, Birk?"

Birk glanced at Jade. "You won't ask questions? Not one? Because we're locked into an NDA. There's stuff we just can't disclose."

"I've known that for at least eighteen months. I get it. After all, this isn't the first time you've disappeared without notice, then reappeared at odd hours. Just don't insult my intelligence with another ridiculous story."

"You're too smart for me," Birk stated.

"Why don't you head home to get some sleep?" Kelly suggested, leaning against the counter. "Both of you. We'll discuss 'next time' when your brain's less foggy."

"I'm about to drop," Beckett confessed. "Just give me eight hours."

Kelly crossed to the table, draped an arm over his shoulder. "Brodie's fine where he is. Go home and take however long you need. You look wiped. Even superheroes need their shuteye."

Jade nodded. "Get out of here, Birk. Turn your phone off and go to bed. Come back when you've recovered."

"You'll be here?"

"I'll be here."

"We both will," Kelly confirmed. "I'll even walk you to the truck."

After the men left, Jade turned to Kelly. "Do you think we let them off the hook too easily?"

"I get the sense you've done this before—let Birk off the hook."

"I love the guy," Jade admitted. "But I don't want to become a doormat."

"I don't see that at all. You're an independent woman who doesn't nag the man she loves. How is that a bad thing?"

"Thanks for that."

"Now come on, let's get back to work. I need to pick up the tracking log where I left off. And you need to focus on going back through all the call logs."

"How soon did your friend say he'd get the cell phone dump?"

"Probably not until this afternoon. That's okay. It gives us more time to broaden our scope."

They spent the rest of the morning slogging through lines and lines of data.

Kelly was on the second time around when she noticed something odd. "This is so weird. Brigid had no less than fifteen different apps running in the background that tracked her movements."

"Do you think it's from her activity on SecretSingles?"

"Some sure, but not all. At least twelve are GIS-related. I'm talking about real-time, online tracking here, Jade. Do me a favor. Could you go back through the CCTV footage from the burger joint, the one you first posted to your blog?"

"There's nothing there, Kelly. It just shows Brigid pacing back and forth in the parking lot like she's waiting for someone to pick her up."

"Review it again. Please. It's important."

"Sure. You got it. Or is this busywork, so I'll stay out of your hair?"

Kelly chuckled. "Of course not. This time, I want you to focus on what's happening around Brigid. Tell me what you see in the surrounding background. What's happening on each side of her? Try to figure out what's happening in the street, that intersection. Count how many cars you see that go zooming past her while she's pacing. And spend time looking at the other side of that intersection for cars entering from another direction. Pretend Brigid isn't the focus. Zoom in on everything else. Sometimes we miss what's right in front of us."

While Jade reran the video surveillance, again and again, Kelly took the raw data from Brigid's Android and turned it into another digital map. She compared it with the map of the pings, then drilled down and overlaid both charts with the data that came from the log.

Since the log followed Brigid's cell phone in real-time, Kelly could verify the woman's movements from how much time Brigid spent walking around the burger chain's parking lot. It was like using a stopwatch to clock Brigid's actions. When that data lined up, Kelly began to focus on the timestamp from the log, confirming each entry back to Brigid's walking speed. It came back at three miles an hour, a typical pace for someone on foot.

"Oh, my God, How did we miss this?" Jade muttered. "See that silver or grayish car? It keeps circling Brigid. It's a sedan, I think. You have to run it back from the beginning to almost the end of the clip. All anybody focused on was Brigid's pacing. But if I look past that and let it run for its full length, you can see what looks like a Toyota Camry appearing at the top of the video. It appears three more times. Tell me that Toyota isn't circling her."

"Let me see all of it," Kelly directed. "From start to finish. I need the timestamp from the last moment you saw the vehicle appear in the video to compare with Brigid's movements in the log."

"It says twelve-oh-five a.m."

"Okay, let's see what the log says is happening with Brigid at that moment."

Jade's breath caught. "What's that jerking motion I see on the video? It looks to me like Brigid stops pacing at the same time she spots the gray car. Then she and the car disappear out of camera range."

"Maybe that's the moment Brigid stopped to get into the Toyota. After that, see how the GPS signal moves through town at a faster clip, then keeps moving further west at twenty miles an hour until it speeds up to thirty-five."

"How the hell are you able to do that?"

"It's not me. It's one of the GIS tracking logs. If that impresses you, look further down at the timestamps."

"What am I looking at?"

"Brigid's phone data shows that her Android makes a Wi-Fi handshake with another mobile phone right before she gets into the car."

"What the hell is a Wi-Fi handshake?"

"It happens whenever one cell phone connects with another. The devices are exchanging data. The logs are all about tracking each exchange."

"That means she wasn't alone."

"Yeah. But her Smartphone shows it happens again with the same mobile device as soon as she reaches Shark Fin Cove. That's two Wi-Fi handshakes in a span of twenty minutes. We need the data from that cell phone dump to compare to her phone calls."

"Unless it's from a burner."

"Doesn't matter. The cell phone dump will reveal every mobile device in the area on that date. Think about it. What's the likelihood of a cell phone connecting with Brigid's on the same night at Shark Fin Cove? That can't be a coincidence. And look at this, at twelve-thirty-five a.m., Brigid stops using her phone. It goes silent. And she or someone else physically went into her settings and turned off the GPS."

"Why would she do that?"

Kelly met her friend's eyes. "I don't think she did, Jade. I think that's the exact moment things went wrong. Whoever turned off the GPS probably thought they were clever. They didn't realize that her phone would still ping off the nearby cell phone towers." She scrambled through the map showing the pings. "These show that Brigid's Android remained on for another fifteen hours after leaving that beach. There's evidence her phone is moving during that timeframe. It moved away from Shark Fin Cove."

"What does all this mean, Kelly?"

"It means—all this time—the family's been looking in the wrong damn place."

"So the cell phone dump should have that same phone number somewhere in the data to match the Wi-Fi handshakes, right?" Jade restated for clarification. "Is this in theory or for real?"

"It's for real," Kelly mumbled as she perused what her friend Isaac had sent her.

Jade's eyes grew wider as she scanned the map filled with tiny cell phones that represented the different phone numbers. "How on earth will we find that one number? It's like a needle in a haystack. There must be five hundred that popped up in that area."

"All we need is to find Brigid's number first with an 831-area code on the chart. Then we zoom out from there. Extend the analysis from her number until we connect it with the target—his handshake—which begins with a 4-0-8 area code."

"That area code should stick out. Four-zero-eight covers most of Santa Clara County, including San Jose. Does that mean he doesn't live in Santa Cruz?"

"He could've been a student back then at UC Santa Cruz and decided to keep his San Jose number.

Just remember, this four-zero-eight number is almost six years old. We're dealing with dated information."

"I still say it's incredible."

"Let's hope it's phenomenal. Oh, man. Look at this. Isaac included internal and external data sources from Facebook, Twitter, and Instagram platforms. Damn. I should've told him not to include social media."

"No. No. That's okay," Jade said. "Think about it. When we identify the handshake number, we'll also know more about the person through their Internet presence."

"Maybe even an address," Kelly prompted, getting stoked. "Yeah. Yeah. That'll work. Thanks, Isaac."

"Wow. This dump covers all the different carriers. The fact that your friend could pull this stuff after such a long time is like a door opening up."

"True."

"There's so much data. How does it do this?"

"Software that's automated the process and figured out how to parse the different data sets to break them down into segments—phones, phone calls, and cell towers." She digitally circled an area. "This is the tower closest to the burger restaurant." She drew another circle. "And this is the one closest to Shark Fin Cove. We're looking for—there's Brigid's number. It appears within both cell tower data. See the link? Let's circle this and move outward. Now we're looking for the handshake number beginning with 4-0-8."

It took another twenty minutes to match up the phone number.

"Now for the true magic," Kelly said. "Let's see what we can find out about the owner of this number."

"Will we need Isaac for that?"

"Nope. We do it the old-fashioned way. We use the Internet. Most background software provides cell phone data now. It might be old information, but it should show up on at least one of them."

An hour later, they had a name—Bradley Wardlaw—an address in Santa Cruz, probably old, and a social media trail.

"This guy is thirty-eight years old. But on his social media accounts, he acts more like he's still a frat boy." Kelly pointed to his employer information. "Look at that. Wardlaw's a teacher in the high school drama department."

"That fits. Wardlaw grew up in San Jose and went to high school there. His family owned a string of convenience stores. He got his bachelor's degree from UC Santa Cruz in 2005. He was married once, with no kids, but divorced six years ago, around the same time Brigid went missing. My gut instinct tells me this is the guy," Jade whispered.

"Your gut and the fact my skin's beginning to crawl," Kelly added. "Let's go check out the address."

Jade cut her eyes to Kelly's. "Is that wise? What if this is *the guy* and we're knocking on the door of a serial killer?"

"We'll take the pups with us. Besides, this address is probably older than dirt. Wardlaw's bound to have moved by now," Kelly said as she keyed the address into her GPS. "It's just a fishing expedition anyway. We don't plan on confronting him."

"Unless he's in a pissy mood and doesn't want visitors dropping by unannounced on a Saturday afternoon."

"There's four of us and only one of him," Kelly reminded Jade. "In a situation like this, numbers count."

Twenty-Three

From the moment Kelly pulled up to Wardlaw's house, Brodie and Journey started to whine and act skittish. The dogs might've been the single indicator that they were walking into trouble.

GPS had brought them eight miles north of Santa Cruz to a rural area surrounded by pines and nestled alongside the soothing, flowing water of a creek bed. A dirt road led past the house and dead-ended near the entrance to a barn.

The frame house had once been a prosperous farmhouse but had long since fallen into disrepair. The peeling paint, the shutters barely hanging on, and the piles of rusted farm equipment littering the front yard were all signs of neglect.

Kelly's pickup bumped along the rutted road until she stopped near a broken gate.

"I guess you were right," Jade noted. "This place looks abandoned, maybe for twenty years or more."

"You'd think, except for the fresh tire tracks leading to that barn."

Jade swallowed hard. "So there's probably someone in there."

"Yep. I hate to bring up even more bad news, but the coordinates fit with Brigid's cell phone pings after Shark Fin Cove." Kelly held up her cell phone.

"Longitude and latitude of the cell tower of the last set of pings are within a two-mile variant."

"How do you do that?"

"Software app," Kelly muttered. "How should we play this? Tell him we're lost and need directions, ran out of gas, or just start poking around on our own?" There was silence until Kelly snapped her fingers. "I've got it. He's all about drama, right? We tell him we're scouting for a movie location. Tell him we need a haunted house."

"Do you know anything about movie locations?"

"No. Do you?"

"I can fake it," Jade declared. "We'll tell him we're doing the West Coast version of *The Amityville Horror*, and if his house makes the final cut, we'll pay him twenty grand for four months of availability."

"I'm not the only one who thinks on her feet. That's good."

"Let's hope I'm convincing enough that he buys it."

"I'll be your assistant," Kelly offered. "While you're doing the sales pitch, I'll poke around. If he asks what I'm doing, just explain that I need to check angles for all the interior shots."

"Good one. I like that. What about the dogs?"

Kelly rolled the windows down more than halfway. "I don't think he'd appreciate us bringing two large dogs into his house. They'll need to stay here."

The women got out, approached the front door, and Kelly knocked, taking a step back and nudging Jade to take the lead.

They got their first look at Bradley Wardlaw, a bespeckled, blond-haired man with dark brown eyes and a goatee who didn't look threatening at all.

Jade went into her spill. "Hi, are you the owner of this place?"

"Yeah. Who wants to know?"

"I'm Ellen Frazier, and this is my assistant Donna Hatcher. We're scouting film locations in the area for a horror movie that begins shooting in August. I think your farmhouse is exactly what we've been looking for, the perfect location. Of course, we'd need to see the inside to make sure it works aesthetically inside and out."

"Why would I let strangers into my house?"

"It pays twenty grand for four months of filming," Jade dangled.

"You're kidding?"

"I kid you not. What Hollywood pays for locations is outrageous. And I ought to know because I've been scouting locations for fifteen years. Everything's lined up. We have our investors on board, the production crew in place, a complete script, and signed the actors. The project's in its final pre-shooting phase. All we need now is the perfect rural, farmhouse setting."

Kelly could tell the moment Wardlaw took the bait.

"I teach drama at the high school level," Bradley explained. "I have an extensive theater background, too. I might be interested if you could find a part for me in your movie, no matter how small. Would that be possible?"

"I'd have to take that up with the director. I'm not saying it's a no, but the director would need to see a clip of what you've done in other films or the theater."

"That's not a problem. My name's Bradley Wardlaw. I have lots of theater experience from college. And since 2005, I've made a name for myself on the dinner theater circuit from Santa Barbara to San Jose."

"Oh, well, that sounds great. I'm sure your experience would go a long way in convincing the director."

"What's the film about? Would I know this director?"

"I'm not at liberty to divulge names, but I can tell you that the overview is a West Coast version of what happened in the original *Amityville Horror* and directed by a noted European director."

Bradley scowled, his enthusiasm waning. "A reboot? Foreign at that? Hasn't that subject been done to death like dozens of times?"

"It won't look like Amityville. It'll look like a California farmhouse horror movie, similar to Hitchcock's *Psycho* reboots."

"Oh. Okay. You might as well come in and look around while you're in the neighborhood. The house is nothing fancy, but it once belonged to my grandparents until they passed on."

Jade hesitated before stepping into the entryway with Kelly close on her heels. She pivoted, tossed an arm out toward Kelly, and said, "Get some shots of the parlor and maybe that dining room."

"Sure," Kelly uttered, leaving the door cracked behind her. She took a left and walked into the living room holding her cell phone out, snapping photos of the dreary, drab space with its peeling wallpaper and dated, dusty furniture. The dining room wasn't much better. Her eyes drifted to the cracks in the ceiling, water spots, and drapes that dated back decades. It felt like she was in a scene from the movie. She could almost picture Anthony Perkins stepping out of his hiding place with a sharp knife.

While Jade kept Wardlaw busy chatting, Kelly perused deeper into the home's interior. She took the initiative, moving down a hallway, opening closet doors, and even sticking her head inside the only bedroom on the first floor.

With that done, she decided to check out the kitchen. It had linoleum floors, metal cabinets, avocado green appliances, and a 50s-style cream-colored Formica tabletop with chrome trim. Across the room, she spotted an open basement doorway with a narrow staircase that looked promising but dark and ominous. As she circled back to where Jade stood in the foyer, she decided that each space seemed more depressing than the last.

Kelly cleared her throat and reported, "Just as you'd hoped, Ms. Frazier, this place is a time capsule inside. There's even a basement off the kitchen that we'll need to check out. If it's as spooky as it looks, it will make a perfect spot for our evil psycho to set up shop."

"The basement is off-limits," Wardlaw announced. "You didn't say anything about using the cellar."

"But we'll need the basement," Jade insisted, cutting her eyes to Kelly's. "Those critical shots are the backbone of the movie. The scariest scenes take place in the basement."

But Wardlaw stood firm. "That's so trite and cliched. It has a dirt floor. There's nothing in that cellar that would add to the film. It's old and musty, unsafe to boot. You could easily substitute the barn for the basement. Trust me. I head up a high school drama department. Staging is part of what I teach my students to do. I guarantee I could do it for your production company, using the barn."

"Could I at least take a few pictures of the cellar?" Kelly proposed. "That way, Ms. Frazier could make a judgment call—"

Wardlaw's demeanor changed. His brown eyes flared to a deeper, menacing black. Clenching his fists, he took a step toward Kelly. "No! What part of no don't you get? You women are all alike. Pushy, arrogant, know-it-alls who don't always get what you want no matter how much you nag. You always screw everything up by pushing, pushing, pushing. You never know when to shut up. Men can't take it anymore, listening to you bitch. Why is it you go out of your way to make up lies?"

With Wardlaw blocking her path to the front door, Kelly backed up toward the kitchen. "Whoa. Where did that come from? We just wanted to see your basement. For twenty grand, we need to see the entire house, maybe even the entire property. You don't get to pick and choose."

"It's my damn house!" Wardlaw sneered, taking a step closer. "I don't need your movie or your money. Get out! Now!"

"What brought this on?" Kelly pushed back. "What could be in the basement you don't want us to see? You don't have bodies buried down there, do you?"

Wardlaw raised his arms and lunged at her, taking a wild swing at her face.

Kelly dodged the punch but lost her balance, stumbling back against the 70s refrigerator.

Journey came charging into the room from the entryway, leaping onto Wardlaw's back. Brodie went after his ankles, snagging the man's pants leg. Wardlaw tumbled to the floor and rolled over to cover his head.

"Call off your dogs, bitch!" Wardlaw screamed. But that comment seemed to give the dogs more incentive, especially Journey. The German Shepherd Husky mix opened her mouth next to the man's throat and ear. Without taking a chunk out of him, Journey kept snarling. Brodie seemed content to hang on to a trouser leg and not let go.

Jade rushed into the kitchen. "I called 911. What do we do until they get here?"

"Look around for something to tie him up," Kelly said as she opened kitchen drawers.

Jade fished around in her bag and brought out a pair of plastic zip ties and a hot pink can of pepper spray. "Will these do?"

Kelly gaped but not for long. She moved to take the zip ties out of Jade's hand and secure Wardlaw's wrists behind his back. "I don't even want to know why you carry those. It's okay, Journey. You can let go now. I've got him."

Journey looked unconvinced and whined but glanced over at Kelly.

"You, too, Brodie. Let go," Kelly directed. "Good dogs."

"Birk told me never to leave home without zip ties and pepper spray."

"Thank God for that. Will you watch him while I look in the cellar?" Kelly said, reaching back in a drawer for a flashlight.

"Maybe I should do it. You stay with the dogs. They do what you say." She handed off the can of pepper spray.

"If you're sure, okay. You'll need the flashlight."

"I'm not sure of anything," Jade uttered as she approached the open doorway, looking for a light switch.

"Above you," Kelly indicated. "It's one of those strings you pull down to flick on the light." Sensing Jade's hesitation, Kelly handed back the spray can. "I'll go down and look. I've dissected sea creatures since I was fourteen. I know what to look for."

"Yeah. I can't go down there," Jade admitted. "I just can't."

"It's okay. Journey, Brodie, watch him. If he moves, rip his throat out."

Jade aimed the pepper spray at Wardlaw's face. "You move a muscle, and I'll fill your eyes full of this stuff."

The dogs stood guard above his head, glaring at Wardlaw, daring him to move.

Kelly started down the stairwell. With every step, the wood creaked. Once she reached the bottom, she stopped. Without going any farther, the musty odor overpowered everything else. She flipped on the flashlight and shined it along the dirt floor. One whiff of decomposition made her feel like throwing up. After counting five mounds, she held her breath and darted back up the steps.

"It's him," she whooshed out. "Bradley Wardlaw is the serial killer. There are graves in the cellar."

Kelly put the dogs back in the truck just as the first sheriff's unit pulled up. The deputy got out and swaggered up to the pickup. "What's the problem here?"

"Go inside the house and down to the basement. It's off the kitchen. You'll find bodies buried in the basement. It's a disgusting smell down there." She pointed to a grove of Ponderosa pine across from the house. "You'll find another two graves under that patch of trees. The perpetrator's tied up in the kitchen. We left him sitting on the floor, leaning up against a cabinet."

"And who are you?"

"Me? Dr. Kelly Ecklund, Ph.D. professor of biology at Redwood State University. My friend and I made the mistake of stopping here to ask for directions. We'd gotten lost and couldn't find our way back to the highway. He invited us in, Mr. Wardlaw, Bradley Wardlaw, that's his name. He was nice at first. But then he went crazy and tried to attack us. My friend and I took him down. Together. With the dogs helping, of course."

The deputy looked like he'd swallowed a whole bag of sour candies. "There are bodies inside the house?"

"That's what I said—buried in the cellar, off the kitchen. My friend's throwing up at the side of the barn. See?" Kelly lifted her arm and pointed. "Jade Weingarten is her name. She's a blogger from Santa Cruz."

"Don't go anywhere. Does this Wardlaw have a weapon?" the deputy asked.

"I saw several sharp knives in the kitchen."

"And you left him alone there by himself?" the deputy scoffed before talking into his radio and requesting backup.

Kelly watched him disappear into the house with his sidearm drawn.

Jade walked over and slumped against the side of the pickup.

"Feel any better?" Kelly wanted to know.

"Not really. Strangely, you don't notice the smell right away until you do. Then you can't get it out of your—" Jade fanned her face.

"Once you've taken it all in, keep telling yourself how this story will play out. It will make one of your most dynamic, firsthand accounts on your blog. You captured a serial killer. What other blogger can boast about doing that?"

Jade laid a hand on her still-queasy stomach. "I might give up the crime angle. This is the real thing. Too real."

Cops from all over began to swarm and fan out through the property.

The two women answered the same questions, not once but repeatedly. Each time a different cop would show up, they all wanted to know the same thing. What were they doing here? Were they related to the killer? How did they find the bodies? How did they take the guy down?

They told the same story each time until, finally, Kelly had had enough. "Why don't you ask the asshole in zip ties why he killed all these people? Why don't you question him?"

After that, the lead detective, a man named Bob McIlneny, left her alone after running her plates. But he checked them both out for warrants through their driver's licenses.

Near the late afternoon, news helicopters began to hover overhead. McIlneny ordered his team to keep the press as far away from the scene as possible. But he did have to walk down to the road and make a brief statement. "We're still actively investigating what looks like a possible dumping ground and possibly a serial killer. We won't have any further statements to make until we've finished our investigation."

Kelly and Jade sat in the pickup with Journey and Brodie. The dogs accepted all pats and ear rubs from the string of cops who passed by.

They watched as the cops opened the barn and discovered a silver Toyota Camry, similar to the vehicle seen in the CCTV footage circling Brigid.

"It's eerie to think Brigid might've spent her last hours out here at the mercy of a man like Wardlaw," Kelly said aloud. "We won't know for sure if she's one of the victims until they exhume all those graves and do DNA testing."

"Come on. We might not be able to convince Birk and Beckett of that, but you and I know Brigid's remains are here somewhere. The phone number, the handshake, the drama department link, the Toyota, the bodies in the cellar. Everything points to Wardlaw. Which makes me wonder, why aren't you happier about it?"

Kelly lifted a shoulder. "It feels surreal. I haven't even texted Beckett yet. How do you notify someone that you've just solidified that their sister isn't ever coming back?"

"They already know that. So do Betty and Craig. This will hurt, but at least they'll finally know what happened." Jade gingerly punched Kelly's arm. "So cheer up. We did it. We freaking took down a freaking serial killer."

Kelly's lips curved. "We did, didn't we? Holy crap. We might as well have tied a bow around him and delivered him to the cops." She thought of Scott's advice and added in a low voice, "All along, the answer was right there in the CCTV footage."

"Yeah, but it took you to find the needle and put the puzzle pieces together. Without you, I'm not sure that guy would be sitting in the back of a police car. He wasn't even on anyone's radar. You saved lives, Kelly. No telling how many. My blog post should be about you."

"Don't you dare make me out to be the hero. I was in this to help the Callahans, same as you. I could never have done this on my own."

"We make a good team. Now let's get out here. I'll flip you for who tells the guys how this went down."

Twenty-Four

Birk listened to the banging on the front door. He thought he heard his brother's voice in the distance through a fogbank—shouting. He snapped awake, sat up, and reached for the Smith & Wesson he kept on the nightstand. Rubbing his eyes, he tried to orient himself to the dark bedroom, giving himself a few seconds for his eyes to adjust.

He pulled on a pair of jeans and marched out of the bedroom to the front door. "I'm gonna kill you, Beckett."

When Birk threw open the door, Beckett stormed past him and into the living room. "Turn on the TV."

"What the hell's wrong with *your* TV? You woke me up to watch TV?"

"Just do it. Where's your remote? You've got to see this. Kelly and Jade are on the six o'clock evening news."

"What the hell are you talking about?" Birk grumbled as he picked up the remote. The big screen flashed to life, but it was on a cable channel.

Beckett jerked the remote out of his brother's hand and changed the channel to the news station out of Santa Cruz. He cranked up the volume as a reporter stood in front of a dilapidated farmhouse. "Just listen to this."

"Two women out with their two dogs on a Saturday afternoon stumbled on a serial killer's lair during their scenic drive through the countryside. So far, the body count is eight. But authorities are still inside, going through everything in this farmhouse behind me belonging to Bradley Wardlaw. Wardlaw is a local high school drama teacher. Sheriff's deputies have already uncovered eight graves in his basement, with another two found on the surrounding grounds. They're looking for anything to connect Wardlaw to the disappearances of eight missing Santa Cruz women over the past six years."

Beckett lowered the volume. "Kelly and Jade solved the case, Birk. They found the bastard who killed Brigid. We should get over to Mom and Dad's and make sure they don't hear about this like I did—on the news."

"You're jumping the gun, aren't you? Kudos to Jade and Kelly for finding this SOB. But I didn't hear the reporter say anything about Brigid Callahan. Or tell us what they found to link Brigid to this Wardlaw asshole."

"You really do know how to throw water on everything, don't you?" Beckett groused as his cell phone buzzed with a text. "Kelly wants us to meet her at Jade's house. She says to bring Mom and Dad. Kelly must've found the link to Brigid. Put on a shirt or do I have to do it for you?"

"You could try. But now's not the time for me to kick your ass." He held up both hands. "Fine. I'm going. But you're buying everyone dinner tonight."

"You should've seen Journey and Brodie come to the rescue. They rushed straight past me and into the kitchen. Journey latched on to this guy and wouldn't let go. Same with Brodie. They were awesome. I'm thinking about getting a dog now," Jade told Birk. "You could make that happen, right? How soon will your parents be here?"

"They texted they were on their way fifteen minutes ago. They were antique shopping and grabbed dinner out. They were right in the middle of enchiladas when we called."

Kelly glanced over at Beckett, who hadn't said much since getting there. "What's up with you?"

"I'm anxious to understand how all this came together so fast. I'm scratching my head over it. We go take a nap, and you guys manage to do what we couldn't do in six years."

Jade crossed her arms over her chest and nodded. "You should've seen Kelly work, untangling the pings, the cell towers, and the Wi-Fi handshake."

Beckett sat up straighter. "The what?"

"That was my reaction at first. I didn't know what that meant until Kelly came up with it."

"It was simple really. There's no reason we shouldn't be able to follow someone's pings with technology today, especially if GPS is tracking them in real-time."

Birk cocked a brow. "Are you saying all this information was there, and we didn't follow through?"

"It's not a criticism."

"No. That's not what I meant. You figured this out in less than two weeks after we studied this crap for five and a half years, looked at it, drilled down to the bone until we were sick of going through it all."

"I just got a cell phone dump, Birk. That's what changed everything."

"A cell phone dump?" Beckett murmured. "Isn't that what law enforcement is supposed to do?"

"Or doesn't do," Kelly pointed out.

"She's got us there. How did you do that?" Birk demanded.

Kelly chewed her bottom lip. "I know a guy."

Beckett traded looks with his brother. "Is she great or what?"

"I underestimated you, Kelly," Birk admitted. "If you ever want to do this kind of work as a full-time job, I'll put you to work for me."

She chuckled. "I'm a researcher. I know how to get around obstacles that keep blocking my way to a result."

"I'll say. I think Mom and Dad just drove up," Birk announced. "They know something big is up. I can tell by the way they're rushing up to the house."

Beckett opened the door for his mom.

Betty hugged her son, then glanced around the room. "What's happened? You found her, didn't you? It's that news about the drama teacher out at his farmhouse, isn't it?"

Craig was just as anxious. He looked at Birk. "We heard the story on the radio. Somebody start talking."

"We'll let Kelly and Jade pick up the story. It's their story," Birk pointed out.

"Somebody start talking," Betty echoed. "Now. Was my daughter there at this awful place or not?"

Kelly sucked in a breath and slowly let it escape. "I can't answer that question. Yet. But all the pieces came together after we got the cell phone dump. Even before that, we discovered the night Brigid went missing, she had fifteen GPS-related apps tracking her in real-time."

"Holy crap. Why so many?" Craig wanted to know.

"When you sign up on an app with an Android phone, certain location features track whatever you buy, wherever you go, whatever you do. Brigid had a Smartphone, a fairly old model. The Androids originally allowed tracking features to run in the background, twenty-four-seven, which is a good thing for us. Because these multiple GPS location features made it possible to track her movements."

"Do you remember the CCTV footage of her in the burger restaurant parking lot?" Jade prompted.

"Sure. I have that image emblazoned on my brain. I must've looked at that video a hundred times," Beckett admitted.

"During that walking back and forth, Brigid's cell phone showed a Wi-Fi handshake with another mobile device. We could follow the GPS tracking and know the moment she got into the car with someone she probably already knew."

"Bradley Wardlaw, the drama department link to the university's wardrobe and costumes," Jade provided. "Back then, he was heavily involved in the college's theatrical offerings. Drama was his major. And he drives a silver Toyota Camry we spotted circling her on the video that night."

Birk frowned and looked over at his brother. "Do you remember a vehicle showing up on the footage?"

"Not the video I viewed."

"It's there," Jade revealed. "Kelly is the one who spotted it."

"She's wrong. Jade's the one who picked up on it," Kelly countered.

"Yeah, after she told me to use the longer, wider version I'd originally posted to my website years ago. The one law enforcement handed off to me once they ruled Brigid had drowned."

Beckett rubbed the side of his jaw. "Then how did we end up with the short version?"

"Early on in the investigation, the police provided a clip of the surveillance footage. That's all it was for the press conference, a clip. Law enforcement always holds back from the public. You should know that. Maybe that's what you guys saw. Kelly pointed out the additional footage, the one I uploaded to my website so long ago I'd forgotten about the post."

"So not only did the police have a longer version to work with," Betty grumbled. "They ruled no foul play was involved in her disappearance. Case closed. Go ahead, Kelly. Finish. It sounds like a breakthrough to me."

"I think it is," Kelly said, picking up the thread. "So now we know the silver Camry starts moving toward Shark Fin Cove. How? Because the GPS tracking is running in the background. Once they reach the beach, Brigid's cell phone shakes hands again with that same mobile device at twelve-thirty-five. Now we have two encounters within thirty minutes of each other. But something happens at Shark Fin Cove. Something goes wrong. The person she's in the car with turns off her GPS, and the phone goes silent. Brigid stops using her phone. But here is where he makes a mistake. He doesn't turn off Brigid's phone. It keeps pinging off the nearest cell phone towers all the way through the rural area north of Santa Cruz."

"To Wardlaw's farmhouse," Jade supplied. "Something about longitude and latitude matches GPS coordinates. Ask Kelly about the way it lines up."

"Wait a minute," Birk began, "who's to say this guy didn't take her phone and leave her there, drive away with the device? You know that's what the cops will stick to."

"We'll get to that in a minute," Kelly promised. "Right about now, this guy probably thinks he's covered his tracks at this point. But making a handshake with someone else's cell phone is a big deal. It means one, Brigid wasn't alone. And two, we don't think she went over the cliffs. Why wouldn't she have her cell phone with her if she fell into the water? No one found her cell phone in the area. You guys looked, right? But it wasn't there. So, where did it go? Data shows the phone pinged off cell towers moving north at a high rate of speed at twelve-forty-one. So she didn't end up in the ocean. Here's why. I used a Google map and overlaid it with every piece of Brigid's cell phone results."

Beckett looked dumbstruck. "You did all this while we were in Mexico?"

"I had to follow through with her cell phone data—the pings, the calls, the contacts, the text messages, the cell towers—they all played a part in the solution. But I used the Wi-Fi handshake at Shark Fin Cove as the starting point."

"But we already knew the beach is where she ended up," Birk said.

"Let her finish," Betty admonished. "We're finally getting somewhere, but you're still stuck back on that stupid beach. Let it go."

Kelly wet her lips, prepared for a debate. "You're not listening to me, Birk. The handshake itself blows the police theory out of the water. No pun intended. It means your sister wasn't there by herself. Her cell phone couldn't have made a Wi-Fi handshake at twelve-thirty-five with another mobile device and exchanged data unless someone else was on that beach with her. Wardlaw's cell phone coordinates mirror Brigid's. And I can prove it. The cell phone data shows Brigid's phone left that area. Left the area," she repeated for emphasis. "So did Wardlaw's at the exact same time. Jade and I think Brigid was still inside Wardlaw's car. Data shows she wasn't at the beach for more than five minutes. Hard to murder someone that fast and then play with the phone settings to turn off her GPS at twelve-forty. Remember, at twelve-forty-one, the car is already moving. Maybe he used those five minutes to incapacitate her and throw her in the trunk. I don't know for sure." She looked over at Betty and Craig. "I apologize for the way that came out."

"No, it's okay," Craig said in a whisper. "We're on the same page. Finally, we're hearing something that makes sense."

Beckett's hands balled into fists. "So you're saying this bastard yanked her phone away, fiddled with the GPS, and tossed her in the trunk?"

"Part of that statement is true. The other part is conjecture. But I think he turned off the GPS to throw off the police—when you think about the last five years—the tactic worked."

"Which means he knew what he planned to do before picking her up," Birk snarled.

"Probably. I know that Brigid's phone stayed on for another fifteen hours after leaving the beach until the battery died."

"Her device pinged off the closest cell tower to Wardlaw's farmhouse," Jade reminded them.

"But the Wi-Fi handshake is the key here, guys. The owner of that mobile device is Bradley Wardlaw. His own cell phone pings mirrored hers all the way to that rural farmhouse. Getting the cell phone dump helped us track the cell phone number back to him. Using the phone number, we came up with his address, his occupation, and where he worked. Wardlaw is the guy who picked up Brigid at the burger restaurant, drove her to Shark Fin Cove under some pretense, then took her phone. Maybe he knocked her out, or maybe he promised to take her to his place and let her go. Whatever went down between them turned ugly. Brigid might've been his first, but what I saw in that basement, maybe not. There could be other victims before Brigid. We won't know for sure until the police ID all the victims."

Betty wiped away the tears that trickled down her face. "I don't know how to thank you. All we ever wanted was the truth about what happened. Thank you for this."

"When do you think the cops will come to their senses and change their theory?" Craig asked.

"Once they start identifying bodies, the pieces will come together. Just as I sorted through the data, they will eventually do the same. It doesn't take a genius to determine Brigid didn't drown if her remains are there on Wardlaw's property. Possibly reluctantly, the cops will correct their bogus theory—better late than not at all."

"Will you turn over what you know about the phone data?" Betty inquired.

"Some of it. But I can't turn over the phone dump. That would get my friend in hot water. Someone in this room should probably suggest that law enforcement pull their own cell phone dump tying the handshake back to Wardlaw."

"I don't mind meeting with the detective and suggesting that very thing," Craig admitted, looking over at his wife. He laid a hand on Betty's shoulder. "For now, this Wardlaw asshole is locked up. That has to count for something. We got here because of persistence from two women—first Jade's blog and then Kelly's ability to generate reliable data."

Beckett lifted a brow and traded looks with Birk. He swept Kelly off her feet and turned her in a circle. "Is she brilliant or what?"

"She's brilliant," Birk agreed, tossing an arm around Jade's waist. He kissed the top of her hair. "You both are. You both did what we couldn't do. And I'm damn proud of you for it."

Epilogue

Four weeks later
Pelican Pointe, California

The month of June along the coast had warmed up, making Science Camp inside the school building feel like a sauna. But the kids didn't seem to mind the high humidity, even though the temperature in the classroom hovered around seventy-five degrees.

Kelly had talked Julianne into expanding the camp to any age student who wanted to learn more about science. As a result, twenty-two science nerds had signed up. Right now, they were laser-focused on the experiments Kelly had assigned them. They stood next to their tables, inspecting the progress of the seaweed they'd planted on Friday.

"It grew four inches over the weekend," Kyra Pierce noted.

"Mine grew five," Hutton boasted.

Maddie Del Rio couldn't let that go unchallenged. "Mine grew six inches."

A few of the boys chimed in—Jonah Delacourt and Tommy Gates—causing debates about whose kelp grew faster and taller.

Kelly clapped her hands to get their attention. "Hey, it's not a contest. If your kelp took off, that's a good thing. It doesn't matter how fast it's growing. The point is, it's growing. And tomorrow, when we take our newly sprouted plants and place them in the water at Sandpiper Marsh, they'll grow even faster outside with photosynthesis. We talked about that, remember? If your seedlings aren't as big as you want today, they'll catch up. I promise you. They will double in size within a week. Once we're in the field, you each will plant your specimens, document the location, and track the kelp's progress in its natural habitat."

"When do we get sea stars?" Hutton wanted to know.

"Sunflower sea stars are all about next week. The rest of this week focuses on getting our kelp planted and taking care of it—as a team. Once the plants are in the water, just know that you've created your own kelp forest, your own ecosystem, growing, thriving, right in your own backyard. We'll use an underwater camera to track its progress. You'll document the fish and animals that inhabit the wetlands, using the kelp for shelter. You'll list everything you see on your worksheets as the kelp takes over the marsh. As long as you live here, you'll watch its progress. No matter what you do, you can be proud that you were part of reforesting the coastline."

Kelly glanced out the window and caught a glimpse of Scott outside, looking on with approval. When he sent her a brief head nod, her lips curved. She turned back to the kids. Never had she felt this comfortable in front of a classroom. She figured Scott must've known that from the beginning.

The first week of Science Camp, he'd left her a note in the top drawer of her desk. It was simple and to the point but scrawled in the most God-awful handwriting.

You've found your calling. Try not to blow it. Our kids are the future. You have a genuine gift, a natural talent for teaching what you love. That love of science benefits everyone. It's a win-win for the kids, the town, and the future. Why would you want to waste your talent writing papers when you could inspire the next generation? Money isn't everything. Join your research abilities with Beckett's. Together you'll bring happiness to the lost. Remember that as you settle in and make a home in Pelican Pointe for good.

She'd wondered at the time how a dead man could manage to write a note. The scientific part of her brain had a difficult time believing it. But the metaphysical side was more inclined to embrace the impossible.

When class ended at three, Kelly gathered her stuff and headed out the door.

Beckett met her in front of the school entrance with the dogs in tow. He handed her an apple. "For the teacher. I'm applying for teacher's pet."

She stifled a giggle and held out her hand. "You're my favorite but don't tell the other kids. Let's take the dogs for a walk. I feel like stretching my legs and getting some fresh air."

The sea breeze stirred the humid air under a canopy of sunshine. They sought shade as they walked down the tree-lined street.

"I've given this some thought," Kelly began as they strolled toward Phillips Park, the dogs sniffing the shrubs laden with summer hydrangeas popping out in huge blooms. "Maybe you and Birk could create a memorial garden for Brigid. You could take the idea before the city council. Ask permission to have a small corner of the park, say a flower bed, and fill it with sunflowers. You could offer to pay for a bench and a plaque."

"That's a great idea. My mother would like that, too. Mom's working on a memorial service as soon as the medical examiner releases her remains."

"I'm sorry, Beckett. I truly am. I wish your family could've had a different outcome."

"You found her, Kelly. If not for you, we might still not know what happened that night. I still can't believe you confronted him like that, a dangerous serial killer."

"I wasn't alone. Jade was crazy enough to go with me. And these dogs, these dogs saved our lives. Who knows what Wardlaw would've done without Journey and Brodie gate-crashing the party?"

"Which brings up a point. I think Journey would make a great rescue dog. We could start her off by training her in the backyard like I did Brodie."

"I don't know, Beckett. Let me think about it. She's been through so much. Some things still rattle her, like loud noises and thunder. We'd need to overcome that first, I think."

"Does that mean you're sticking around here past the summer?"

"I'm loving teaching this age group. Julianne and Keegan were right. The job fits better than I thought it would."

"What about your dream job at Coastal Blue Trust?"

She thought of Scott. "Let's just say I've found what makes me happy. I talked to my mom last night. It seems everyone knew what I needed except me."

"So when your lease is up—you and Journey—will move in with me?"

"There's nothing for me back in Hayward. My future, our future," she corrected, looking over at Journey, "is right here with you and Brodie."

"I'm relieved to hear it." He spotted his brother and Jade walking toward them. "Look out. Here comes trouble."

Instead of waving hello, her attention turned to a mewling sound coming from the shrubs. Journey had her nose stuck under the bushes inspecting whatever she'd found.

"What is that sound?" Kelly asked, going over to see what Journey had uncovered. She dropped down to her knees and spotted a pitiful-looking malnourished puppy, quivering and shaking, cowering in the underbrush. The gray and white pup's matted fur and skinny frame told her the poor thing was close to death. She scooped him up, nuzzled him against her chest. "It's okay. You're okay. Beckett, we have to do something."

"We'll take him to Cord," Beckett said, eyeing the starving dog. He rested a hand on the pup's head. His palm dwarfed the tiny creature's skull. "What kind of a person tosses away a puppy?"

"How old do you think he is?" Jade asked.

"Six, seven weeks maybe," Kelly guessed. "I can't even tell what kind of breed he is."

"Looks like some kind of miniature shepherd," Birk offered. "My truck's parked back at the house. It'd be quicker than walking."

"The animal clinic's just down the street. But we should probably get there before Cord leaves for the day," Kelly pointed out, still cuddling the pup.

"Come on," Beckett encouraged. "We'll get him checked out, get some milk into him. He'll be okay."

"I hope so," Kelly said as she headed toward the clinic. The closer she got, she heard the sound of barking dogs coming from the kennels. "I wish I could give them all homes. What about you, Jade? You said you wanted a dog. Has that changed?"

"No." She looked over at Birk. "You promised."

"I did, didn't I? We'll go through the place and see what happens, see if we find one to bring home."

"This is the perfect time to pick one out before the shelter closes for the night," Beckett said, slapping his brother on the back. "You did promise Jade."

"Bite me," Birk mumbled as they entered the clinic.

The waiting room had only one other patient—a woman sitting with her cat.

"We have an emergency," Kelly explained to the receptionist. "We found this little guy under a bush in the park. He's barely hanging on. He might need an IV or something."

Ellie Woodside, who usually worked in the kennels walking and grooming the dogs, took one look at the puppy and said, "Oh, no. He looks in bad shape. I'll get Jessica. Dr. Bennett is finishing up with Sasha's surgery for Ms. Bigelow's other Persian cat. But don't worry. Jessica St. John will know what to do."

Ellie rushed down the hallway and brought back Cord's technician.

"This looks like she belongs to the same litter that Colt found a few weeks ago out at Cleef Atkins' old place," Jessica said, holding up the little pup to get a better look. "The markings are the same."

"It's a he," Beckett corrected. "Where are his other siblings?"

"All adopted out. Seth and Ophelia took the last one. We didn't even realize there was a seventh puppy out there. Colt only found six. This guy might've been the runt of the litter."

"And his mother?"

"She's an American Shepherd mix."

"See? I guessed part miniature shepherd," Birk bragged. "Where is his mama?

"Still here, hoping for a good home," Jessica replied with a wink and angled toward the hallway. "We'll start an IV on this little guy and get some nutrients in him. How does that sound?"

"Whatever it takes to save him," Kelly noted. "Could we look around in the kennel? Birk and Jade are looking to get a dog."

Jessica smiled. "Music to our ears. We have plenty in need of homes. Ellie, maybe you could start them off with the American Shepherd mix. We call her Mia. She's the sweetest little girl and smart as a whip."

Birk nudged Jade. "Let's go take a look."

Kelly exchanged looks with Beckett. "I've got to see this."

"Same here."

They followed the couple out through the kennel, walking past a line of cages, each one occupied with more dogs that looked sad.

Kelly laid a hand over her heart. "This is just so depressing."

"Are you thinking of a name yet?"

"I don't know what you're talking about," Kelly feigned.

"You certainly do. The puppy you found. I say we call him Jax."

"I like that. It's a deal. He'll pull through, won't he?"

"Sure. Any dog named Jax is tough as nails." He bobbed his head toward Jade and Birk. "Looks like they've fallen in love with Mia."

Kelly grinned and hooked her arm through Beckett's. "I've fallen in love, too."

"Something tells me saving every stray means we're gonna need a bigger house."

"A bigger house, our house," Kelly repeated. "I like the sound of that."

Cast of Characters

Promise Cove - Book One

Jordan Phillips—The widow of Scott Phillips living on the outskirts of Pelican Pointe in a huge Victorian with her baby daughter. She's trying to fix the house up to open as a bed and breakfast.

Nick Harris—A former member of the California Guard who served with Scott in Iraq. Nick suffers from PTSD. He tries to adjust back to civilian life after Iraq but finds that he can't ignore a promise he made during the heat of battle.

Scott Phillips—Died in Iraq while serving with the California Guard. In life, Scott was best friends with Nick Harris. Scott doesn't let death stop him from returning to his wife and child and the town he loves. He appears throughout the series as a benevolent ghost helping new arrivals settle in and overcome their problems.

Patrick Murphy—The mayor who owns the only market in town.

Lilly Seybold—Another newcomer with two children living alone on the other side of town, isolated and struggling to get by. Lilly is recently out of an abusive marriage. Lilly and Jordan form a bond.

Wally Pierce—Owner of the gas station and the best mechanic around. He's instantly attracted to Lilly. Their relationship blossoms throughout the series.

Carla Vargas—County social worker and Murphy's longtime girlfriend.

Flynn McCready—Owner of McCready's, a mix between an Irish Pub and a pool hall.

Sissy Carr—Spoiled daughter of the town's banker. Sissy is having an ongoing affair with local developer and shady con artist Kent Springer. Sissy went to school with Scott and gives Jordan a hard time every chance she gets.

Kent Springer—Local developer and sleaze, always working on his next scam. He wants the property owned by Jordan Phillips and will do whatever it takes to get it.

Joe Ferguson—Owner of Ferguson Hardware. Grouch. Complainer.

Jack "Doc" Prescott—Former ER surgeon from San Francisco. Retired. But since moving to the area, he's actively providing medical care for residents.

Belle Prescott—Doc's wife who wants him to retire for good.

Reverend Whitcomb—Pastor of the Community Church. Wife's name is Dottie.

Hidden Moon Bay - Book Two

Emile Reed/Hayden Ryan—Arrives in Pelican Pointe during a storm, stranded at the side of the road. She's on the run from a mobster who has defrauded people out of millions of dollars.

Ethan Cody—Native American. Works as a deputy sheriff but longs to be a writer.

Brent Cody—Sheriff of Santa Cruz County and Ethan's older brother.

Marcus Cody—Father of Ethan and Brent. Marcus possesses psychic ability.

Lindeen Cody—Mother to Ethan and Brent.

Margie Rosterman—Owner of the Hilltop Diner, a 1950s throwback to a malt shop.

Max Bingham—Cook at the Hilltop Diner and Margie's boyfriend.

Julianne Dickinson—A first-grade teacher who lives in Santa Cruz in the same neighborhood as Marcus and Lindeen Cody. Lindeen often invites

Julianne to supper, hoping Brent will take an interest in her.

Janie Pointer—Owner and stylist at the Snip N Curl and best friend to Sissy Carr.

Abby Pointer—Janie's younger sister. Her boyfriend Paul Bonner is serving in Afghanistan

Wade Hawkins—Retired history professor

Dancing Tides - Book Three

Keegan Fanning—Marine biologist running the Fanning Marine Rescue Center her grandparents founded.

Cord Bennett—Former army soldier and California guardsman who served with Nick and Scott in Iraq. Because Cord feels guilty about his fiancée dying in a spree shooting, he wants to end it all.

Pete Alden—Keegan's right-hand man at the Fanning Rescue Center.

Drea Jennings—Owner of the flower shop. Her family owns the Plant Habitat, a landscape nursery in town.

Abby Anderson—Works at the Fanning Rescue Center.

Ricky Oden—Founder and lead singer of the local band, Blue Skies. Married to Donna Oden.

Bran Sullivan—Veterinarian, owner of Pelican Pointe Animal Clinic.

Joy Sullivan—Receptionist at the animal clinic and wife of Bran.

Lighthouse Reef - Book Four

Kinsey Wyatt—An up-and-coming lawyer who comes to Pelican Pointe to prove she's the real deal.

Logan Donnelly—Sculptor and artist who relocates to Pelican Pointe with an agenda.

Perry Altman—A five-star chef from Los Angeles who opened The Pointe, the fanciest place in town to eat.

Troy Dayton—A young carpenter who works hard at surviving everything life's thrown at him.

Mona Bingham—Max's daughter from Texas.

Carl Knudsen—Owns the pharmacy in town he inherited from his family. Married, but not happy. In his younger days ran with Kent Springer.

Jolene Sanders—Hostess at The Pointe. Works part-time as a clerk at Knudsen's Pharmacy.

Megan Donnelly—Logan's sister.

Starlight Dunes - Book Five

River Amandez—Thirty-three-year-old archaeologist who arrives in Pelican Pointe harboring a secret. She's in town to excavate the Chumash encampment uncovered during a mudslide.

Brent Cody—Forty-year-old sheriff of Santa Cruz County with a bad marriage under his belt and a not-so-stellar dating record. Brent has someone in his past who wants him dead.

Zach Dennison—Picks up odd jobs around town, trying to make ends meet. Zach lives with his sister, Bree Dennison.

Bree Dennison—Goes to community college in San Sebastian and works as a waitress at McCready's.

Ryder McLachlan—Cord's buddy from the army. New in Pelican Pointe from Philadelphia and looking to make a fresh start.

Ross Campbell—Pharmacist from Portland, relocates and buys the local pharmacy. Renames it Coastal Pharmacy.

Jill Campbell—Ross's wife.

Last Chance Harbor - Book Six

Julianne Dickinson—First-grade teacher, slated to be the principal of the newly renovated Pelican Pointe Elementary.

Ryder McLachlan—Cord's buddy from the Army. New in Pelican Pointe from Philadelphia and looking to make a fresh start.

John Dickinson—Julianne's dad.

Bree Dennison—Goes to community college in San Sebastian and works as a waitress at McCready's.

Malachi Rafferty—Owner of the T-Shirt Shop and single father with two teen girls, Sonnet and Sonoma.

Cleef Atkins—Lives south of town in an old farmhouse. His barn is stuffed with things he's collected over the years.

Drea Jennings—Cooper's sister.

Caleb Jennings—Cooper's brother.

Landon Jennings—Cooper's uncle and adopted father.

Shelby Jennings—Cooper's aunt and adopted mother.

Layne Richmond—Father of Cooper, Caleb, and Drea.

Eleanor Jennings Richmond—Mother of Cooper, Caleb, and Drea. In prison for murdering Layne Richmond and Brooke Caldwell.

Archer Gates—Son of Prissie Gates.

Sea Glass Cottage - Book Seven

Isabella Rialto—Known as Izzy, Logan's mysterious renter who shows up in town and starts people talking about her past.

Thane Delacourt—Ex NFL linebacker who comes back to Pelican Pointe to raise his son.

Jonah Delacourt—Thane's six-year-old son.

Fischer Robbins—Thane's best friend from New York and a chef who helps Thane open Longboard Pizza.

Tommy Gates—Jonah's best friend and Archer's son.

Bobby Prather—Jonah's bully at school

Greg Prather—Bobby's dad. Works odd jobs to make ends meet.

Sydney Reed—An ER nurse in St. Louis and Hayden Cody's sister. Sydney relocates to become Doc's nurse.

Lavender Beach - Book Eight

Eastlyn Parker—Ex-army helicopter pilot, crashed her chopper in Iraq and lost the bottom part of her leg. She hasn't adjusted to civilian life very well.

Cooper Jennings Richmond—Son of Layne Richmond and Eleanor Jennings. Photographer who traveled the world but now owns Layne's Trains.

Drea Jennings—Cooper's sister.

Caleb Jennings—Cooper's brother.

Landon Jennings—Cooper's uncle and adopted father.

Shelby Jennings—Cooper's aunt and adopted mother.

Eleanor Jennings Richmond—Mother of Cooper, Caleb, and Drea.

Jonathan Matthews—Eleanor's son.

Sandcastles Under the Christmas Moon - Book Nine

Quentin Blackwood—Doctor replacing Jack Prescott.

Sydney Reed—Sister of Hayden and Jack Prescott's nurse.

Beckham Dowling—Teenage boy, resourceful, savvy, and smart, worried about his grandmother's health.

Charlotte Dowling—Beckham's grandmother who's lived in town for years.

Faye DeMarco—Beckham's girlfriend.

Andy DeMarco—Faye's older brother, who takes care of her after their parents die in a car crash.

Winona Blackwood—Quentin's grandmother, also known as Nonnie.

Stone Graylander—Miwok tribal medicine man. Boyfriend of Quentin's grandmother, Nonnie.

Douglas Bradford—Former professor, moved to Pelican Pointe and became its mayor before Murphy. Owner of Bradford House.

John David Whitcomb—Pastor at the Community Church.

Dottie Whitcomb—John's wife.

Beneath Winter Sand – Book Ten

Caleb Jennings—Brother of Cooper and Drea. Works at The Plant Habitat with his parents, Landon and Shelby.

Hannah Summers—Owns a cleaning service. Picks up extra money on the weekends working as a waitress at The Shipwreck.

Micah Lambert—Hannah's little brother.

Cora Bigelow—Postmistress.

Lilly Pierce—Wally's wife who helps him run the gas station and auto repair shop.

Jessica St. John—Works for Cord at the animal clinic.

Jonathan Matthews—Eleanor's son.

Tahoe Jones—Caretaker of the Jennings' cabin.

Delbert Delashaw—Boyfriend of Eleanor Richmond.

Barton Pearson—Funeral director.

Geniece Darrow—Jill Campbell's little sister.
Ruthie May Porter—Neighbor to Tandy.
Tandy Gilliam—Neighbor to Ruthie May.
Durke Pedasco—Friend of Eastlyn from Bakersfield and owner of The Shipwreck.

Keeping Cape Summer – Book Eleven

Simon Bremmer—Ex-Army Ranger. Sniper. Twelve years in the military.
Amelia Langston—A woman Simon met on Cape Cod.
Gilly Grant—Nurse at Charlotte Dowling Memorial Hospital.
Delaney Bremmer—Simon's daughter.
Jayden Grant—Gilly's son.
Connie Grant—Gilly's mother.
Gretchen Bremmer—Simon's mother.
John Dickinson—Julianne's dad.
Gideon Nighthawk—The new surgeon from Chicago.
Ophelia Moore—Daycare director at the Community Church.
Aubree Wright—Nurse who works the day shift at the hospital.
Sheena Howser—Nurse at the hospital who fills in for everyone else.
Seth Larrabee—New minister at the Community Church.
Brad Radcliff—Owns a used car lot.

A Pelican Pointe Christmas – Book Twelve

Naomi Townsend—Vice-president at the bank.
Colton Del Rio—Ex-Army Ranger. Sniper. Eighteen years in the military.

Tabitha Porter, nicknamed Tibby—Foster child.

Madison Lee, Maddie for short—Foster child, whose mother has died.

The Coast Road Home – Book Thirteen

Marley Lennox—A newcomer to town from Wisconsin, she's stuck in town after a car accident damages her vehicle.

Gideon Nighthawk—Surgeon from Chicago

Shiloh Jones—Tahoe Jones's granddaughter who's moved to town and now works at The Plant Habitat.

Keva Riverton—Julianne's friend from Modesto who works at Reclaimed Treasures.

Bodie Jardine—Waitress at the Hilltop Diner.

Hollis Crow—A mild-mannered garbage man in love with Ellie Woodside.

Ellie Woodside—Part-time dogwalker and groomer. Works at the animal clinic with Cord. Part-time house cleaner. Works with Hannah Summers cleaning houses.

Bette Magnuson—A woman whose husband left her who Marley befriends.

Lorelei "Lolly" Acoma—Gideon's aunt who adopted him.

The Boathouse – Book Fourteen

Tucker Ferguson—Runs the hardware store.

Bodie Jardine—Waitress at the Hilltop Diner.

Ellie Woodside—Part-time dogwalker and groomer. Works at the animal clinic with Cord. Part-time house cleaner. Works with Hannah Summers cleaning houses.

Hollis Crow—A mild-mannered garbage man in love with Ellie Woodside.

Keva Riverton—Bodie's friend from Modesto who works at Reclaimed Treasures.

Oliver Tremaine—A troubled kid.

Kris Mallick—Oliver's uncle.

Lucien Sutter—Artisan and local furniture maker, an all-around handyman.

Adam Harkness—Lawyer, visiting from San Sebastian.

Owen Kessler—Part-time worker at the hardware store.

Matty Cruz—Part-time worker at the hardware store.

Novah Hensley—Part-time worker at the hardware store.

Arthur Gaylord—Neighbor to Tucker. Birdwatcher.

Astor Gaylord—Married to Arthur. Birdwatcher.

Clive Ogilvie—Retired Army man who works the saw at the lumberyard.

Vernon Jackdaw—Junkyard owner.

The Beachcomber – Book Fifteen

Brogan Cole—CEO of Brinell Steel. Daughter of Rory Rossum Cole legendary rock star.

Lucien Sutter—Artisan and local furniture maker, an all-around handyman.

Rory Rossum Cole—Brogan's rock star father, singer for the band Indigo. Rory was murdered in his studio while he worked on new material.

Graeme Sutter—Father of Lucien, lead guitarist for the band Indigo.

Kate Ashcroft—Lucien's mother.

Nigel Brighton—Drummer for the band Indigo.

Gordon Mayer—Keyboard player for the band Indigo.

Maeve Calico—Rory's longtime housekeeper and Brogan's surrogate mother.
Sloane Cole—Rory's fifth wife. Brogan's stepmother.
Milo Lomax—Sloane's son from a previous marriage. Brogan's stepbrother.
Felicia Watts—Graeme's Irish cook. Lucien's surrogate mother and Maeve's younger sister.
Angus Eden—College friend of Lucien's and an actor.
Big Jack Milliken—Head of security for Rory Rossum Cole.

Sandpiper Marsh – Book Sixteen

Beckett Callahan—Ex-Navy SEAL, half owner of Terra Search & Recovery.
Colleen "Kelly" Ecklund—Professor of biology at Redwood State University, in town for research and to reforest the area's kelp beds.
Birch "Birk" Callahan—Ex-Navy SEAL, brother to Beckett, half owner of Terra Search & Recovery.
Tess Knightley—New hairstylist at the Snip N Curl.
Cassidy Kennison—Jordan's new chef at the B&B.
Paula Bretton—Owner of The Perky Pelican, a coffee shop next door to the bookstore.
Jade Weingarten—A true-crime blogger, websleuth, and resident of Santa Cruz trying to find out what happened to Brigid Callahan.
Debra Rattlin—Head of the Coastal Canine Search Unit.
Betty Callahan—Mother to Birk, Beckett, and Brigid.
Craig Callahan—Father to Birk, Beckett, and Brigid.

Brigid Callahan—Sister to Birk and Beckett. She disappeared five and a half years ago after drinking at a bar in Santa Cruz.

Don't miss these other exciting titles by bestselling author!
Vickie McKeehan

The Pelican Pointe Series
PROMISE COVE
HIDDEN MOON BAY
DANCING TIDES
LIGHTHOUSE REEF
STARLIGHT DUNES
LAST CHANCE HARBOR
SEA GLASS COTTAGE
LAVENDER BEACH
SANDCASTLES UNDER THE CHRISTMAS MOON
BENEATH WINTER SAND
KEEPING CAPE SUMMER
A PELICAN POINTE CHRISTMAS
THE COAST ROAD HOME
THE BOATHOUSE
THE BEACHCOMBER
SANDPIPER MARSH

The Evil Secrets Trilogy
JUST EVIL Book One
DEEPER EVIL Book Two
ENDING EVIL Book Three
EVIL SECRETS TRILOGY BOXED SET

The Skye Cree Novels
THE BONES OF OTHERS
THE BONES WILL TELL
THE BOX OF BONES
HIS GARDEN OF BONES
TRUTH IN THE BONES
SEA OF BONES
FORGOTTEN BONES
DOWN AMONG THE BONES
BONE MESA

The Indigo Brothers Trilogy
INDIGO FIRE
INDIGO HEAT
INDIGO JUSTICE

INDIGO BROTHERS TRILOGY BOXED SET

Coyote Wells Mysteries
MYSTIC FALLS
SHADOW CANYON
SPIRIT LAKE
FIRE MOUNTAIN
MOONLIGHT RIDGE
CHRISTMAS CREEK

A Beachcomber Mystery
MURDER IN THE DUNES
MURDER IN THE SUMMER HOUSE

ABOUT THE AUTHOR

Vickie McKeehan has thirty-one novels to her credit and counting. Vickie's novels have consistently appeared on Amazon's Top 100 lists in Contemporary Romance, Romantic Suspense and Mystery / Thriller. She writes what she loves to read—heartwarming romance laced with suspense, heart-pounding thrillers, and riveting mysteries. Vickie loves to write about compelling and down-to-earth characters in settings that stay with her readers long after they've finished her books. She makes her home in Southern California.

Find Vickie online at
https://www.facebook.com/VickieMcKeehan
http://www.vickiemckeehan.com/
https://vickiemckeehan.wordpress.com

Printed in Great Britain
by Amazon